SANDRA SCOFIELD was born and raised in West Texas. Her first novel, *Gringa*, was nominated for the First Fiction Award given by the American Academy and Institute of Arts and Letters and was selected by the NEA/USIA for a 1990 New American Writing Award. Her second novel, *Beyond Deserving* (Plume), underwritten by a Creative Writing Fellowship from the National Endowment for the Arts, was hailed by critics around the country, was a finalist for the 1991 National Book Award, and won a 1992 American Book Award. *Walking Dunes* is her third book. She currently lives in southern Oregon.

W9-DDN-485

WALKING DUNES

A NOVEL BY

SANDRA SCOFIELD

For
Rainshadow
Books

Sandra Scofield

A PLUME BOOK

PLUME
Published by the Penguin Group
Penguin Books USA Inc., 375 Hudson Street, New York, New York 10014, U.S.A.
Penguin Books Ltd, 27 Wrights Lane, London W8 5TZ, England
Penguin Books Australia Ltd, Ringwood, Victoria, Australia
Penguin Books Canada Ltd, 10 Alcorn Avenue, Toronto, Ontario, Canada M4V 3B2
Penguin Books (N.Z.) Ltd, 182–190 Wairau Road, Auckland 10, New Zealand

Penguin Books Ltd, Registered Offices: Harmondsworth, Middlesex, England

Published by Plume, an imprint of New American Library,
a division of Penguin Books USA Inc. This is an authorized reprint of a hardcover edition
published by The Permanent Press.

First Plume Printing, September, 1993
10 9 8 7 6 5 4 3 2 1

 REGISTERED TRADEMARK—MARCA REGISTRADA

LIBRARY OF CONGRESS CATALOGING-IN-PUBLICATION DATA
Scofield, Sandra Jean, 1943–
    Walking dunes : a novel / by Sandra Scofield.
        p.   cm.
    ISBN 0-452-27027-8
    1. Teenage boys—Texas—Fiction.   2. Texas—Fiction.   I. Title.
[PS3569.C584W35   1993]
813'.54—dc20   93–3801
                                                              CIP

Printed in the United States of America

PUBLISHER'S NOTE
This is a work of fiction. Names, characters, places, and incidents either are the product
of the author's imagination or are used fictitiously, and any resemblance to actual persons,
living or dead, events, or locales is entirely coincidental.

For Oleta and Evelyn,
then and now

With thanks to Bill Danley
for his generous spirit
and fantastic memory

1.

It was an afternoon in late August, when people who could stay indoors did so, while others sought shade along the edges of buildings or other structures where they were obligated to be. The sun this time of year seemed to have bled its yellow, to have drained the West Texas sky and spilled almost without boundary onto the scruffy ochre plains. People dreaded the wind that came up hot and gritty. It obscured the last pale patches of sky. In August, color was forgotten. There was no blue, no green, no true yellow. Sand was a color, heat was a color.

A man was leaning against the side of a pickup bed, one foot propped against the wheel. He wore jeans, a blue plaid shirt with rolled-up sleeves, wine-red ropers, and a bleached, once-black cowboy hat with a curled front brim. His visible flesh—hands, face, lower arms, the back of his neck—was burned a tan the hue of a dirty bruise. Anyone would know him for a roughneck. He was thirty-eight, slim-limbed, with a beer drinker's sloppy belly. He spat in the dust and packed a plug of tobacco under his lip, staring out over the mesquite in the direction of a pump jack. With his left hand he held a .22 rifle, propping the butt against his raised thigh.

Behind the man and his truck, thirty feet away, lay a dry stock pond, gouged out of caliche, four to four and a half feet deep in the center. It was about the size of the man's bedroom on North Buckhorn back in Basin. Off-center, toward the lip opposite the side of the pit where the man stood, a trickle of water came from below ground and darkened the rock for a few feet, then dried. In the spring, if it rained, the pit became again a "pond," but now it was no more than another scar on the face of an ugly landscape.

At the apex of a triangle, its base the line from man to pit, a girl sixteen years old sat on the ground cleaning rabbits the man had shot. She was turned away from him. Several times she shielded her eyes and stared out toward the pump jack. Once she did this at the same moment as the man, who was her father. Then she went back to her bloody work. She was making two piles. One, on a rectangle of torn plastic sheeting, was of cottontails, which they would take home to eat. The other was of jack rabbits. Some of the jack rabbits were whole, merely tossed aside, of no use past sport, but there were a few that, shaken, spilled bladder and bowels onto the sand. The girl skinned and gutted the cottontails, working carefully.

She wore clothes much like her father's, except that her boots were brown, and she was hatless. The sun glinted off her pale hair, like off metal, and washed out the features of her face. The man, staring past her, saw a long stripey patch of blue wavering in the distance. Glimpsing a couple of rabbits in the brush, he lifted his rifle and shot several times, barely to his daughter's left. One rabbit leaped away. He yelled at her to look for the other one. "You fetch it!" he called. He held his arm straight out.

The girl rose obediently, dropping the knife but not bothering to wipe her hands and arms. The front of her shirt and her pants were splattered. When she was on her way, he took a burlap sack from the pickup bed and went over to the place where she had been cleaning the rabbits. He put the cottontails in the sack, loaded them in the truck, placed his rifle in the rack in the cab, and wiped his hands on a rag from the floor. Only then did he look up, watching for the girl's return.

She was walking quickly now. She seemed to be headed toward the blue shimmering mirage, toward the horizon, which was far away. At first she carried the jack rabbit by its long ears, so that it dragged and bumped along the ground. When it caught in brush, she jerked it free; shortly, she pulled it up and draped it over her arm.

Her father yelled her name, Sissy. Wind was gusting, and as he yelled again, perhaps half a dozen times, his mouth was lined with dust, and his voice broke in hoarseness against the fierce wind. He coughed and spat furiously. The girl strode on, towards the north, beginning to look small. She was a small girl, about ninety-five pounds on a delicate frame. He grabbed his gun from the rack and fired it, not quite up but not really in her direction, either. She might not even have noticed, her pace was so steady and unchanged. She began to veer toward the east, perhaps spying the turnoff of a lease road where the walk would be easier. Her father spat again, then turned and fired straight into the pit, at the wet spot, spraying splinters of rock and clumps of dirt. He racked the gun and scrambled into the truck, pulling away fast in a cloud of dust. The horizon was smudged out by the rising storm. He thought urgently of a beer, a cigarette, his head and hands under a tap running cold water. He drove east, back toward Basin, away from the girl.

2.

In town, the air was a dirty yellow, and the wind threw sand against the houses. David Puckett caught himself grinding his teeth. He was anxious to get away. It was Sunday, late afternoon, and he would be driving to Fort Stockton, a few hours away, as soon as he could leave. For one more week, he would be on his own, and then the school year would start again. Though he had only been home three days this trip, he had the sense of having needed to fill time. Boring and lonely as his work was in Fort Stockton, it was *his,* and at eighteen he had felt, for the first time, really, the dignity of unassailed privacy.

He was just finishing a chess game with his father, Saul Stolboff. Or the game was finishing him. At first, as always, David had agonized over each move, though he sometimes found himself forgetting the pieces, thinking only of his father across the kitchen table, waiting to pounce. Now he simply could not maintain attention; the sound of blowing sand was more compelling than the game. Then David noticed the particular tension in his father's arm before checkmate, before he actually saw the move itself. His father took great pleasure in these games, and the best part for him, David was certain, was yet to come.

The analysis.

"By God!" David said as his father crowed his win. He thought if he could pretend to be excited, to be impressed, he could carry the next few moments, then eat the meal his mother was preparing behind his back at the stove; he could maintain his patience, and *be gone.* There was no real reason to quarrel with his father, and there was no winning if he did. The purpose of quarrels, for Saul, never seemed to be to settle anything anyway; it always had to do with stirring things up. Anything could provoke him; he seemed always poised on the cusp of a tirade.

Almost immediately David realized he had sounded not impressed but surprised, an open invitation to a lecture. "Good game, Pop," he added weakly.

Saul leaned forward on his elbows. "You were a fast kid, back when you were first learning chess, son," he said, almost amiably. Teaching David chess had been Saul's first order of business when he returned to the family after his last long separation. David was then thirteen. David had felt singled out, special, madly eager to learn. Now David knew that behind this seemingly affectionate allusion would be something savage. His chest ached, waiting.

His father jabbed his finger in the air. "You've got a good memory for the moves, and if you concentrated, you could visualize—"

"What's for supper, Mom?" David asked, leaning back in his chair, tipping the legs, and stretching his arms over his head.

His mother turned at the stove to give him a smile. "I'm frying potatoes and onions, Davy," she said. "And sliced tomatoes—"

"Goddam!" Saul shouted. "Can anybody finish a SEN-TENCE around here?"

Marge turned back to her cooking. David let his chair down gingerly.

"You confuse tactics and strategy, son," Saul said across the board, as if David had just seated himself in readiness for a lesson. "Sure it's tactical to hit fast and hard, but, you don't have a strategy, you make a fool of yourself; you've got to know what's got value, and where you want to be, not just now, but across the board, moves ahead. You've got to know what you're willing to sacrifice."

"Like tennis," David said, unable to keep a tinge of longing out of his voice. He would much rather be outside, hitting balls, but of course you couldn't do that in this wind.

"Yes, like tennis!" his father said. "All the more reason for you to THINK."

"It's just a game, Pop," David said meekly.

"You missed it, sonny, back here—" Saul rearranged the pieces, positioning his own rook and queen, then David's, a few moves back. "Here's how it could have gone."

The whine of the wind made David's skin crawl. Inside the house, he felt trapped, but really, he liked driving in a storm. It was like driving into the sea. Once, in Lubbock—he and his father had gone to the mills there to buy fabric seconds—a terrible dust storm moved in like a bank of water. They could see it coming up the street, blocking the light, blacking out the buildings and the streetlamps. As it reached them, it was like being blotted out, like disappearing, and he had been very excited, not scared at all. He had known to cover his eyes and wait.

Saul shifted the pieces around, now intent and superior. "If you'd have disposed of the check here—See this?" David followed the movement of his father's hand, aware of the dark curls of hair on his arm, the stringiness of the tendons from his wrist down into the fingers. *He's so hard on me,* he thought, unable to think why. Why all the lectures? Why all the criticism? Why couldn't he just let me *be*?

Why did David seem always to disappoint him?

"Black couldn't have stopped the passed pawn from queening. You'd have been a whole rook ahead."

Suddenly David saw what his father meant. The slightest hint of the possible move had actually flitted across his consciousness back then, but he had dismissed it as simple. He had been looking for something trickier. Had he overestimated the queen? Underestimated the pawn? Or had he simply not paid attention, as his father accused him all the time?

"In the proper position," Saul went on, full of himself now, "the queen has many ways of queening the pawn."

"Lucky pawn," David said bitterly.

"Is it so bad, losing?" Saul said.

"Is it so great, winning?"

They glared at one another.

"Five minutes," Marge announced. David realized she had been standing there, shuffling one foot back and forth, for the whole time Saul was lecturing.

"I'm starved!" David said gratefully.

A mask of anger came and went on Saul's face, something considered and rejected, and he said, "Time for a drink, then, eh, Ma?"

"One," Marge said. The phone rang.

Saul swept the pieces into the cardboard box he kept them in. Marge looked toward the phone on the wall over by the arch into the living room. "I'll get it in my room," David said. His father had had a fit when David put that extension in. He made David pay two dollars a month for it.

"Oh good, you're not gone yet," Glee Hewett said when he answered.

"I'm eating, I can't talk," David told his girlfriend. He hated for her to call the house. Sometimes her sly, whimpering attempts to sound sexy did have an effect on him, but he could not bear the thought of his father commenting on her breathy little voice. "You know I don't like for you to call."

"*You* weren't going to call *me*."

"I talked to you last night."

"Talked, Davy, just *talked*," Glee fussed. "I *miss* you."

David had worked on his mother's shift at the hospital, where she was charge nurse for the psychiatric ward at night.

"Yeah, well, I'll be home next weekend for the year, Glee. I can't help it if I have to work out of town." Glee's problem was she had nothing to do all summer but lie around the municipal pool working on her tan, or practicing cheerleading splits.

"What about now?"

"What about it?"

"Oh, why are you acting like this!"

He sighed. "Because I need to eat and go. I'm sorry, I don't mean to hurt your feelings."

"I know," she said, forgiving him at his slightest conciliatory effort.

"I'll see you in a week or so, Glee. I can't talk now."

"Don't blow away," she said, as if she were telling him to take his pants off. She had a real gift for tone.

She made him laugh, relax a little. "Save up," he said.

His father had fixed them all gin and tonics. Marge set hers on top of the refrigerator and went about her cooking. Saul held his up to David for a toast.

"To my Big Shot Son, the Tennis Star," he said. "To my Devil Son, the Girl-Eater."

The rib of insult in each toast made David bite his cheek, but he said nothing. He even smiled. He acted as if his father meant well. They stood under the ugly arch while Marge set the table. "Look at that!" she exclaimed. There was a fine layer of dust settled on the table. She ran a finger through it, then put the plates down without wiping it up.

From his chair David could see a band of sky through the kitchen window. The thick look of it was oppressive. They sat down. "Looks good, Mom," David told his mother. For some reason, this made Saul smirk, first at him, then at Marge. Marge looked down at her fork as the tines sank into a pyramid of potato slices. David felt caught in a crawlspace with his mother and father. Could he belong to both? Or only be crushed between them?

David scraped the last of the fried mess onto his plate, to please his mother. She looked fretful. "I don't know if it's a good idea for you to go out in this," she said.

Saul pushed his plate a few inches toward the center of the table. "It's not that bad. It's not one of your famous west Texas storms that scour cooking pots and make barbed wire blister-hot." His teasing had a mean sound; he often reminded his wife that she was the one who lived where she had grown up. He never mentioned New York.

"I'll be okay," David said. He hated his mother's worrying, but as soon as he left town he would forget it.

Saul gave him a six-pack of Lone Star out of the refrigerator. "This isn't for the road," he said.

At the edge of Basin, heading west, David pulled off on the shoulder of the road, dug out a church-key from the glove compartment, and opened a beer. He drank it slowly, steadily, letting the comfort of it gush through him. When he had drunk half of it, he tucked it between his legs and drove on. Not far down the highway he spotted a black Highway Patrol car along the line of a slight rise, and he glanced at the speedometer, careful not to get stopped with an open can of beer in his crotch.

The beer went straight through him. In a few minutes he felt the urgent need to urinate, and turned off onto a lease road. He got out of the car and stood for a moment beside it, staring west. There was a lot of sand in the air, but the wind had died down. It was not yet twilight. The sky and land all seemed one reddish color. It was as if he were suspended in an ocean of settling sand. It was quiet, almost eerily so; he couldn't even hear a pump jack anywhere. He chewed on a thumbnail and tasted the residue of greasy onions, and the grit of sand. He had his hand on the car door when he saw someone coming from a ways off, someone small, maybe a child. The person—he couldn't see if it was a male or female—was swerving and lurching, then walking for a moment or two at a time perfectly straight, then swerving again.

He stood watching as the person came toward him. In a few minutes he could see it was a kid, carrying something. The kid stopped, seemed to see him, then sat down.

David walked quickly toward the kid. He did not see that it was a girl until he was right on top of her. On the ground beside her she had dropped the thing she was carrying, a skinny jack rabbit with long blood-streaked ears, huge dangling feet.

"Here, now, what's the matter? Are you all right?" He dropped to the ground in front of her, kneeling on one knee. He tried to take her arm, but she jerked away. Her shirt was caked with blood. For a moment he was scared, really scared; he had never seen anybody seriously injured. He had heard stories, people beaten up in fights, oilfield accidents, passengers mangled in cars, but he had never seen anything like that himself. He had never been in the emergency ward, for all the times he had been to the hospital. He felt vaguely nauseous, the peppery aftertaste of his supper now a sour hot phlegm in his throat, the beer a churning in his stomach. "Look," he said sharply, "you're hurt, I've got to do something." He thought, she's just a kid, I've got to be in charge. She looked up at him, frightened, and not, he thought, quite all there. He had seen that look before, on faces in his mother's ward.

"Where are you hurt?" He reached for her again and she let him take her hand. He didn't want to pull at her; he didn't know what to do. If she had been a boy, he might have patted her all over, like someone looking for a weapon. How else did you check for wounds? But a girl, a young teen-ager, he thought: he didn't want to paw at her. His chest was hurting crazily. He had to stop for a few seconds and attend to himself. He had to talk to himself in his head: Calm down, it's okay, breathe, breathe. He put his hands on his chest. The girl was on her feet, her hands at her side, staring at him. The blood on her clothing was dry. She did not seem to be hurt.

She reached down and picked up the rabbit. The blood was from the rabbit, he realized. He was confused, wary. He took a step back, and as he did, she stepped around him and walked in the direction of his car. God, he thought, there'll be blood on the car seat. His father would kill him.

The girl went right past the car and off into the bunch

grass. "Hey!" he shouted. "You better wait up! You crazy, or what?" but she didn't even seem to hear him. He took a moment to think this over. Was he going to run after her, tackle her, drag her to his car? He remembered the patrolman, maybe five or six minutes away.

He could see that the girl was headed for the highway. She trudged along like someone on her way to do a despised chore. He took the beer and carried it around to the back of the station wagon and put it under a pile of jeans jackets, then gunned the motor and spun out of the sand.

The cop was sitting in the same place, hiding behind his mirrored sunglasses. He hardly looked up as David pulled fast across the road and up beside him. "Man, you aren't going to believe this," David told him. He leaned out of his window a little, his arm dangling along the hot chrome.

The cop grinned. "Who died, son?"

David grinned back. He knew he had the punchline. "Would you believe a rabbit?" he said.

3.

David Puckett had lived much of that summer of 1958 in an old beauty parlor in Fort Stockton. His father had rented the building as a store for the third year in a row, but this time he hired his son to spend half of each summer month there alone, doing business with the local people, both Anglo and Mexican. David sold yard goods (mill ends and damaged fabrics), clothing (discontinued or imperfect), and some Army surplus goods. Four or five days a month he traveled to outlying towns like Iraan and Rankin, sleeping at night in the station wagon and setting up sale tables wherever he could. He liked being out from under his father's eye. He liked feeling he was on his own. And he told himself, as his father had told him, that he was doing a service to these communities, selling cheap goods nobody else wanted to people who needed them, for bargain prices they could barely afford.

The beauty parlor still had its name painted on the stucco above the outside door: Pearl's Curls. Pearl had moved her business into her own house's parlor, as his Aunt Cheryl had done in her Monahans home. Inside and out, the old building was a faded salmon color. All the chairs had been removed, but there were mirrors and counters along two walls, and two deep, black ceramic sinks at the rear of the store. He rented tables from a church. He slept on a cot beneath the mirror. He ate from cans, or went to the Brite Spot Cafe two blocks up the street. Sometimes he walked at dusk out on the edge of town where it was so hot and dry and barren, it might have been some farflung planet. At night he listened to country music on his little radio, and read. He had begun keeping a notebook, too.

He had been listing the events of his life. It was merely a way to combat boredom. He had thought of the list as an inventory, and he had been amazed at the ways he could vary it. It gave him an odd sense of power to realize that what he left off and what he put on the list changed the quality of his history. Did he say, for 1947, "Dad left us."? Or did he say, "Dad went back to New York to work."? Did he record his grandmother's death, in the house she had been helping pay for? And what did he make of his many childhood illnesses— the mumps and measles, croup and chicken pox? What of his asthma attacks, which his father dismissed as phantom, his father being an expert after a lifetime of "real" asthma that had kept him out of the war. David saw that the details of his life were petty, but he sensed that if he amassed those details, they would add up to something, that their density would amount to a life. He was fascinated with the way stories and novels were built of particulars, how small details lingered in his mind for a long time after a book was put away. He would never forget, for example, the moment when Hardy's Tess, having changed into shoes to go into Clare's house, hears Clare and his buddy laughing at her poor, ugly, hateful boots. And when he read *The Great Gatsby* months before his first visit to the Basin Country Club, he found himself dreaming of girls in dresses cut low on their breasts, of chandeliers, deep carpets, food arranged on platters like the petals of flowers. When he read "Winter Dreams," he heard himself saying, *"yes, yes,"* even though the story was set in a part of the country far away, with white winters and summers of lakes. He understood Fitzgerald's special talent at conveying long-ing, because it evoked his own yearnings, so that his own pain—what did he want so much, except, like Dexter Green, the possession of beauty in all its forms?—was as real and acute as if someone had been sticking pins in his chest. The more he played with memory, and with recording his own life, however sketchily, the more he burned to go on with it. He wanted to get to the good part, which he associated with independence, and which encompassed all those things for which he longed. He felt impatient, because he was sick of being a boy, and he did not know how to set his life in motion. Then he reminded himself that this year, his last in high school, was for that very thing, for commencement.

His father's name was Saul Stolboff, and David regarded him as a good subject for character study, for he was an odd man in Basin, Texas. Any good explanation of the man would be complex. But as David pondered what he knew of his father, he realized how little it was. He did not know enough to build stories; he did not understand enough to explain anything, but things he had always taken for granted began to take on new resonance. There was, for example, the matter of their names. David's name was Stolboff, too, of course; David had seen it on his birth certificate. He had gone through a phase when he was convinced he was illegitimate, and his mother had produced proof that he was not. There was a sister, too, fifteen months younger. Saul had abandoned them when the children were five and seven. He returned to New York, where he had grown up. He had met David's mother when she was a nurse in a hospital on Long Island. Marge had intended to nurse for the Army when the country entered the war. (Such audacity! David thought, wondering how she had found the courage to leave her family.) Of course by the time the Army wanted her, there was her unlikely marriage, then there was David. After the war they had gone to Texas. The thought of that fascinated David. Maybe, when they stepped off the train, the sight of that vast featureless landscape had triggered in Saul ancestral memories of Russian wheat fields, but such ideas had been erased by drought and hardship, by the Protestant culture and his wife's family. Saul had truly gone abroad. He had not lasted two years before he fled, going back to work for his brother, who owned a pants factory in Queens. In a while David's mother changed their names to Puckett, her family's name. When Saul returned in time for David's thirteenth birthday, mumbling about Bar Mitzvahs but doing nothing, the names stayed changed, a constant reminder of who the parent-on-the-front had turned out to be, a constant reproof of the man who had run away. Only recently had David wondered how it made his father feel, to have a son who did not use his name.

David tried to imagine his father's life, but he had little to go on. If David asked questions, Saul said, "You don't need to know," or "What's it to you?" Once, drunk, he said, "So much to know, all the way back to Russia, and it dribbles out with you like an old man's piss." There was a vast chasm between father and son, and David did not know how to bridge it. He was a child of the plains, his father a city boy. He tried to learn about city life. He read *Studs Lonigan* twice, but it was another city, after all, another kind of family. His immigrant grandparents were dead, his mother's parents were dead. The family floated on a sea of estrangement. At least Marge had her sister, and her daughter, though Joyce Ellen was out of the house now. His father belonged to another world entirely, and he had left it for his family of Pucketts.

It was not difficult to imagine his parents falling in love. David had a strong romantic streak; he understood that attraction can feel like fate. There was a photograph of his parents on his mother's bureau. His mother had been a handsome young woman, with her long rolled hair, her marble green eyes. His father would have been so different from the boys she had known in Texas. Now David's parents' first feelings had drowned in disappointment and anger. David would realize that days had gone by and his parents had not spoken in his presence. He would wonder, what did it this time? Sometimes they shouted, and David would not know why. Often it was money. Marge didn't see much of whatever Saul earned as an alterations tailor; there were hints that he gambled, though David imagined only penny-ante stuff with his barber and the junkman. For Marge, there were debts from her mother's illness, and the house always needed something. Then too, Saul's messy habits drove her wild, though she was sloppy at home, herself. David's sister, Joyce Ellen, was always good for a row, too. Saul struck her a couple of times after he came back: she was lazy, provocative. Marge told him flat out that if he ever did it again she would throw him out; *it was her house*. After that Saul used his better weapon, sarcasm, but Joyce Ellen could rouse him to a shout. The night she ran off with her boyfriend, there had been slammed doors, some broken dishes. Marge said she would never forgive him. It seemed she *had* never forgiven him. Once David heard her scream, "I could have gone to the war!" Yet, surely, there had once been something larger between Marge and Saul, and the disintegration of that something would account for a great bitterness. But David saw his parents sliding toward the stagnancy of indifference. He thought: One day my father will go away a second time, and I will never see him again.

How he envied the lives of ordinary families! He had dated a nice, pretty girl for a while the year before. Sarah Jane Cottle. She had a clean bright beauty, plump chipmunk cheeks, a quiet air of courtesy and shyness. She lived in a white frame house that had curtains and rugs and an elm tree in the yard. Her mother sewed skirts and blouses for her. Her father was the owner of a restaurant supply company. He showed David his freezer in the utility room, stocked with New York strips, fat prawns, quartered chickens, for the family. Once when David was at their house for dinner, Mr. Cottle told his wife, "This is an excellent pot roast, dear." David simply could not bear it; why did it seem so easy for them? How were they different from his family? *What is wrong with us?* He had quit dating the girl.

Little by little David realized that all the questions you had about your life could serve as a kind of inspiration, a springboard to whatever fiction you preferred. Of course David did not know how to construct stories yet. A story had to have a shape. His favorite teacher, last year's old Miss Bodkins, said great stories were about moments in people's lives when they saw everything clearly, if only for an instant, and so everything changed. Real life, for a boy, was a tedious unraveling, the rolling out of a ball of string. If David could have such a moment of apprehension as Miss Bodkins described, if he could see, if only for a moment, where he was headed, how his young life had meaning, he felt he could seize it—the meaning, the life. Miss Bodkins suggested books for him to read. She smiled when he said how he loved the passion of A. J. Cronin and Erich Maria Remarque, the largeness of their visions. She said all the great questions had been explored, the great characters had been written, that life now was smaller, and his generation would have to learn to write new stories. She said the atomic bomb had made them all insignificant. She said most people would pass their lives without a moment's serious reflection, but David could be a writer if he wanted. He had language, ambition, and something she called his "fine sensibility." Still, he did not ask Miss Bodkins how to make stories out of his family's life. He would have been humiliated to discuss it. Miss Bodkins urged him to write stories about teen-agers. She said there was a lot of drama in kids' lives. "I've learned that if I've learned anything, teaching all these years. Teen-agers live on the edge of a knife." Miss Bodkins found him in the library during her free period, and had these talks with him. She sat across from him at a table with her hands flat on the surface in front of her. The skin around her knuckles was loose and he wanted to tug at it, to see it come away from the frail mass of her hand. She spoke matter-of-factly, even when she said dramatic things. "You wonder why they do it," she said, pointing at the newspaper, where it told that someone had committed a terrible crime. She was an old maid, with tight pin-curled hair. She wore the same two suits over and over again. He wondered what she would write about if she tried. He thought she probably had tried, and failed, and so she would spend forty years teaching dolts the difference between assonance and alliteration, and the meaning of Ozymandias.

In Fort Stockton, David got the idea for his first real story. There was a girl there. A woman, Teresa. She was twenty years old. Her parents had been killed when their car was struck by a freight train the winter before, while she was a student at the college in Alpine. She had come to stay with her mother's parents until she felt like going on. They owned the pharmacy, the laundry, and the beauty parlor.

David had met Teresa in late June, when he took his laundry in one day. Shorts, socks, shirts.

"Sibilant laundry," she said when he came back to pick them up. She was pretty, with straight dark hair pulled back in a plain pony tail, dark eyes, a slim body—a type he admired. But she was older, and he thought she probably saw him as a kid.

He laughed and said, "Now clean, thank you very much." He felt wonderfully sophisticated with his repartee, but when he saw her again, he felt oafish. He was afraid they had exhausted their wit with one another.

A few weeks later she came to the shop while he was folding shirts. She pushed some cloth back on one of the tables and hopped up to sit there. "My grandfather says your father is Jewish," she said.

"My father is a Jew."

"I think I'd like being Jewish, feeling that I go back so far."

"Everybody does that. Goes back. Everybody comes from somewhere."

She peered at him. "I thought you could tell me what it's like."

"What are you asking?"

"Being Jewish! Doesn't it make you different?"

"I don't think about it." This was not altogether true. "I don't think of it as the reason I feel different."

"You do feel different, though?" she persisted.

"Maybe, in some ways. But from what? Different from rich kids? Hah, that's obvious. Different from dumb ones? Let's hope so. I'm not weird. I have friends. I play tennis, I'm on student council." He felt a flush of hostility toward her. He hardly thought of himself as a curiosity! The only thing strange about him was that he read so much. He didn't know other kids who did. His tennis partner Ellis read auto and sports magazines, his buddy Leland read science fiction and the newspaper. Glee read girls' magazines. Saul read Tolstoy, Dostoevsky, Chekhov, the same books over and over. He kept them in the bedroom. Of course he wasn't a kid.

"The only thing different about me is I'm alone," Teresa said. "I suppose I should be glad I'm grown, and there's a little money for me."

"You should be glad, if there's money!" he said quickly, then blushed deeply when he realized it would have come from her dead parents. "Were you away when it happened?" He knew it was a terrible question. There was no right thing to say. He had this crazy thought: I've never said anything serious to a girl.

She stared at him a moment. "I might get married. A rancher's son I know in Alpine. My grandparents think I should. They think I'd cheer up if I had a baby. What do you think?"

He sat down on the cot across from her. From her perch on the table, she looked down on him, grasping the table edge and swinging her legs. She wore a long Crayola-green cotton skirt. He said, "People should marry if they're in love and they want to." He felt silly. She was making fun of him.

"Do you have a girlfriend? You look like you would."

"I guess so."

"Don't you know?"

"I'm not in love with her. I like her."

"You don't date other girls?"

"Not right now. I could, if I wanted to."

"Do you sleep with her?"

He shifted on the cot and stared at the floor between his feet. What the hell, he thought; he would never see her again after this summer. "Yeah, sure," he mumbled. When he lifted his head, she was going out the door.

That was when he had the idea for a story. That was when he really started his notebook.

Three or four buddies are on their way somewhere (where?), and they're coming to a train crossing. The kid driving is always the careful one. It's a joke with his buddies. He studies for tests, he begins assignments the same night he gets them. The other boys razz him. In an instant, he decides to show them, he decides to play chicken with the train. They are all killed.

Teresa's parents' car stalled. Couldn't they have gotten out and run? Did they sit there while her father tried to turn the key? Did they think the train would stop in time?

Were they completely stupid?

He went for weeks without seeing Teresa. He passed her on the street. Her eyes were red, her face drawn. She didn't seem to see him. Well, why wouldn't she cry? She had lost her parents.

He lay on his cot at night and dreamed of making love to her. His father had once warned him: *Never fuck a crying woman, it will obligate you,* but his father could not have foreseen this.

He thought of her with her blouse open. Her bra would be very clean and white. He would be scared. He would whisper, *Why?* and she would answer, *I'm so sad.* Then, gently, he would push her down on the cot. He would kneel and touch her reverently; she had lost her parents. Making love with her would ennoble him, draw him into her grief. It would be wonderful.

He kept thinking about the boys in the pickup, the train wreck. Each of them would have a story. One of the boys just found out his girlfriend is pregnant. He loves her. He doesn't really realize it until that last instant, that tiny part of a second when he knows he can't ever tell her. If he had lived, he would have married her.

He wondered: The girl who was pregnant, when her boyfriend is killed, would she kill herself? Or would she defy her family, keep her baby, remember him always? He didn't think many girls had that kind of grit. They buckled under.

Of course his own sister had eloped, hadn't she? With Big Pete Kelton.

He kept thinking about the pregnant girl. He thought about her when he drove away from the cop and the girl with the rabbit. He thought about her later that night in the beauty parlor. But when he sat down with his notebook, intending to write about her, he wrote instead:

A woman, heavy with grief, goes to a young man, to touch his innocence, to feel young again.

He was very excited. The mind, the unconscious mind, has its own way! *Here* was the story. This woman, she would be much older, of course. In her thirties. It would be her child who had died. And he, the boy, would be innocent. It would be his first time. Not like with Glee, who had teased him and led him along like an animal, then turned simpering, as if it had not been her idea.

In the story, the woman would kill herself. He could not think just how.

He had been eager to see Teresa again in this last week in Fort Stockton, but now he realized that making love to Teresa didn't really matter. Knowing her didn't matter. *She* didn't really matter. It was the idea that counted. So, on Wednesday, when a man in a red pickup truck came for her, and David saw them drive away, he did not feel bad that they had never talked again. He did watch to see if the pickup came back, but he had to go to Iraan for a day, and after that, pack up, and go back to Basin.

He went home on Saturday. In Monahans, he stopped at the A & W and ate a cheeseburger and drank a root beer float. He felt queasy afterwards; it was too hot for so much food.

He drove to the sandhills and pulled over for a while. The dunes stretched across the plains for sixty miles, a gleaming, sugary, shifting whiteness. Some of the dunes were fifty feet high. He had heard his uncle say how hard it was to work the sandy areas, how at the bottom the ground was hard clay, but above, where the sand had not been anchored by grass and mesquite, the dunes resisted man and machine, gave way and closed around intruders. The winds kept a trickle of sand moving on their peaks; some days the sand shifted so fast they said the dunes walked. On the other side of the dunes, the plains stretched out. Once they had been thick with buffalo grass, a sea of flat sameness that the Spanish marked with stakes as they traversed it, afraid they would not find their way back again. Monahans was a finger, a peninsula of the plains. By the time he reached Basin he could, theoretically, look due north and see Canada.

For just a moment, he wondered what it might have been like if he had been the one driving away in the red pickup with Teresa. They would go to Santa Fe, he thought. He had always wanted to go there. There were kids in Basin who went to Ruidosa and Taos, plains kids who knew how to ski, had seen horses race, owned shoes made especially for walking. In Santa Fe, he would find work in an inn. He would work at the front desk, giving people their keys. At night he would write stories, like F. Scott Fitzgerald. One day he would move on.

He laughed aloud and started the car. He was glad nobody had any idea about the notions that flooded his head, what a fool he would seem. He dismissed Teresa. When he left west Texas it would be on his own, he would be in pursuit of something better. He would not go away hanging on a girl's skirt hem. Leaving would not have anything to do with girls at all.

4.

"Your girlies have been calling."

David was startled by his father's voice coming out of the
darkness of the closed-up living room. As he stepped in from
outside, he was blinded for a moment. The house was sti-
fling.

"Your mother talked to one," Saul said. "She left you a note
in the kitchen. Your mother, not the girl." He barked a laugh.
"The other was your little chickadee, wanting to know when
you'd be in town. If you're going to have her on your string,
you need to jerk it now and then, son. You shouldn't leave
her in the dark." He was sprawled in an easy chair, his feet
propped on an ottoman. He was wearing boxer shorts, and a
wet washrag was draped over his scalp. On a rickety side table
he had positioned a small fan so that the air would hit him
directly. He had one hand on his chest, plucking at his thick
hair, and with the other hand he held a brown bottle by the
neck. "I told her you might not come back, you were thinking
of moving to El Paso. She shouldn't count on seeing you, she
should get on with her own life."

"I hope you're joking."

"With her I was joking."

"She's nobody for you to razz, Dad. I told you. She doesn't
understand your sense of humor. And I told her not to call
here."

His father waved David's protest away with his hand. "I
told her she should come and wait in your room if she wants.
She should squat in the alley to catch you the minute you
return. She should pull your mother's weeds, to pass the
time." David's mother grew tomatoes, all harvested or dead
by now, and sunflowers, along the fence, in the alley.

David's chest hurt sharply. He bent forward slightly and
took a deep rattling breath. "Now you're giving me a load of

shit," he managed to say. He pushed air out of his lungs and coughed noisily.

His father snorted in laughter. "So I told her, what do I know, my son comes home from the sticks? All the rest, I lied. I told her, I don't know."

"There's stuff still piled in the car," David said as he walked into the kitchen just beyond the chair where his father sat. He had backed the wagon onto the yellowed lawn so that it wouldn't be so far to haul goods into his father's workroom. His father's shop—with his sewing machine, an ironing board, shelves, and many boxes—was a second-thought addition made by the original owners. To get into it you had to go out of the house and in the door from outside. Nobody ever told what other owners and renters had done out there. David's room was another afterthought. It was, at least, truly attached, entered through what had once been the back door out of the kitchen into the yard. Only a tiny bit of space remained between the alley and the house. The room had been built as a mother-in-law studio. It had had a stove and refrigerator, both tiny and malfunctioning. His mother had had them removed and replaced with a washer and dryer. There was a toilet and shower, cold as ice in the winter. His grandmother had lived in the room until she died a few years ago, in the same bed where he now slept. It had been Saul's idea to give his son the room. He had said, "David will be needing his privacy already." Though this made David happy, it was an awkward moment, Saul pontificating about the dispersal of space in a house his wife had bought while he was away, gone so long she changed his children's names.

David felt that moving into the room was a passage into his young manhood. He didn't care that it had only a portable gas heater. There was the private entrance. The tiny house proper was merely a green-shingled box sliced into four small rooms and a bathroom not much bigger than a closet. Saul and Marge's room was cozily carpeted and painted a deep blue. Marge had decorated the room for herself, while Saul was in New York. David and his sister had shared the second bedroom, he in an upper bunk. After his father's return, in David's early puberty, he had become agonizingly aware of night sounds: his father heaving himself onto his mother, making a sound at the end like a sick man clearing his throat; his sister turning, rearranging her legs under the sheets, sometimes making light clucking sounds or popping her lips like someone blowing a kiss. He had masturbated dozens of times in absolute silence. When Grandma Puckett died, he had thought his parents would move into the larger room and give their blue room to Joyce Ellen. But the prize was his, and the irony was that his sister was gone anyway, and the back bedroom nothing but a storeroom, with his mother's ironing board left standing all the time. Neither of his parents ever slept there, even in the worst of their quarrels, probably afraid that whoever moved would never get back into the double bed.

His mother had scrawled a note to him:

Somebody Kimbro called. Something-Ann, hyphenated. I didn't get it. La-di-da voice. She'll call u Sun. Davy, I cd. use some help tonite.

He glanced at the wall clock by the door. It was smeared with grease and dirt. A little after four. They would be bringing supper up soon. If he was going to help, he ought to go right now. Supper could be an ordeal in a mental ward.

He did not recognize the name of the caller. He did not know any girls besides Glee who would call him.

In his room he saw that his mother had changed his bed. He felt a stab of resentment—his mother did these things as an excuse to snoop—but he was soothed by the thought of lying on clean sheets. She had swept, too, and shaken out his shabby rag rug and laid it again on the linoleum right beside the bed. Piles of laundry were heaped in front of the folding doors that hid the washer and dryer. One of her white uniforms hung droop-shouldered and slack, making him think of her posture at the end of a shift.

He lay flat on his back on the bed and flung his arms out straight from his body. His shoulders ached. His father would yell at him in a minute to unload the car. Saul was probably half-drunk already; he would have started in the minute Marge went out the door at 2:30. At least he was still on beer.

He closed his eyes. He should call Glee. He expected to see her in his mind's eye, the way he always could if he tried. He could always see her tiny wide tits with their rosy nipples. Her belly button made almost no indentation at all in her flat abdomen. That was how she came to him in these musings: a torso with no head. She was an attractive girl, in a peculiar, broad-faced way. Her eyes were spaced too far apart, her face was square, her shoulders wide. She would have made a good-looking boy, though she was feminine enough, for she used makeup expertly, and curled her hair, cut just above her chin line. She aspired to be voted "Most Beautiful" in their class, though they both knew some rich girl would win. The girls with money had beautiful teeth and hair and clothes. He had teased Glee about fussing with her hair, and the wish for adulation had come out accidentally. She had said, "This is how Annette Carlton wears her hair, remember? She was Senior Most Beautiful last year." He had felt painfully sympathetic for her; she had indeed chosen a goal that was appropriate for her while still utterly unlikely. He had told her, "You're a cheerleader, isn't that enough? And you made it because you're pretty, and because you look good out there." Truly it had not been because she was "in"— she was a waitress's daughter—but as a cheerleader she automatically assumed a new and better status. "Don't let it go to your head," he had said, to cut back on his sympathy. He had been made nervous by the moment of fondness; he liked to keep his feelings for her carefully bounded by his mix of gratitude and resentment that she let him make love to her, that she was always there and willing. Of course, she wanted sex from him. It was the least thing she wanted, and the easiest to give. He would not let her name the other things, they all came down to love. "Talk doesn't make love," he told her. He picked his moments. Then he had just been entering her, and she would tell herself he meant *that* was love, though he didn't.

If he thought of her face, he saw her mouth. She looked best smiling, and knew it, and so smiled nearly all the time. He had had U.S. history with her last year—that was where they had first spoken, where he had yielded to what he now knew was her campaign—and at any moment he looked her way, she was smiling. She beamed at Mr. Yarborough, the teacher; she beamed at the blackboard, at her textbook open on her desk, even at test papers. She was very tan. He had learned that even on a cold day of winter, if there was sun, she sat out in her back yard—her house had a little pink brick patio—and turned her face up to catch it. Over the summer she had grown progressively darker until, the last time he saw her, early in August, she looked like someone from India. She kept her toenails scrupulously groomed, and painted them pearl white. Of course he would see her, if he tried. But the face that floated before him was Teresa's. He could see her thin upper lip and the line of her nose. He could see her blouse open, the white brassiere showing. He felt a thick warmth in his chest. His imagination was a hot fist in there.

His door was banged open. "You're not through, sonny boy!" his father growled. He had put on a pair of worn flannel pants. Even in summer Saul wore wool. He did not own jeans or khakis, though he sold plenty of both. David wore jeans because he liked them, and they were what kids wore, but he was conscious that doing so was a small act of defiance.

He opened his eyes and pulled his arms up, bending them at the elbows, pressing down on the bed but not yet getting up. "Mom wants me at the hospital. Do you need the car tonight?"

"All summer I walk. Now the car is mine again."

"You'll have to take me." David thought how ridiculous his father looked standing there with his hairy chest showing, being stubborn about the car.

"You could walk. Your legs don't work already?" It was over two miles to the hospital. David had walked it lots of times.

"It's supper that's the craziest time," he argued. "If I'm going to help, she needs me now." He pushed himself up and swung off the bed. "I'll unload in the morning." His shirt was soaked under the arms. "Just let me pull on a clean shirt."

"Clean up for the loonies," his father grumbled. He went through the house ahead of David and out to the car, still bare-chested. "Where's the cash box?" he asked when David scooted into the car.

David jerked his hand back and pointed with his thumb to the piles of clothes. "Under the green wash pants."

They didn't speak for the first ten blocks. Saul's arms glistened with perspiration. Finally David said, "I'm sick of summer."

Saul grunted. "Just wait for winter dust," he said, meaning the wild storms when the wind blew dust so hard it was like ground glass, sometimes mixing with rain to splatter mud. His father hacked and wheezed all winter. It was not the dust, or the cold, that brought on David's attacks. His bad moments always came from moments of stress; he was deeply ashamed of his weakness.

"At least we'll get rain then," David said, "if we're lucky. He was happy to have his father talk to him about anything.

"I'll pay you in the morning," his father said at the hospital. "After you unload."

"Sure, Pop." David thought Saul looked foolish, driving half-dressed. "Where am I going tonight?"

The air was perfectly still. He could smell dust. It was hot and bright, the orange brightness of late afternoon. He looked out at the town. Most buildings in Basin were a single story, except the hospital, the high school, a couple of office buildings, and the Alamo Hotel, at eight stories the city's only "skyscraper." Looking into the sun, David saw the city fade and waver like a mirage. In half a moment he saw only sky and light. The sky was vast; it would hold light until ten or later. Once it was dark he always felt the city had sunk even farther away from the sky, making it seem larger. He felt, at certain times, that he lived in the very bottom of a huge bowl, aptly named Basin. Yet the truth was he lived on a high plain, and the basin was below and inside it, the heart of an ancient sea that extended all the way to Kansas. And in that sea, pooled in the rocks that had accumulated over timeless time, was clear and bountiful water, so that, if you got at it, you could live here, where it looked as though nothing could live. And there was oil, which seemed to matter more, so that the people in this city—more than 20,000 of them—could live small lives digging and refining it, and the lucky few whose oil it was could live in the next city over, which was neater and prettier, or in Dallas, which was a real city, or if in Basin, then in a part of town that was an oasis of trees and grass and elegant houses, some of them surrounded by stone walls.

He shook his head to clear it. If he thought about it—and "it" was nothing more than luck, fate, to be born what you were born—he would grow bitter, like his father, or stoic, like his mother. He would become crazy, like the old geezers he was going to see right now. It was not right to seethe; anger dragged you down. It was only right to hope, and strive, and escape. He had not lost yet, he was not defeated; he had not entered the battle.

His father knew he would, and knew he might win—something—what?—*something better than this.* Saul needled him ceaselessly. What if it was not meanness or jealousy? (Sometimes David longed to say, Can't you get it up anymore, old man?) What if it was exactly what Saul had to give: permission to try for more than either of his parents would ever have? What if his father was driving him away, so that he could go?

Or did his father like it when he lost? Saul laughed at him in the spring when he came back empty-handed from the tennis tournament. He tapped David's head and said, "If this gets too big—" and he hit his ass—"or this—" and he laughed again—"you can't keep this—" and he mimed a back stroke—"you can't keep this going where the goddamned ball is!"

Like father like son. Was that Saul's ambition for him? David had spent many hours sitting in his father's little shop, doing homework while Saul hummed, altering some rich man's trousers. Would a son who repeated his father's sorry life validate it?

"Not me, sport!" David said aloud to no one, shaking his fist in the direction his father had driven. The shrill squeal of an arriving ambulance brought him back to himself, standing in the side entrance of the hospital. Does anybody think like me? he wondered. He knew other boys had dreams, of course they did. Leland Piper wanted to go to Rice and become a scientist. Ellis wanted to play professional tennis. He heard a kid once in the hall at school say that he could die happy if he ever owned an eighteen-wheeler. Sure kids dreamed, but did the longing feel like something searing their souls? Was it bigger than anything?

5.

As he pushed the buzzer at Ward 2-West, the supper cart rattled up behind him. He said hello. The pudgy woman pushing it nodded curtly. He hoped it was not the food making her look so grimly determined. A strong, steamy, unidentifiable smell wafted out from the cart. "Can I help?" he asked, as the door opened. She shoved the cart past him without answering.

It was Nurse Benke who let him in. "It's you," she said. Benke always seemed befuddled to David, which at first had surprised him. In time he had come to expect personnel on the mental ward to have their own eccentricities. His own mother often looked sour, but could be very kind. Sometimes hysterical at home, sometimes morose, she never lost control at work. And she was tough; even a small person could be difficult to manage on the ward.

She was on the phone behind the desk. She wore a name tag on her left breast pocket, PUCKETT. He went into the day room. There were a lot of patients on the ward today. Pajama-clad men huddled at a big round table, awaiting their supper. The food server gave them their trays without speaking and then, consulting a list, set more trays in front of empty chairs around both tables. Other patients shuffled into place. A woman lay sprawled on the vinyl couch over by the television, which was off. She was talking to herself, twisting her head this way and that, and kneading her knuckles. Another woman patient went over to her. "You come eat," she said loudly, and led the way back to the table. As they sat down, David heard an elderly man say his wife had cooked the supper. A tall fellow with a long bony face was working his way down the corridor, touching one wall with the palms of his hands, then turning and going to the opposite side. He was standing behind a chair, holding onto the back of it, when two women came on the ward. The older woman looked uneasy. Her eyes darted from patient to patient. The younger woman called, "Daddy!" and ran and hugged the man. He pulled the chair out and sat down without reply. David went to the desk.

Marge came out from her place and gave him a quick hug. "I came on shift, and only four patients had dressed today. I don't know what the day nurses thought they were doing. There was no afternoon therapy group. I've got a 180-pound woman in lock-up. She's worn out but we'll be hearing from her. And my orderly's hung over." It helped, if the load was heavy, to have David come in for part of the evening shift, and Marge had an understanding with the hospital that she could use him so many hours a month. Sometimes she came home with bruised shins and scratches on her face and arms. She liked to talk with David about the patients. She thought he had a knack with them. They could tell he was interested in them; he might be the only person they knew who was. David had said, "It's more fun than church," which made his mother smile. Her sister was hardshell Baptist, but Marge had quit religion after her mother died.

Benke rolled a woman by in a wheelchair and pushed her up to the table, then turned and trudged back down the hall. The woman laid her face on the table. Marge gently pulled her by the shoulders back to a sitting position.

"Go get the girl in seven," she said. "Take a wheelchair."

David was surprised to hear his mother refer to someone as a girl. He hurried to find out who she was. She was sitting on the edge of her bed, staring at her lap, her head ducked so that he couldn't see her face. She was a little thing, with light fine hair and wrists like sticks. He asked her if she was hungry. He said, "I didn't see what supper was, but the carts are here. I'll sit with you while you eat, if you want."

She looked up. She really was just a girl, maybe only fourteen or fifteen. It took him an instant to register the familiarity of her face. Of course! She was the girl on the highway, the girl with the rabbit. Without the blood, the rabbit, the dirty hair, she was nothing but a waif, someone you would never notice. He thought he had seen her at school, too, though in a bleached blue hospital gown and scuffs, he could not tell much about what she really looked like. She had a little sunburn across her nose and cheeks. He held his arms out and helped her into the chair. "My name is David," he said cheerfully. He had often thought that you could get along with disturbed patients by treating them a lot like you did teachers, with hearty good spirits, a false but well-meaning respectfulness. You had to make them think they were okay, no matter how much they were not. The ones who saw things, though, the ones who thought you might do them great harm, were different. They were not in the hospital very long; they had to be moved along the system.

She began to scrub her arm vigorously. She held it out in front of her and ran her other hand up and down the length of it. By the time they were near the day room she was making squeaky sounds as she rubbed.

Marge hurried over and knelt by the chair. "Sissy, dear, I want you to eat your supper. We're having macaroni and cheese, everybody likes that." She stood up. "If you don't eat, I'm going to have to do something." David looked at the girl again. Sissy. He thought being forced to eat must be one of the worst indignities a patient could suffer, and he resolved to keep it from happening to her. Her arms were relaxed now, but the one she had been rubbing was a bright chafed red. He thought again how mild and unremarkable she was. She was the kind of girl who grew up and became a clerk at Woolworth's, a girl you would never consider had a complicated or errant mind.

He pulled a chair up for himself and set it alongside hers, then went to get both of them a Coca-Cola from the refrigerator behind his mother. The woman from the couch, now at the table, pointed a long finger at the Coca-Colas and screeched, "Mine!" David ignored her and she screamed again. Benke pulled her arm back and spoke sharply. "Your dinner is right in front of you, Wanda June. You pay attention to your own dinner and you can have pop later on." Benke gave David a dirty look.

The girl ate. It was a slow business, but she ate some of the macaroni and a few bites of carrots. She drank the Coke. While she ate, David talked quietly, telling her about his drive into Basin today from the west. "I couldn't believe how hot I got. I hope this heat breaks. Think how it'll feel, sitting at a desk all day. Though I'm glad school is starting. It's my last year, and I want to get on with it." He touched her arm where it was red. "I bet you burn if you stay out long. You have really fair skin."

Sissy put her spoon down in the applesauce, turned her head slightly to look at him, and smiled. Big tears were oozing out of her eyes and sliding down her cheeks. He cleared away her tray and asked her if she would like to play cards. She watched but didn't say anything. "Do you know how to play gin rummy?" he asked. She shook her head no. He felt relieved; there was something he could do. He moved her away from the clot of patients in the middle of the day room, some of whom were beginning to quarrel about where to sit, or about dessert, or what television show to watch. There was a side table where he laid out the cards and began explaining to Sissy how the game worked.

She hugged herself. "I can't."

"Oh sure," he said. "Anybody can learn to play this." He gathered up the cards and made a big show of shuffling them.

"Can't go," she said, a little louder.

"Go where?"

"There."

"I hope you won't have to then," he said, and dealt the cards. For the next half hour he played both their hands, talking all the time. She watched. The patients calmed down. A few visitors came and went.

Marge came and said, "I've got your meds, Sissy." Sissy didn't look back as Marge pushed her down the hall. David found some checkers and a board and looked around. One old man looked at him hopefully, and David found a place where they could play. The old man was very happy to play checkers, and very attentive. He told David that his father had died while playing a game in a checkers tournament in Lawton, Oklahoma, forty years ago. "Died happy," he said. David wondered whose idea it was for him to be on this ward. He didn't seem any more out of it than most people. David could not help wondering about his own father at sixty or seventy. Now Saul played checkers and chess with his barber and a clerk from the men's store where he did alterations. At least once a week he played pinochle with the junk dealer, Chasen. Sometimes the four of them got together for poker. Who would play with Saul when he went off the deep end?

He did not plan to be around to see it, but it was painful to consider. It seemed inevitable. He was afraid for his parents. They did not eat well, or sleep well, and they did not take care of one another.

At ten his mother called him to her desk to drink a cup of tea. "The highway patrol picked her up. Sissy. She was bloody, carrying a dead rabbit." She lit a cigarette and inhaled deeply.

"That must have been a sight." He thought this was going to sound a little fantastic. He wondered about the cop in the fancy sunglasses, how he had handled the girl after David drove on. Had he put her in the back, behind the mesh barrier, like some old drunk? Had he tried to be gentle? He wished he had not abandoned the scene so readily. He could imagine himself in the patrol car with her, comforting her, soothing her, on the ride into Basin. What had he been afraid of? Maybe of the cop, the cop's car. It was one thing to imagine his arm around the girl—and she had been skittish as a rabbit, herself, hardly asking for solicitude in that moment of encounter in the brush—and quite another to imagine himself locked up like something in a can. Anyway, he had forgotten her. He had been so wrapped up in his little Fort Stockton fantasies, he had forgotten. Christ.

"Mom, I was going to tell you about it. I found her out there. On my way out of town. She was careening all over the landscape with that damned rabbit. She was scared of me, and I didn't want to grab her like some crook, I went and got a cop, and went on to Fort Stockton." He felt sheepish, ineffectual. He felt like a reporter who had missed a scoop.

"Wonders never cease. You know, she was rigid as a board, eyes off to wonderland, when they hauled her in here." Marge regarded her son through eyes half-closed to slits. David thought he saw contempt at the corners of her mouth. What did she expect! He wasn't the nut-nurse in the family! "She'll probably be here into the week, until she feels stronger. She's actually a lot better today. I was beginning to wonder. We staffed on her, talked about shipping her off to Wichita Falls. I'm glad we gave it a little more time. Kids are tough, in their own way." She stubbed out her cigarette. "Something happened out there. She'll be okay, though. She's lucid. Come up and see her."

"Okay."

"Coming up here—it brings out the good part of you, son."

"Gosh, I hope this isn't what it takes." He was relieved to hear his mother's warmer tone return. He felt like a real horse's ass, but he could make up for it. He would visit Sissy. He would give her some of his TLC. Wasn't that what all girls wanted, attention? Why wouldn't it help one that had had her toe in deep water for a while? Give him small enough company, and he was a big shot, just like Saul was always saying.

His mother was looking at him curiously. Sometimes he thought that she could read his mind—maybe not the words, the actual thoughts, but the caliber of his thinking. She could see his self-centeredness. The way he looked at it, though, he had to be concerned about himself. Nobody else had the same stake in him. Everybody has a streak of crap in them, he thought. Either you hide it, or you find a way to use it.

"Her father had taken her out shooting. He says she got away from him." Marge put her hands at the top of her forehead and pulled her skin back and up, easing the depth of her wrinkles, giving her the look of someone in a bathing cap. She let go, and her face crumpled back into place. She looked tired.

"Sounds like something you'd say about a dog. Maybe he's the one who's nuts."

"May *be*. The county is going to put her in a foster home. I suspect there's a story there."

"Mom, I saw your note about the call."

"I wrote down what the girl told me. Should I have asked her to spell her name? She was so—not exactly snotty, but— *distant*?"

"I don't know who it could be."

"She'll call you back. Kimber—"

"Kimbrough!"

"Yes, that's it."

"Kimbrough's the name of the fellow who had Ellis and me out to play tennis last May, remember? At the country club?"

The phone rang and then the woman in lock-up began beating on the door. Marge was busy until they left. David stretched out on the couch in the day room and watched the television with the sound low, until the news was over and Benke turned it off. The man with the long face wandered down and sat in a chair near David. "Sombitches took it all," he said sadly.

David said, "I'm sure sorry to hear that, sir," and closed his eyes. Right away now he could see Glee, naked and sweet, just the way she would be with him as soon as he felt like himself again.

6.

David took a quick shower and went to find something to eat. His parents had already settled in at the kitchen table. Saul, now wearing a garish Hawaiian print shirt, had started on a bottle of gin. Marge, in a rayon wrap, had her bourbon. Her robe was an old one, bright green and blue, with snakes crawling up the trim, their heads caught in the facing and turned in on her breasts. She wore it unbelted, and her bra and half-slip showed.

David asked what food there was.

Marge shrugged and reached up to loosen her bra straps. Her large breasts slid down like filled balloons. David opened the refrigerator to inspect the contents. A chicken had been stripped of the meat. There were eggs, a plate of soggy sliced tomatoes, jars of chow-chow, olives, and pepperoncinis. He slammed the door shut. "What do you eat!"

His mother said, "There's stuff in the cupboard." She drained her glass and made a face. "Get me some ice, Davy." She poured an inch of whiskey into the glass.

The ice tray was thoroughly stuck in the tiny freezer compartment, which looked like an ice cave. It had been his sister's responsibility to defrost it, and it probably had not been done since she left last New Year's Eve, never to return. He used a table knife to hack away at the tray. He made a lot of noise.

"Ice we can do without!" his father said.

"You do without ice, I want it," his mother said.

"I got it, I got it, jeez." David ran water over the tray, plunked a couple of cubes in his mother's glass, put the rest in a bowl in the refrigerator, and refilled the tray. He knelt to inspect the canned goods. He chose a can of bean with bacon soup and held it up for inspection. "Anybody?"

Saul said, "I'll have a cup of that." David scraped the soup into a pan, added water, set it to heat, and turned on the iron skillet. He spread a piece of bread with bacon grease from the crock on the stove. His mother had bacon almost every morning. He put the greased bread down on the skillet to fry.

"Piece of this, too?" he asked his father.

"You should live so long, to see me eat pig grease."

"There's bacon in the soup."

Saul flipped his hand. "And you need a microscope to find it."

David gave his father soup in a cup, and ate the rest from the pan. He set it in the sink to soak. The phone rang. "I'll get it," he said, but his father had already stepped the few feet it took to reach the phone. He held it out away from him and pointed to it. "Your girlfriend, so late."

David went into his room and picked up the phone. "You can hang up now," he said.

"Davy, weren't you going to call me?" It was Glee.

He could hear his father breathing. "So *hang up,*" he said again, and Saul did. David sat down. "Don't start that."

"I knew you were home. I drove by a little after five and there was the car. I went home in case you called. Then I figured you must a gone to the hospital. But now it's mid-night—"

"I know what time it is. Don't your folks mind you blabbing on the phone in the middle of the night?"

"That's what I called to tell you. They're not here. They went to Greg's sister's for the weekend. Big Spring. You could come over."

"I'm too tired. Too much driving today."

"Davy—" she whined.

He felt as if she had run her manicured fingernail down his spine. "I'm too tired," he said, more softly.

"I can come over there."

"My folks—"

"When they go to bed."

He did not want to try to explain. "They'll be up a while."

"I have things to tell you." She spoke so breathily he could hardly hear her.

"Tell me."

"In person, Davy."

"*David.*"

"You're in a bad mood!"

"I told you, I'm tired."

"Sorry." She did sound contrite. "I haven't seen you since August 12, 11:20 PM. I missed you."

"Tomorrow, okay? I'll call you tomorrow. I promise." He hung up and lay back heavily.

It wasn't long until he heard scratching at his door. He wondered for a moment if it would be possible to lift his head. He felt anger flash through him; of course it was her. Then he had an instant to think of her, before he opened the door.

"I had to," she said. She was wearing white. Her blouse had puffed sleeves, a scooped neck, and elastic under her breasts. Sometimes she wore old clothes of her mother's from the forties. Her shorts were pleated and full and a little yellowed with age. She looked like a starlet from an old movie. She smelled of vanilla. "Don't be mad," she whispered. Her bare midriff was smooth and brown. Her light brown hair was streaked almost white, by sun, or peroxide, or a combination of both.

He put his arms around her and moaned as she moved her body against the length of his. Suddenly he wanted to touch her everywhere. He did not know why he fought this so much. She was sleek as some fine animal. How could she be so hard and lean, and yet so soft?

She was trying to pull up the sheet. He laughed at her. "It's not exactly cold in here." They were both shiny with sweat.

"What if they come in?"

He laughed again. "You don't have to worry. They don't come in here. They're busy."

She looked perplexed at his sardonic tone. He made a motion, *chug-a-lug*. Her expression shifted to one of sad concern. "Forget it!" he said sharply. "It's none of your business." He moved his leg so she could cover up.

They lay side by side. He thought, she's not going to put me down on account of my parents. She has her own history.

He laid his hand on her thigh.

It had been a great relief to connect with Glee, whose mother had been a waitress in the cocktail lounge at the Alamo Hotel for years, until she recently married an accountant and got pregnant again. Glee didn't know who her own father was. If anyone asked, she said he died in the

Pacific. After she had been with David all winter, she told him she thought it was more likely her father was one of those cowboys you see going in the roadhouses in the early evenings, wearing filthy boots and cheap shirts. David, in a rush of pity, said, "He must have been good looking, though, look at you."

"Stu and Angie, Buddy and Ray-Jean—"

"What?" He was half-asleep.

"They're all going."

"Going where?"

She raised up on her elbow and glared at him with mock disappointment. "Now you've got what you wanted, you don't even listen to me." She grinned at him. He could not believe she was so confident. You always heard that girls were afraid you would dump them after you screwed them, but Glee obviously saw it exactly opposite; once you slept with her, you could not get away. There was something to it. He had necked with a few girls, but nothing very serious, before Glee. Maybe he did owe her, and he would not want to hurt her, but he knew he could not give her what she wanted most, some kind of pledge.

Leland Piper had told him, Guys like me kill guys like you. David objected. He was lucky. He had met a girl who wasn't hung up. Oh yeah, Leland said. Girls meet me, they become virgins again. I know just how they used to become martyrs in the old days. They simpered and turned away and said, you'll have to kill me first.

David ran his finger along the bare slight rise of her breasts. "I need sleep, that's all, Glee."

"They're going to go out to Red Bluff Monday to water ski. Stu's got his daddy's boat. I said we'd go. I mean, I said I thought we would, if you were back. Can we?"

His scalp prickled. He could not stand for her to assume things, to make plans for them. But he had been gone. Be fair, he told himself. She always did what he wanted to do. "I guess so, sure," he said. "Maybe." He closed his eyes again.

"Shirlee Ames left town yesterday. Carl Stuckey ought to have something to say about that!" she said primly. He opened his eyes and watched her smooth the sheet over her chest. He wished she would go home. He was having a difficult time staying awake. He felt wary. He would like it if she would shut up, turn around, and tuck her firm brown body into the curve of his.

"She is going to a home in Sweetwater run by Church of God. To have it."

He rubbed his eyes. "Glee!"

She grew more excited. "She's pregnant, dumbie, and Carl wouldn't marry her."

"Of course he wouldn't marry her!" Carl Stuckey was the son of Avis Stuckey, *Incorporated*. His parents had half a million dollars if they had a dime. And Shirlee Ames did not.

"Maybe Lu Anne can take her place cheerleading. She was a close runner-up last year." Glee was delighted to have his full attention at last. She let the sheet slip down off her nipples.

"Glee," he said, all he could think to say.

"He was using her."

He knew she was fishing. What could she possibly expect from him? "Glee, you aren't going to get pregnant. I'm seeing to that, in case you didn't notice."

She clicked her teeth together. "Well, shut my mouth!"

"You're not going to get pregnant, and I'm not going to marry you."

"I never!"

"Come here." He made a space for her in his arms. "I've got to go to sleep." She nestled close, mewed. "I love you, Davy Puckett, you ole mean thing." He was too tired to scold her.

His mother stumbled into his room early the next morning. He woke to see her stuffing clothes in the washing machine. She poured in a cup of powder and started the cycle. "Mom," he said, before he could think.

She turned around in a kind of pirouette. She was still half-drunk, wild-eyed, her hair a mess. She had taken off her brassiere and tied the robe. Her breasts bounced under the clinging cloth as she turned. She seemed to be dripping dirty clothes, pants hanging off her arm. "I forgot you were here," she said. She saw Glee and fixed her eyes on the girl's buttocks. She looked back at her son. "You piece of shit," she said. The wash cycle kicked in and made a clatter, then a roar.

Glee rolled over, saw Marge, and shrieked. She jumped up and ran to the bathroom.

Marge was still by the washing machine.

"Jesus, Mother, you KNOW not to come in my room. I've told you a thousand times, I want PRIVACY!"

She shook her head. "Piece of shit."

He got out of bed, pulling the sheet around him, dragging it on the floor as he crossed to her. "Go to bed now, Ma, really, you're dead on your feet. Go to bed. I'll make coffee. I'll go to the store and come home and make breakfast. I'll run the vacuum and do my own laundry. You'll see. Just go and get some sleep."

She left.

Glee peeked around the door of the bathroom, her eyes slyly narrowed, as though she might not be seen if she could not see. "She gone?"

"Go home," David said wearily. "God, this hour of the *frigging* morning."

Glee stepped out into the room and erupted into giggles.

"Why are you laughing?"

She put her hand up to her mouth. "I never got caught before. It's embarrassing." She looked, thought David, quite pleased with herself. Who would she tell about this? She was one of those girls everybody liked. Before David, she went with (slept with) Tyler Johnson, who graduated and went away to Texas A&M, and in no time she looked around and landed on David, and nobody talked about her, nobody said nasty things, like they did about a lot of other girls. "You hear?" he said. "Go home. *I* will call *you*."

"Oh Davy," she whimpered. She touched his chest lightly. "I loved sleeping by you. You know you're not mad." She saw the look on his face and scurried to get dressed. He sat on the side of his bed. She buttoned her shorts and said, "Your mother was so—so sleepy—maybe she won't remember, huh? See you later? Maybe this afternoon?"

He looked up and shook his head yes, to make her leave.

"I'm sorry if I got you in trouble."

"Don't be silly."

He stood under the shower until the water cooled, then gave himself a blast of cold. He had just stepped out of the bathroom, a towel around his waist, when Saul burst into his room.

"You asshole! You don't do that to your MOTHER!"

"Aw, Dad, it's not so big—"

"FIRST YOUR SISTER ELOPES WITH A FUCKING BIG MOUTH DISC JOCKEY AND NOW YOU BRING YOUR SLUT INTO THIS HOUSE. YOUR HOT LITTLE KURVA."

"Calm down. She's not a slut."

Saul stepped up to his son and punched him in the chest with his fist. David was so surprised, and it hurt so much, he staggered, his hands to his chest.

"You don't bring your whores into this house. You don't do that to your mother."

David gasped and sucked as hard as he could for breath. When his chest felt like this, there was always a moment when he fought terror.

"And don't play that asthma shit!" Saul cried. He leaned toward his son and took a long noisy breath. He banged his own chest with both fists. "You don't tell ME about asthma, you little prick."

"Who's mad about what here, Dad?" David asked coldly. "Who wishes what about pretty little Glee?"

His father glared at him and held his fist belly high.

"You don't touch me again. Ever." David kicked the towel that had dropped to the floor and walked over to his dresser. Without turning around, he dressed deliberately, as if for an occasion. He heard Saul leave the room. He went to the Stockman Cafe and ate three eggs, ham, hashbrowns, and a cinnamon roll. Then he drove to Ellis' house to see if he could play tennis.

7.

David had played tennis all that summer with his doubles partner, Ellis Whittey, anytime they could juggle their obligations, but those times had been fewer this summer than in years before. Ellis was working with his dad, as a roustabout; there were seven Whitteys, and they needed his income. David had been gone more than half of each month, selling his father's goods in church halls and basements, in parking lots, and in the old beauty parlor in Fort Stockton. Tennis was an oasis in a sea of tedium for both of them.

David liked to play hard in the terrible heat—the concrete courts were fiery slabs, scarred with cracks and pits and buckles—and then sit under an elm tree and swig liquids, whatever they would have brought: water out of the tennis ball cans, jugs of tea from home, warmed in the heat, a purloined beer if he could manage it. He could feel quite content with Ellis, their skinny legs stretched out on the bristly grass; there was nothing David had to be, or say, with him. Their friendship went back to seventh grade, both of them new in McCamey School, a little lost. Ellis had had a thick East Texas drawl; he was a dirt-poor kid, friendly and pleasant. They were too small for football; it was David's idea to play tennis. He had been whacking balls against backboards for a year or so, virtually alone. He was thin and gawky, and crazy to see his father who had written to say he was coming back. He thought, Wait till he sees this, slamming each ball with all his strength. David took Ellis to the public court, and in no time at all, when he sent a ball across the wire net, it came back. Ellis was a natural, he loved it instantly. They played the game like a giant ping pong match that lasted two years. Tennis was a wonderful secret, a two-man club they had from then until high school, where the coach was shocked by the level of skill they displayed (along with a total lack of strategy). Now they were older, taller, accomplished. They talked about taking the state title this year, which meant they had to beat Dallas and Houston teams who played real tournaments and practiced on courts at country clubs or in their own back yards. A big win would mean scholarships. David would be able to go away, instead of staying at the junior college as his parents expected him to do. Winning would mean a moment of glory. Tennis was not in the same class as football and basketball, but a win is a win. On his own, David beat balls against the backboard at the high school. At night he ran through the streets, panting and reliving his last lousy shot in the spring state doubles semifinals. He could still see the smirk on that Spring Branch player's face when the ball hit the ground, not three inches off the line, on the wrong side.

David pulled up in the dusty front yard. The Whitteys lived at the place where the town paving stopped. The street asphalt ceased fifty yards before their driveway. The house seemed so small, it was always hard to believe how many people lived there. Now children were trooping out of the porch, moving toward the Whittey station wagon that was older even than Saul's. Ellis and David had made jokes about their family cars, how the junkman Chasen would be the last owner.

There were four kids younger than Ellis, and his mother was pregnant again. Catholics.

"Hey man," Ellis said, bringing up the rear like a sheepherder. They socked one another on the shoulders. Ellis' father would be asleep in the house. Ellis and his father did not go to the wells on Sunday. Mrs. Whittey would have a Catholic fit. But Tom Whittey slept through Mass. Ellis said he heard his father tell his mother any God who paid attention would understand a roustabout staying in bed.

Ellis was dressed in a starched and ironed white shirt and stiff twill pants. He had a fresh haircut, and a line of white skin showed between the edge of his mowed hair and his dark oilfield tan.

"When you're done, we'll go smack a few, huh?" asked David.

Ellis looked up at the glaring sun, shading his eyes with one hand. The family was going to 9:30 Mass. "It'll be eleven before we get home. It must be ninety now. You want to die on the court?"

His family was in the wagon, kids piled on top of one another in the back, Mrs. Whittey sitting primly in the front, waiting for Ellis to drive. She fussed with her hat, an old yellow straw with a wide green ribbon.

David slammed his fist into his other palm. "I need to play," he said intensely. "We need to practice."

Ellis slapped his partner's arm. "We've got months to get back in training, old buddy. It's August, man. Listen, I'll meet you at the college courts at seven, how's that? We'll play till it's dark if you want. But it's too hot now, Puckett. It's too darned hot." He was the color of leather. Under his bright white shirtsleeves, David knew, his arms were knotty with hard muscle. He liked to say, Working is good for something besides money.

David drove slowly through town. He followed the route they drove when they "did the strip" on Friday and Saturday nights, up the main drag past the junior college, through the Dairy Queen, up to Dewey's Drive-In, around back of the playing fields. Nobody was out, of course. The world was at church.

At home his father was shaved and dressed and frantic to get the car. "How's it going to look, I have to walk to my poker game?" he asked. His pals liked to play while the women went to church. Marge went to Monahans to see her sister Cheryl on frequent Sundays. On Mondays she visited her daughter.

David could see that Saul wanted to snarl at him. His father clenched his fists, holding his arms out away from his body half a foot, but he only gave David a dirty look, and stormed out of the house. He backed out so fast the tires squealed.

"You could go with me, Davy," Marge said, coming out of the bedroom. "You could do the driving," she said, as though it were a long way and not just thirty miles. "Cheryl's so disappointed that you never stop, all these trips right by Monahans." She had done her hair. It was naturally curly, and sprang out when it was washed. She wore a little lipstick, and had dressed in a light green dress with pale red strawberries all over it. The dress had large buttons from the neck right to the hem of the skirt. She wore a bright red patent belt. With her figure so well-defined, David had a sudden vision of her twenty years ago. She must have been a knockout. "Their house is nice and cool," she pointed out. Aunt Cheryl had central air conditioning, instead of fans and window coolers like they made do with here. Being cool was not enough to bribe David into his aunt's house. The thought of her shrill nosy questions and her hysterical religious pronouncements was like the memory of fingernails down a chalkboard. And his pukey cousin Leona, sixteen and stolid as a fence post, was worse.

"I'm going to sleep," he said rudely.

"Davy—"

He could guess what was coming. He shifted his weight from foot to foot. He told himself other parents paid a lot more attention to what their kids did; other parents lectured all the time. Leland said his father had to give him a daily dose of advice, like a vitamin. Leland liked Saul, and was the only friend David had who came and went in the house comfortably. Behind his back, Saul referred to him as "Pecker Piper," thinking he was very funny to think of it. He had no way to know how much sex was on Leland's mind, how he was always wanting to talk about it.

"I don't have anything to say about what you do away from the house," his mother began. "But that girl, in my house—"

"Don't start in on it. I'm sorry you came in, sorry she was there for you to see. She's just a girl, though, a nice kid. She's not something awful, and neither am I. And you're no holy-roller. You know what goes on in the world."

"The damage is done," his mother said flatly.

"Shit." David walked past her into the kitchen.

She followed. "Assume I'm the last to know what you've been doing with her. Or maybe her own mother is. Other kids must know."

"What's it to you?" He swung around to confront her. "What do you know about teen-agers, anyway? What have you learned, with two in the house?"

"I know girls suffer when they get talked about."

"So don't tell anyone."

"She loves you? That's it, is it? She loves you, so she'll do whatever you want?"

"It was her idea! Crimeny, Mother, what do you think I am? Your Son the Girl-Eater? *She* started it! She's the one who started *me*. Get it?"

She was hurt. It wasn't Glee she cared about. She was thinking about Joyce Ellen, who had not been in this house, had not laid eyes on her father, since she eloped with "Big Pete" Kelton, local DJ and all around jerk. Saul had called her a tramp, she insisted they had not "done it", that they were in love and wanted to get married. Marge bawled. What a scene.

Kelton had never met Saul.

"Maybe Joyce Ellen can go with you," he suggested.

Marge shook her head. "If Pete's home, she has to be home too."

"So? What did she get married for if not?"

"What do you know!" His mother looked like she'd like to spit at him. Instead, she stormed out of the house, too.

Alone, David felt he could breathe for the first time that day. He switched on the cooler in the window above his bed. He smoothed out his bed and lay down with his notebook. He thought he would write about the woman who seduced the young man. He needed a name for her. The story was not about Teresa, and he needed a name, to break the connection.

He doodled with rows of warm-ups—ovals and slashes, from his Palmer practice days—and began listing possibilities. Carolyn. Paula. Susan. Virginia. He liked the nickname, Ginny, but it was too young for his character, who would be matronly. Rosemary, that would be good.

I can name some other character Ginny later, he thought. It sent a delicious chill down his neck. He imagined a stack of books in a bookstore with his picture on the back, and his name on the spine. David Puckett. David Stolboff. That sounded good for a writer. What would his father think then?

The phone rang.

"David Puckett, that you?"

"Yes. Who's this?"

"Hayden Kimbrough here. I'm glad I caught you."

"Yes, *sir,*" David said.

"You've been out of town, I hear." Kimbrough made it sound like David had been on vacation.

"On business for my father."

"I called to issue a little invitation. It's late, I know, but it can't hurt to try."

"What is it, Mr. Kimbrough?" David asked in a steady voice. The perspiration on his face felt icy in the gush of air from the window unit. He brushed his hair with the flat of his hand. "What can I do for you, sir?"

8.

The last time Hayden Kimbrough called it was early May, and David and Ellis had just won the regional school championship. They had won the West Texas Relays in March, exulting in their home court advantage on the concrete, playing in high gritty wind. They had won the Southwest Invitational in El Paso, too, although none of the Dallas or Houston schools sent teams, diluting the sense of victory over lesser districts. Basin was barely big enough to fit the AAAA category, with few of the advantages of the bigger schools. The team had bought new rackets with money cadged in parking lot car washes. The city had always poured money and enthusiasm into the football teams, which had a wildly fluctuating record, and had ignored everything else except basketball, but this was the first time anybody from Basin High had performed significantly in tennis apart from the Relays. The paper splashed the boys' photograph across the sports page: WHITTEY-PUCKETT TEAM SWATS LUBBOCK OUT OF REGIONAL TITLE SLOT. At school, guys said, Good going, Puckett. Hang Houston. Girls smiled and said, Great going, y'all.

It felt good to win. This year, it was more important. If David and Elis could win state, there would be scholarships. Every time he drove by Basin Junior College, he gulped to think of two years there. Two years nowhere.

David and Ellis had gone out to the country club to play with a group of Kimbrough's friends. Kimbrough said he was trying to build sponsorship for a county meet at the club; too late for '58, but he thought '59 was possible. "Let's show you off to the fellas," he told the boys. So they played exhibition sets with Kimbrough and the tennis pro, moving fast to win each one, quicker and more aggressive and more alive than the older men. And of course David and Ellis were a real team, moving like one organism that spring, and, that day, richly confident. They won the match 6–2, 6–4, and Kimbrough split them up to play other combinations. Kimbrough and his daughter played his wife and David. It was a surprisingly vigorous, enjoyable game. The women were evenly matched, and Kimbrough had improved through the morning. David, cut off from Ellis, played a less spectacular, more sociable game. He found himself smiling, even humming. Mrs. Kimbrough and Beth Ann wore fetching outfits with short skirts that swirled around their slim hips as they dipped and ran. They were quite tan. Mrs. Kimbrough wore her hair in a short cap-like style, uncurled, with a stretchy band on her forehead. Her hair rose when she leaped, and fell back perfectly in place. It shone like taffeta in the sun. She had the same clean features as her daughter, and she did not look twenty years older, either. Beth Ann wore her hair pulled straight back in a curvy pony tail. David noticed how long her throat was, and how strong her legs. She probably had her own pool, and swam every day.

After they played, there was a nice buffet laid out on a long table in the shade of the portico. The table was banked at each end with bowls of cut flowers. Someone handed the boys bottles of Nehi Orange Crush, not what David would have chosen to quench his thirst, but he drank his greedily anyway and wiped his mouth with the back of his hand. He suppressed a belch, and caught his partner's look; Ellis, familiar with David's mighty burps, winked. They set their bottles down on a round glass-topped table and moved toward the end of the buffet to pick up plates. David was starved, and exhilarated to be in this company. Just then Kimbrough came over and somehow seemed to gather them in like children, close to him. He pumped their hands, and gave them hearty pats on the back. He thanked them for coming and promised they would do it again. "It does us good to see our youngsters so healthy and able," he said. Other men, most of them now showered and dressed in golf clothes or swimming suits with matching shirts, gathered around to say thanks and goodbye and nice job. Good luck at state, they all said, and turned back to their friends. David saw girls and boys he knew from high school, sitting in clusters at tables or on lounge chairs near the pool. None of them seemed to have noticed him, except Beth Ann, who waved a light, fingery goodbye and turned away. David looked around. New people had arrived. The buffet was something else, not to do with the tennis at all. It was not for them. Ellis looked confused. He was dangling a paper napkin from his left hand. David gave him a sign with his eyes, and they left hurriedly.

In the car they expelled the held-back air, cried "Shee-it!" and then shook hands jovially and mocked their hosts. "Such fine YOUTH!" they laughed. "So HEALTHY!"

"Did you see that fat guy in a turquoise bathing suit?" Ellis was bent over with laughter.

David went along with his brave humor. He said, "And how about Sue Hunnicutt's black bathing suit? I mean, puhl—unge. She sits near me in chemistry. Always dressed to the gills, little silk scarves tucked around her throat. Now I'll see those big smashed boobies, no matter how she hides them!" He felt hot and anxious, stirred up. He beat his hand against the steering wheel, then backed carefully out of the tidy parking lot. Sounds of chatter and laughter sprayed the air.

Now here was Kimbrough, calling again, and David's chest seemed to fill with happiness. He wanted to go to the club again. He had always known that tennis was a gentleman's game. Although he had started with a three-dollar used racket on a public court, he had often imagined himself in expensive clothes, dangling a cat-gut racket while he waited for his opponent to crawl out of a little black Jaguar. Even as a little kid he had seen himself in better circumstances, play-ing tennis for fun. For *leisure,* as people do who have the money to call their fun a word like that.

But he wanted to set himself up for a less humble exit. "Sure, I can spare a couple of hours," he told Kimbrough. "I'm going water skiing later." Actually, the gang would be long gone for Red Bluff by eight in the morning. Sure enough, the kids did come by for him early, and he waved them away sleepily. He said he wasn't up to it. He often begged off from group events. He skirted the edge of being stand-offish. He knew it, and tried to make up for it with his pass-by friendliness at school. Down the halls he went, raising his hand in a palm-forward, raised salute. Hi, hi, and hi.

Glee's protests were aborted by the other kids' urgency to be under way. "Oh goodie," Dickie Huber said, hugging Glee and giving her a smacking kiss on the cheek. "Two girls for me, my good luck, huh?" His date looked peeved. David thought to himself that Dickie Huber was a creep who wanted to get under Glee's skirt; he could hardly bear the minute it took for them to pull away. His last view of Glee was of her glaring angry face as she looked at him through the back window of Buddy's pink BelAir. They really are her friends, he thought. Why does she like me?

He raced to shower and dress. He had washed his tennis shorts after Kimbrough's call, adding extra bleach to make them as white as possible. He wore a white polo shirt with a pale blue collar and ribbing at the armholes, a birthday gift from his mother. He could kiss her for it now. He had scrubbed his tennis shoes, too.

No women were at the club courts. The players were all men and boys. Sons and fathers, David guessed. He seemed to be the stand-in for Kimbrough's lack of a son. The other boys were older than David, young men about to go back to college. He heard the schools' names floating in the air all morning: Baylor, Texas, Yale. Bobby Birdsong, who had been All-State, and nominated for All-American, who might have picked any of a dozen schools if he had played football, was at Dartmouth, for the rowing team. The other guys kidded him. He said he had seen a photograph, and had wanted to leave the prairie for water. Still a team player, he pointed out. David felt a moment, just a moment, of complete rapport with Birdsong.

The boys treated David with neutrality. He was someone's guest, that was all. They did not seem to remember him, and why would they? As a freshman and sophomore, when they might have known him, he was still a skinny and unremarkable little boy. Even now he was small in the chest, with thin arms, no matter how much he worked out. The two or three years the others had on him had filled them out. He felt dwarfed, outclassed.

David played seriously, but until the last couple of sets, he avoided the smashing drives that characterized his best games. He was—face it—awed by the company. He studied the haircuts of these boys who had been at schools in the East.

The styles were different, a little longer. Somehow, Eastern. He made himself concentrate on the ball. He was really glad he had on a new shirt.

They shook hands all around. In a moment David realized they had all gone off to shower and change. So here I am again! he thought, damning himself for not bringing clothes. He stood bewildered at the edge of the court, sweat running in rivulets down his face and neck. His shirt was soaked. Kimbrough handed him a towel, and then with another, began mopping his own face and neck and thighs. "Almost too hot for this, isn't it?" he asked David amiably. David dabbed at himself. "The heat doesn't get to me too bad, sir," he said. "I like feeling I've worked hard." He fought the urge to raise his arm and check his odor.

"Sure you do!" Kimbrough barked. He threw his hot arm across David's shoulder for a moment and steered him across the broad patio, past the pool, to a table with a large umbrella. Kimbrough was putting off a healthy smell himself. David felt better. "Have a seat there, young man," Kimbrough said, "I'll hurry up something to drink." He took their towels.

Mrs. Kimbrough and Beth Ann were already at the table. Mrs. Kimbrough was smoking. In front of her on the table were an ashtray and a tall frosted glass beaded with moisture. She wore wide-cuffed navy linen shorts and a pink silk shirt open low at the throat. She smiled and gestured for him to sit. He sat beside Beth Ann, leaning toward the empty chair on the other side of him.

The girl looked cool and regal in a white sundress. The material was soft and fine, like good handkerchief cotton. At the shoulders, her straps had wide epaulets flapping onto her upper arms. She sat slightly stretched out in her chair, her rear end scooted up toward the edge and her legs extended into the sun. Her body was turned away from him. She looked at him over her shoulder. Light struck the down on her neck. She had tugged her dress skirt up to the edge of her knees. Her legs were glossy with oil. "Hi," she said, and David felt something close to shock.

He had never really looked at her before. She was someone he knew slightly at school. They were on Student Council together. She was often elected to things; he saw announcements in the school paper. Y-Teen, Junior Board. She was part of the special, almost magical inner circle of students for whom school was a wonderful experience, girls whom Glee was dying to join. (If one of them spoke to her, she would say, So and so was really nice to me today. So and so said she liked my skirt. It was sickening.) Beth Ann had always seemed remote in meetings, as if she were there as a favor to her constituency.

Now, at the sound of her greeting, a single syllable, it struck him that there was a wonderful shyness about her. Modesty. The word sprang to mind. Beauty and modesty, the stuff of medieval ladies, of women in old English novels, of saints. He tried to see the round flesh of her shoulder; the cloth that obscured it was maddening.

"You saved me from being humiliated today," she said. Her whispery soft voice lacked Glee's nasality, though their attitudes toward the words they spoke were a lot alike, gentle and breathy. She turned around and leaned her elbows on the glass table. She raised one hand to her head and spread her fingers in her hair, at the back of her neck.

"I did?"

"Daddy was going to make me play in that awful ole— tournament—or whatever it was. Me, and all those college boys!"

"You play well enough, you could have done it." He remembered that she had an admirably steady, dependable style, the product, he was certain, of many years' practice. She was athletic just the way a girl ought to be, lean, graceful, and quick. And beautiful.

"Oh *sure*," she said, dipping her chin, saying with her face, Yes, I know I could have, but I like it that you said so. She surprised him. What was his opinion to her? He was gawky, naive in the company, however removed, of *college* boys. She played with a long strand of her hair, pulling gently, sliding her finger down it, out at the end, and then, after holding the very tip between her thumb and finger, she let it go, and let her arm down onto the back of her chair. The pose opened her shoulders and exposed her throat.

There was a long moment of silence. Beth Ann was still and almost solemn in her expression. David felt his ears redden as he searched for something clever to say. He swallowed, and was mortified when the swallow was an audible gulp.

"I think Hayden would have had to sit it out," Mrs. Kimbrough said, "if we had not thought of you." She looked at her daughter indulgently. "He could not have made Beth Ann play tennis if she didn't want to." She spoke in a lazy but well-articulated drawl, more Southern than West Texas. She seemed amused.

"'What a good idea,' I told him," Beth said. She looked to her mother. "I said, 'He can play with Daddy, and then have lunch with Mommy and me.'"

Her mother nodded. "So, here you are."

"Indeed he is." Mr. Kimbrough set a tall glass of iced tea in front of David. It was garnished with a sprig of bright mint and a delicate slice of lemon. Kimbrough sat down with his own glass of beer. He lifted the glass in a toast, and the others lifted theirs. "To summer's end," he said. His daughter said, "To good sports," smiling at David. "Hear, hear!" Mrs. Kimbrough said, and they all clicked glasses and drank.

David wished for a photographer, to capture the moment for him. He could not believe he was there. Kimbrough had not mentioned Ellis in the invitation. When David told Ellis about coming—if he told him—he would say, They said it was too bad you were working and couldn't make it. David had this disloyal, amazing thought, that Ellis would not have fit in.

"I took the liberty of ordering our lunch," Kimbrough said. His wife had taken out a fresh cigarette from a silver case on the table. He leaned to pick up her lighter and offer her the flame. The whole shared gesture was like something from a movie with Cary Grant. Actually, Kimbrough might even be better looking than Grant, with the same square jaw, smooth skin, Greek-god nose, and tall athletic build.

"I am starving," Mrs. Kimbrough said. David could see the curve of her breast pressing against the pink cloth of her draped shirt. He felt his own flesh stir. He readjusted himself in his seat, leaning onto the table on his elbows.

Beth twirled her straw in her glass of Coke. "I could eat a roasted goat," she said. Clearly, she could not. She was thin but very healthy-looking, and elegant, like her mother, not so thin as Audrey Hepburn, but much more like her than like the lush Elizabeth Taylor type. Her long mahogany hair, pulled back and caught up so that it cascaded onto her back, was waved around her head, balancing the largeness of her dark eyes and thick straight eyebrows, her large white teeth in a wide mouth. She had been voted Junior Prettiest the year before. Her skin was flawless, except for a tiny brown mole below her left eye, a "beauty spot" like some girls applied with a pencil. Her long brown arms moved languorously; her long fingers were tipped with oval nails the color of apricots. He thought, dismayed, that she was probably taller than he. He remembered seeing her with Walter Fleetwood, who was over six feet. He had never stood right beside her, himself. He was 5'8", if he stood up straight; he hoped he had a last surge of growth in him.

He thought of the times he had sat with Glee in her kitchen while she did her nails. He had liked the intimacy of it. They listened to her 45's. She liked Buddy Holly, Tommy Edwards, Johnny Mathis. He lifted the stack to reset it while she waved her wet nails around in the air. He pulled her to her feet and they danced to "It's All in the Game."

Beth had surely never groomed her own nails. They were perfect. The amazing shininess of her hair was like her mother's though the styles were different. They wore no spray, their hair always fell back into place. That, he realized, was the beauty of a cut. They could go to the beauty parlor all they liked. Everything is better, done by an expert. He had a sudden, clear picture of Beth Ann and her mother, side by side, in black plastic chairs and pink bibs at Pearl's Curls, their throats exposed as they lay arched, their heads back in the deep basins, their scalps obscured by suds. The girls who washed their hair looked like Glee and his sister, Joyce Ellen.

An arpeggio of laughter from the Kimbroughs made him aware that they had been talking while he drifted away. He smiled, hoping it was fitting, and that he did not need to say anything. He was aware of the particularity of his observations; he almost smiled again when he realized he wanted to go home and write them down.

"Ah, here is lunch. You did a lovely job of choosing," Mrs. Kimbrough said to her husband. The waitress laid before them bright white china plates and silverware, a plate of chicken salad and another of yellow cheese spread, flecked red with pimentos, a narrow silver platter lined with bread slices, and a bowl of olives and pickles.

David found he was almost panting with hunger. "It sure does look delicious." He was dry now. He reached up with the flat of his hand to smooth his hair, knowing his cowlick made it stick up after exercise. He kept an eye on Mrs. Kimbrough, and dipped the salad onto his plate in small mounds as she did on hers. He used the bread to slide food onto his fork, and ate it in alternating bites, instead of making a sandwich, as he would have if he were alone. The crispness of the celery and onion and apple in the chicken salad was delightful. To be polite, he ate a little cheese spread, though he did not like the gooey sauce that held the ground cheese together.

"How did you spend your summer, David?" Beth Ann asked. She had a trace of her mother's cultivated Southern accent.

David felt himself flush. He chose his words carefully. "My father owns a small store in Fort Stockton. I ran that, and made trips for him to other towns in the region." What else was there to say? The Kimbroughs would know nothing of shopping in beauty parlors, church halls, and parking lots. His cautious explanation would not conjure up embarrassing images. To them he would be what he was, or what he wanted to be: ambitious, energetic, dependable.

As if he were applying for a job with the Kimbroughs! He felt yet another flush, a long, deep surge of resentment. He set his fork down and took a drink of tea to quell the feeling. The ice in his glass shifted and wet his mouth too much; quickly he dabbed with his napkin. "What about you?" he asked before they could demand any more information from him. He addressed no one in particular; he was looking at his glass. Mint clung to a shard of ice like moss on a rock.

Beth chatted for a few moments, never hurrying her words. Here was a way she was different from Glee. And why was he comparing them, anyway? They were in more ways unalike than like. Beth never got lost in the gush of her own verbiage. She trotted, ladylike, through a long description of her visit to San Miguel de Allende, "in the highlands of Mexico," where her mother's sister had a house. Her parents looked on. David saw how much they liked their daughter, how pleased they all were with one another. He almost wished for it to be false; it was too smug to watch. Like the scene at the Cottles, it was painful for him.

Karen Riley ran lightly across the patio and reached down

to hug Beth and then her mother. She was trailed by Carl Stuckey, looking glum. The girls were caught up for a moment in a gush of words. David took the opportunity to stand and say it was time for him to go. He was shaking hands with Mr. Kimbrough as he heard Carl say, touching Karen lightly on the shoulder, "See you by the pool." He trudged across the patio, shedding his shirt, then his shoes. David glanced at him standing for a brief moment on the diving board. Carl looked down at the water unhappily. Mrs. Kimbrough gave David a light tap on the cheek. He felt the faint tang of her nails. "See you, dear," she said. Beth Ann smiled, David smiled back, and he fled.

If he told Glee about going to the club—and he probably would not—he would tell her how unhappy Carl Stuckey looked without Shirlee.

He drove to Leland's house and said if Leland would come by and pick him up later they would drive around. He said he would like to go visit somebody in the hospital, and Leland could come, too. Leland scratched at a pimple on his chin. "Weird," he said, but he was game for just about anything.

David had a strong urge to tell Leland he had fallen in love. It was a silly idea. He made himself think again of the girl Sissy; he did wonder how she had done through the day. *There* was a girl who was not sitting around the country club, not today or any day. He wished he knew what she had been doing on the highway carrying a bloody rabbit. Gosh, he thought, that's probably a great story, if you knew.

9.

"I already know you." Sissy interrupted David when he tried to introduce himself again. She had been so dopey Saturday. "Everybody knows David Puckett." She didn't seem to remember him from when she was picked up.

"But not you," she said to Leland, rather solemnly. She sat on the daveno near the television, looking limp and pale. She smiled at Leland. She was wearing rolled-up bluejeans and a plain white blouse with a dingy collar. Her fine hair was caught back on each side above her ears with crossed bobbypins.

The boys had pulled up straight-backed chairs to sit near her. Leland grinned. "Heck, nobody knows the brainy kids," he drawled easily. "Leland Piper." He winked at David so that Sissy could see. "Last year in chemistry, who was it figured out his mystery compound in only twenty minutes, when other kids took three class periods?" He patted his chest. "Yours truly, ole Leland Piper. And who won county Ready Math at the spring meet?"

Sissy giggled. "Ole Leland?"

Nurse Mayfield looked up from her desk and shot them a sour look. When David and Leland had asked admittance, she told them David had the wrong night. Didn't he know when his mother was off? He politely explained that he was there to see the teen-ager, Sissy. He had come because his mother asked him to. That was when he learned the rest of her name. Cecilia Dossey. The nurse had to think about it a minute, but she let them in. Not for long, she told them. "She only got up and dressed today. I don't want you wearing her out." David supposed Mayfield didn't mean to sound as vulgar as she did.

"I'm a sophomore," Sissy said. "Oh my!" She clapped her fingers to her mouth. "I'm a junior now. Here it is next year."

She clouded up and tears welled in her eyes. "That's why you don't know me," Leland said, as if they had been puzzling over it. "We'd never have had classes in the same hall."

To David, Sissy said, "We live on the same alley."

"Pardon?"

"I live on North Buckhorn, and you live on Lamar. So you face west off the alley, and I face east. It's like being neighbors, except two blocks apart. I see you sometimes, cutting down the alley off Fourth. You walk right by my bedroom window."

"Shoot, I only live a couple blocks furthern you," Leland told Sissy. "Coming from David's. Seventh and Myrtle? Brown house, red trim?"

Sissy was fiddling with her blouse. The top button was loose.

"I bet the nurse can fix that," David said. His mother would have, if she had time.

Sissy hid the button with two fingers. "I can't lose it. My mama would be mad. She brought this blouse up to me specially this morning."

"She won't know." David leaned toward her. "Unless she's coming back. Is she? You could change." Around them were patients and visitors. There were odd bursts of laughter, a woman in tears, much whispering, as though people were asleep in the room. When relatives came to visit people in the mental ward, they acted like the crazy ones.

Sissy said, "Mama can't come back. There's baby Moses at home, and Daddy won't babysit."

"Maybe your daddy will come," Leland said cheerfully. The sore place on his chin had a crust now, and a bright red halo.

Tears oozed out of Sissy's eyes.

"Shh." David poked Leland. "Go get her a Kleenex at the nurse's station."

David told Sissy, "You don't have to be scared of anything in here. That's what this place is for, to make you feel safe. See, I even come up to visit, myself. I like it here." He had often tried to imagine what it would be like to wake up in one of these pale green rooms. Sissy nodded slowly. He thought she was getting tired. "You can sleep, and not think too much. You aren't supposed to worry."

"Miss Chester says—" Her voice crackled.

"Who's Miss Chester?"

"From welfare? She said they're finding me a family to go live with. Away from my daddy."

"They'll probably be really nice."

"I miss the baby. A baby is so pure."

Leland handed her a tissue and sat back down. "The nurse says two minutes is all."

David said, "Want me to come tomorrow, Sissy?"

"Sure."

"Want me to bring you a Baby Ruth or something?"

"Why would you?"

"We're neighbors, aren't we?"

"I don't like candy. I need a notebook."

"Oh yeah? To write in?"

"A lined notebook, regular kind, yay big—" She shaped it in the air. "I have one at home almost used up. It's under my mattress. I'd be in lots of trouble if they found it. But I miss it—I'm used to writing every day."

"Really! I keep a notebook, too."

"If you don't have your notebook, your secrets crowd up in your head."

"They'd give you paper."

"It's not the same, all loose."

"I'll come by after school."

"School," she echoed. He could see her attention fade in an instant. She was clutching her hands together so tightly the knuckles were white and the tops bright pink. "Sometimes I wonder, would it be pretty on the other side? Peaceful, and pretty?"

"Other side?"

She squeezed her hands. He could barely hear her whispered reply. "In heaven."

Leland whooped as they got to the car. "She's a sad little chick, ain't she?"

"She is a little like a chick," David said. "Something tiny, without feathers."

"She's cute. I mean, if she felt better, rolled her hair and all, she might be worth a try."

"I didn't think of that. Of you liking her." She had said she was a junior; she was older than he thought at first.

"She's never done it, you can tell that a mile away."

"She's not always going to be in 2-West," David said. He sounded so sly, he felt ashamed.

"Didja read about the hula hoop contest in Cleveland, Ohio?" Leland's long legs, crossed at the ankles, looked tangled.

"I guess I missed that." David knew he was going to be the straight man for a joke or a horror story. He thought that was why Leland read the paper every day, to look for wild things to tell him.

"This little girl almost had it won, but then her panties fell down."

David chuckled. "That it?"

"Think about it," Leland said. "Oh man. Her underwear down around her ankles, her heinie bare as butter under her dress."

"It doesn't do a thing for me, Leland, thinking that."

"Hell no. You get to see 'em for real, big enough to poke."

"Not twirling hula hoops." Sometimes Leland was downright disgusting, but he only said these things to David. They had been friends since third grade; they'd even moved to Basin the same year. His father had bought an Ace Hardware store.

"A girl eleven years old won. She spun three hoops for nearly fifteen minutes. Don't that beat all?"

They would not put in the paper if a kid dropped her panties, David thought. He made it up. "You're the one beats all," he said, and laughed.

"Whooey!" said Leland.

David went into the house from the alley. He checked the washing machine. There was a washed load in it, not very wet. It was probably the same laundry his mother had put in the morning before. He set it to rinse again.

He walked through the house to the front door and checked the street. His mother's car was gone, and his father's was parked on the edge of the yard.

The front room was closed-up and hot. He unbuttoned his shirt and fanned himself with a folded newspaper. He lifted the shades partway and opened windows to try to get some ventilation. The air was not moving. The sills had a thick coat of dust. Only the bedrooms had coolers. The door to his parents' room was shut, so he assumed Saul was in there, staying cool.

His mother had been to the store. There was hamburger in the refrigerator, and on the counter, a box of spaghetti, two cans of tomato sauce, and a packet of seasoning mix. He made supper. He had been making spaghetti since he was eight years old. He also made a fair stew, a tuna and green bean casserole, chops, and omelets. He got sick of sandwiches, cereals, canned soups, and had learned to cook rather than wait on his mother's occasional bursts of domestic fervor. The one good thing about Aunt Cheryl's was that there was always a lot of food.

Marge appeared and blurted, "I didn't mean for you to do that, honey." She wore loose trousers and an old man's shirt, tied at the waist. She threw her purse on the floor and began buttering bread. She sprinkled on garlic salt, and put the bread in the oven to toast. Two pots sat on the back burners.

He took one of his father's beers and sat at the table. He watched his mother watch the bread toasting; she kept the oven door cracked for the few minutes it took. He could not imagine that she really thought it was worth sending that broiler heat into the kitchen, but when she scooted the toast onto a plate and set it on the table, he broke one in half and wolfed it down in three bites. "Go on," she scolded. "Go get your father." She set the table.

Saul came to the table wearing the bottoms of a pair of soft flannel pajamas and a white undershirt cut deep at the armholes. The hair on his chest was thick above the scoop of the tee shirt. David had the awful thought that someday he would turn into his father. Despite his drinking, Saul was still a relatively thin man, with a firm chest and ropy arms. He had bright black eyes, bushy brows, and a hooked, although not large, nose. David took his size and shape from his father rather than his mother—Marge was taller, and larger-boned—but he had the sandy coloring of a Puckett, and his face did not really resemble either of them. Both his parents had curly hair, but his own was coarse, stiff, and straight. He kept it cut short, though not mowed down as many boys did. If it grew too long, his cowlick made it stick out in two directions at the crown. He combed the very front straight up, and had a habit of brushing at it with the palm of his hand.

David waited for his father to yell at him about the beer. When Saul did not do so, David took another long swallow, and set the bottle on the floor by his chair. They ate in silence. Never able to bear the tension that hung in the air when the three of them spent time together, he tried to tell them about the matches he'd played that morning. His mother interrupted, the way you might cut off a child retelling a long movie plot. "Did you have a *good time?*" she asked. He said he did. She had never learned enough about tennis to know what was going on. Win or lose was her whole vocabulary, and all his father cared about.

"So who wanted you out at the clubby club?" Saul demanded. "That girl who called?"

David told him what Kimbrough had said about wanting to get a tournament going. "It would be good for tennis in the whole county." He added, "Maybe good for me." His father smirked. David bent closer to his plate and ate quickly, then put his dish in the sink behind him.

"You wait a minute there," Saul said. "Sit down."

David stood behind his chair, his hand on the back of it. He gripped the wooden slat, and, for a moment, remembered the good feeling of the racket in his hand when he played a nice lob volley. His father would appreciate the surprise of a good shot, if he took the trouble to understand the game. "I thought I'd read a while," he said. He noticed how tired his mother looked. He did not want to quarrel with his father in front of her.

"You've spent the whole summer out of the house!" Saul shouted. David was indignant. You'd think I was out catting around, he wanted to say. He slumped into his chair, and knocked over the beer bottle. It clanged and rolled across the floor a few feet to the stove, leaving a trickled trail of beer.

"Shit," he mumbled.

"Never mind, son," his mother said, reaching for a towel.

"Wipe it up!" his father thundered.

He grabbed the towel from his mother and got down on his knees to clean the mess. His face burned. He threw the towel at the door to his room, and sat back down sulkily.

"Well, summer's over now, isn't it?" his mother said with false cheerfulness. "We have to get used to one another again!"

Saul took a crust of bread and sopped up the last of his

tomato sauce, leaning close to the plate to stuff it in his mouth. David and his mother watched him eat. He caught their stares, and laughed. "Nice meal, Mama," he said.

"Davy made it," Marge said.

"Good *boy*." Saul leaned back in his chair and tipped it onto two legs, the way Marge often asked him not to do. "Lucky son of mine, to spend Labor Day playing tennis."

"I work at it," David said sullenly. He never understood why his father demeaned his every accomplishment. Was he not the same man who said, Stand up straight, Wear clean clothes, Speak clearly, Study hard? Did he not say, Every son's duty is to do better than his father? Did he not say, No son of mine is going to be an ORDERLY!

"Your partner went out too? Ellis?"

"He had to work with his dad."

"Oh ho. To *labor?*"

"Am I supposed to understand something here!" David snapped.

"Davy, honey, be nice." His mother pulled Saul's plate over onto hers and stacked the silverware on top.

"*Sir*," said David.

"No holidays in the oil patch," Saul snarled. Marge, who often reminded Saul that he knew absolutely nothing about oilfield work, rolled her eyes and got up to begin banging around dishes at the sink. Saul paid her no attention. "Union contracts would provide for holidays, with extra pay if you have to work. If any holiday ought to be honored, it's LABOR DAY. These desert jackasses think they're too independent and rowdy to be collected, even if it is for their own good."

"Saul, really," Marge said after all. Her father had been a rig builder, and David had grown up on stories about the trouble union organizers caused before the war. "You don't understand, it's not like other work, you live and die a boom and bust life."

"I heard Ellis' dad say they're trying to organize the carbon black plant," David said quickly, hoping it would placate his father. He did not say how worried Mr. Whittey was. The year's work had been spotty; Whittey said a drilling depression was setting in. There were a lot of Whitteys to feed.

"Not roughnecks," Marge said firmly, and plunged her hands into soapy water. "Never."

Saul put his hands on the table and leaned into them. "Your grandparents were sweatshop slaves for years. They fought to get fair treatment. I know something about labor! When my brother Karl built his business, he *invited* the union in. He put his own father to work with a contract. Then me."

Marge said to David, "Your father was in a union at the hospital where we met." She did not say, an orderly's union.

"Dark *ages*, Pop," David said.

"That's right!" his father exploded. "Anything that's not right in front of your nose! Far away and dead history!" He stomped into the living room and turned on the television. It was time for Highway Patrol.

"What's his problem?" David muttered. "What's he want?"

His mother sighed and pulled the plug in the sink. The water would take five minutes to drain all the way out. Then she'd have to rinse the dishes. "He should have worked today. *He's* not bound by anybody's schedule. He only has to organize himself. Idleness makes him moody." She smiled sadly. "The only cure for melancholy is work, son."

"What's wrong, Mom?" David said, suddenly aware of his mother's immediate misery.

She began running water again, swishing each dish under the faucet and stacking it on the drain. She kept her back to him. "Joyce Ellen." The water was rising in the sink.

David put his hand on her shoulder. His sister was unhappy. Big Pete Kelton had not turned out to be such an improvement on Saul Stolboff. Joyce Ellen was only sixteen years old. She did not have the sense of a road runner. Suddenly David could not bear the misery in the room.

He moved the laundry to the dryer, then he went out the back door. Walking alongside the house, he noticed that the siding buckled in waves, like a long stretch of frozen cloth. He did not know how he had failed to notice it before. One of these days it would probably split and peel off like a dried onion skin. There they would be, one flank exposed to the weather.

He took his father's car to go see Glee.

10.

David swung by to pick up Leland, and then went on to Glee's.

"How's she going to feel about this?" Leland asked, when he learned where they were headed.

"I'm not staying. I'll ask if she wants to go for a little ride."

"With you and good ole Leland."

"She'll probably be pissed. But she won't act like it if you're along. She won't want you to know she has a reason to be. She'll be Miss Sunshine."

"She sits in the middle?"

"Where else?"

"Her nice creamy thigh alongside my hot hip?"

"You're a piece of work, Leland." David laughed.

Glee was not at home. Her mother, the now Mrs. Joe Ranger, smiled when she saw who it was, and leaned against the door jamb. She was holding a glass, maybe iced tea. "Your name is mud around here, David," she said pleasantly, and took a drink.

"I couldn't make it," he answered with like politeness.

"She's not here."

"Tell her I came by?"

"She's just down to Dewey's Drive-in, I imagine. With some of the kids from today."

"I might swing by."

Mrs. Ranger pulled her arm down from the door frame, switched her drink to that hand, and rested her free hand on the slight rise of her belly, right about navel high. David was acutely aware of her condition. Behind her, a television was blaring in a dim room.

At Dewey's, Glee was in the back seat of Buddy's BelAir, with Dickie Huber sitting so close to her, another person could have still fit in on his other side. In the front, Buddy and Ray Jean were turned around so the four could visit. As cars came around slowly, one or the other or even all of them could wave and call out to their occupants. It was the night before school started again, and people were out.

David drove around once slowly. When Glee saw him, he said to Leland, "Wave, ole Leland." Leland, laughing, blew Glee a kiss.

The second time around, he parked a few cars away and ordered a Dr. Pepper and onion rings. Leland, who said his own dinner had been light, ordered steak fingers and a chocolate malt.

"Well," David said as the car hop left with their order.

"I can stand to wait," Leland said. He had a gawking, happy expression.

David grinned. "I did come to see Glee, didn't I?" He climbed out of the station wagon and leaned into the car next to his, on the side away from Buddy's car. He chatted with Jason Strickland, who had worked pipeline in Hawaii all summer. Then he went to Buddy's car.

"You missed a good time," Buddy said as David approached. Buddy had a streak of white goop across his sunburned nose. All four of the car's occupants were in stages of burns, although Glee, being the most tan, merely looked flushed. "Ole Jedsel brought a tent." David knew what that meant. There had been a place for couples to "retire to," a hot, still, canvas cave for fucking. "We barbecued, and swam our guts out."

"Jeez, I don't know why I stayed home," David said. He knew Buddy was enjoying Glee in the back seat with his best buddy Dick. Glee had scooted as far against the side of the car as she could, but Dickie had not bothered to add a spare inch between them. David thumped the car with the flat of his hand. "Thought I oughta say hi," he said, and pulled up straight.

Glee got out of the car, and walked around to the back. She leaned against the trunk while David took his time joining her. Dickie, Ray Ann and Buddy stared a moment, and then went back to visiting among themselves.

"Doesn't look like you missed me," David said. He did not care one bit, but he knew Glee would be hurt if he did not say that.

"Of course I did!" she fussed. "But you weren't *there*, and I wasn't going to *mope* all day."

"Course not." He moved closer to her, and brushed at her bangs with two outstretched fingers. Wisps of hair were white as lint. She slid her butt along the trunk to find a comfortable spot where she could look like she was lounging.

"I skied on one ski really good."

"Congratulations."

"And I raced and beat the other girls. Then they were mad, because it was my idea."

"How could I have missed it."

"Davy, why didn't you go, really?"

"I had to do stuff with my dad."

"Liar, liar, pants on fire." She giggled weakly.

"With my mother."

She hit his chest with her little fist. "You're so awful to me, Davy."

He leaned and gave her a peck on the cheek, right on the bone. She smelled of shampoo. She wore tight white shorts and a sleeveless lime green blouse with a stiff pointed collar. "You smell nice," he whispered.

"You want to take me home?" She was relaxing, feeling good. She would not pursue the matter of his guilt, because she knew it would not get her anything.

"I'm with Leland."

"Oh *shit*," she said, and drew back. You did that on *purpose*."

"He's my good buddy, like Dickie Huber is yours." He spoke with no intonation, to see what she would make of it.

"If you didn't want me to go today, you should have said."

"I couldn't stop you."

"You don't want me anywhere with other boys."

"How was Jedsel's big green tent?"

"Oh stop."

"Did they all sympathize? Did the girls coo and say, That David Puckett, he's a bastard?"

"Did not. I didn't act like it was anything. I said you couldn't come, like it was nothing."

"*Was* nothing."

"I never have as much fun if you're not there." When he didn't speak, she added, wise little girl, "But I do have fun."

"That's what I like you for, don't you know? You're the cheerful one."

"You're sure not! You're always moody. You want to act like nobody could guess what's on your mind."

"Nobody could."

"I know, sometimes,—" She grinned. "Don't I?"

He put a little more distance between them. She was expecting him to touch her, or kiss her, here in front of all creation. She could hardly keep from roaming her eyes around to see who was watching.

"Nobody says you can't have other dates," he said.

"What are you *talking*? It wasn't a *date*." She punctuated with little gasps of breath.

"I'm just saying it could have been, nobody says you're my girl only."

"Everybody knows!"

"I never said."

"Davy!" She looked ready to cry.

"When I ask you, and you want to go. That's all. We're not engaged."

"Going steady," she whispered. "That's what I thought."

"I never said."

She had her chin down. She seemed to be studying her blouse's first button. "But you know what you *do*, Davy. You know what."

He lifted her chin with his finger. "Your idea, sweetcakes."

"Why are you being mean to me!" she said loudly. She bit her lip. "You want to break up."

"Nothing to break up. I told you, there's no contract."

"So what, there's somebody else you want to date?"

He looked over her shoulder. Two cars down, Sarah Cottle and another girl were drinking Cokes and talking. "I used to go out with her," he said, without pointing.

Glee turned around. She could see Sarah, but she probably did not know. "Who? Who are you talking about?"

"Sarah Cottle."

"So WHAT."

"You go out with Dickie Huber, I go out with Sarah. It doesn't mean anything. Doesn't change anything."

"You are being hateful. You wouldn't."

"Wouldn't I?"

"You'd ask that girl out?"

"Why not?"

"I dare you, David Puckett! Go do it right now! Go on! See

if I care!" She got back in the car and crammed herself into the corner. The other kids in the car were staring at him. They could not have heard much.

He walked slowly, casually, over to Sarah's mother's nice Buick. "Hi there," he said, leaning against the car, draping one arm on top.

"David," Sarah said, surprised.

"Long time no see."

"I guess so." The girl with Sarah leaned across to look out and see who was there. He did not know her.

"You have a nice summer?" he asked Sarah.

"Sure. We went to Oregon to visit my mom's sister. It was awful pretty there."

"I bet."

"Hi," the other girl said. "I'm Mary Holloway. I was in your algebra class sophomore year."

He had no such memory. Faceless Mary Holloway. "Hi there, Mary Holloway, are you up to trig now?"

She giggled, and swung away to sit up again. "Trig," she giggled again.

"I saw you, and wanted to say hello," David said, and thumped the car.

"Nice to see you." She wasn't giving him much. She was really a very cute girl, very neat and pretty and sweet.

"Call you?"

"I beg your pardon?"

"I said, maybe I could call you?"

She was not at all flustered, as he had thought at first. She was actually quite cool. He admired that. She smiled sweetly. "I thought you were all tied up with a cheerleader."

"I date her. We're not married."

"Course not."

"So can I?"

"Free country."

"Don't you want me to?"

She bit her bottom lip, then said, "I have to think about it. And I got to go, now." She set her glass and Mary's glass on the tray, and rearranged herself. She smiled politely. "See you, Mr. Puckett." She tapped the horn.

He banged her car again. "You will, Miss Cottle!" He was delighted with the way she had handled him. He had imagined her crying when he never called again, with no explanation. He had imagined she wondered, and asked her girlfriends, What did I do? Then later she learned he had a new girlfriend, that he was in real tight with Glee Hewett. He used to see her in the hall. She would go by like he was invisible. Not like she was snubbing him, or making anything of it. She did not see him, anymore.

The car hop took the tray away.

He grinned and watched Sarah start the car and back out. Going by Buddy's car, he banged on the trunk hard with his fist. Their heads swung so they could see him. He smiled and waved. As he walked away, he pinched the bridge of his nose.

11.

To avoid the packs of kids he knew would be all over the front lawns, David walked toward the school a block over, and came up the back side, but the doors to the huge brick building were locked there. Rather than wait for them to open, he took a deep breath, smoothed his hair, and walked around to the front.

Students stood in clots, mostly boys with boys and girls with girls. They were further divided by that elusive but unmistakably effective system that created layers of popularity and status in the school's society. Shy kids of no particular description seemed to hug the sides of the building, tucked into the shadows cast by the recesses of the structure, or clinging to the huge concrete pillars along the walkway between the two main entrances. Out in the center of the lawn stood girls from pep squad and student council, girls who belonged to clubs and to each other. Nearby, in tight formations like huddles on the football field, stood the boys of like caliber, mostly athletes, along with those boys who for various reasons were buddies of athletes though they had not distinguished themselves in any particular way. David headed to one of these groups, spying Ellis and other members of the tennis and swimming teams, boys not quite up to the football players who occupied nearby territory. These boys, for the most part, wore their hair cut very short, "burred," and plaid shirts or polo shirts with jeans. A few wore snap-buttoned cowboy shirts and boots. Ellis wore a starched khaki shirt, rolled twice at the cuffs, and new jeans and loafers. He looked scrubbed and gangly, and happy to be escaping the summer's grueling labor. Someone was telling a story or a joke, and Ellis was laughing and switching his weight back and forth on his legs, as if the tale were too funny to stand still for. He had a way of making everybody around him seem to matter, without drawing any real attention to himself. Seeing him now, David realized how much he had missed him in the past months.

Around the edge of the brown brittle grass stood neatly-dressed kids who made up the fans and compatriots of the central figures. These were girls and boys who dressed like those they admired—the girls with more style and money—and who dated among themselves and were usually occupied making signs for the elections of others, working in minor roles on the newspaper, the yearbook, and various projects throughout the year. The caste of kids who most clearly did not belong—they did not bother even with Future Farmers of America or Distributive Education clubs—stayed off campus until the bells rang. They sat on the bumpers of souped-up cars, or on the seats of motorcycles. Girls hung off of boys like appendages, draping themselves in poses that showed their round rumps. David was amazed to see, as he rounded the corner, that Leland was in this company, standing with Stripling, Nesmith, Eckhard, and other hoods who wore their hair long, slicked back into ducktails with high waves on the top, their tee-shirts rolled at the sleeves, their pants so tight there seemed to be no room to allow them to sit down. There were no girls on Leland's arms, but he was in their company, girls with blackened or hennaed or bleached hair, wearing tight short skirts and provocative blouses some of them might even be sent home for.

"Davy, hi!"

He turned and saw Glee fifteen feet or so away. She was in a cluster of girls who had, collectively, probably put in a week's work getting ready for their entry into the year. Every hair on every girl's head was in place. Skirts were crisp, little low flats were polished to a high shine. "Oh hi, David," a couple more of them called, and he had no choice but to call back, "Oh hi, Doris, hi Twyla, hi Janie." He took an instant to consider whether he would go up to them. It would launch Glee's day right—maybe even her year—to have him trot over to her like a pup on a leash, but he could not. To make up for it, he smiled hugely and called out, "See you at lunch?" He saw her expressions, like a sequence of snapshots: the flash of disappointment, a gloss of anger, then, at his wave, the relief at his date-making. "Yes, sure!" she answered, but then a thought darkened her look again and she broke from her friends and ran up to him. "But *which lunch?*"

He wanted to shake her by the arm and tell her, keep your shirt on. Instead, conscious of her friends, of all the eyes watching her—pretty and popular sweet cheerleader Glee— he smiled and tucked his head a little in a way he knew looked tender, and in a low, almost menacing voice he said, "I'll meet you at the entrance to the library at break and we'll compare schedules, Glee. We'll see if this is going to work out. Now go giggle it up with your friends while I go talk to mine, *this isn't a date.*" It struck him that she was utterly confused. All she had to do was look around: however tight couples were, they had separated for this first-morning rit- ual. In later weeks you could check out the pairings by looking at the morning arrangements, especially on Mondays and Fridays, but today was something larger than courtship. And if you stood around like lovebirds, either you were engaged or you were totally out of it, a joke you didn't catch.

Glee's whole face tightened. Her wide eyes flickered. "Do I embarrass you?" she whimpered. "Or are you trying to em- barrass me? Are you going to start my year out like this? *Did I do something wrong?*"

He put his hand on her shoulder. Her blouse was crisp and sun-warmed. He pecked her on the cheek. "The library at break," he said, and turned before she could as much as take another breath.

When the bell rang at 8:15, the temperature was already hovering near ninety, but the building itself was fairly cool. Only those rooms receiving direct sunlight would be uncom- fortable early in the day. Everyone trooped through the gym, sending up an incredible din, and picked up their schedules in lines, divided by their last names. His sheet had a note to see the counselor at eleven, after break. By ten, most kids were in their assigned home rooms, accomplishing nothing more than finding their rooms, hearing their names called, making corrections, exiting in herds to shove their way to the next station. Teachers weren't even passing out books. Most acted bored. There was time only for the most cursory intro- ductions. Teachers tried to show that they were strict, or jolly, a good guy or a serious type, as if every senior didn't already know every teacher, didn't already have stories out of the lore of past classes. The assistant football coach in civics told two stupid jokes and led a lame mock cheer for the team before dismissing. Only honors English seemed serious. Mrs. Schwelthelm had the carriage of a queen. "We will read and learn," she told them. English would carry the year for David.

He and Glee did have the same lunch, first shift. They met at the cafeteria, where they bought lunches of gray macaroni and tomatoes and carried them out to sit on the stiff lawn. Now seated, students looked different from the morning. They were less arranged and more colorful, like scarves blown onto the ground. David and Glee joined other kids, and everyone compared schedules and complained, talked about the heat, and speculated on the outcome of the first game, with Abilene.

David still had not seen Leland. He looked up over the heads of his companions and scanned the crowd. He spotted Sarah Jane Cottle, and got up so abruptly he spilled the remains of his macaroni onto the lawn. "What's the matter?" Glee asked, startled by his sudden move.

"Here," he said, shoving his tray toward hers with his foot, "take mine back, will you? I'll catch you later." He didn't give her a chance to protest, and he didn't look back to catch the alarm and anger he knew would fill her face when she saw where he was headed.

"Wait up, Sarah!" he called as she started into the building. Inside, she leaned against a wall, her arms at her sides, her palms flat against the wall, looking very small and neat and prim. He put an arm on each side of her head and smiled close to her face. "I wasn't kidding," he said.

After school he went to see Sissy at the hospital. She was looking even better, and she was pleased to see him. She was glazing a ceramic ash tray, painting on tiny pansies around the edge. "My daddy can use this," she said.

He let himself in at Leland's, said hello to Mrs. Piper, who was folding laundry on the couch, and went into Leland's room. There were at least a dozen model airplanes hanging from the ceiling, leftovers from years before, and on the floor, piles of magazines. Leland had a big bulletin board on one wall, covered with clippings from the newspaper, and photographs of Kim Novak.

"What's with you and the Johnny Black Knights?" David demanded. The name was his invention. He didn't know if the crowd he had seen that morning had a name, but he'd heard of some of the gangs: the Dust Devils, the Cougars, the Mesquite Snakes. He had heard about brutal fights, not gang to gang, but single combat matches, fought until one or the other was pulverized. And drag races, the favorite diversion of teen-age boys in Basin, were always won by hoods if they bothered to appear. Those boys seemed only to menace one another. At school they were distant, cool, except when one would get pushed too far, or come to school stoned. David had been in a class his sophomore year when Clint Stripling pulled a knife that must have been eight inches long in old lady Trupp's English class. He made a show of sharpening his pencil, and when she commanded him to "Put that thing away!" he set to carving in the desk top like she was telling him to do that instead. And what had come of that? He could not remember. Probably Stripling's transfer to a male teacher's class, nothing more.

"Listen, Puckett, those guys know how to party." Leland launched into a speech about the sandhills, beer busts, girls with creamy thighs. Stripling's brother worked at the Pearl Beer warehouse. Wanda somebody was said to have given twenty blowjobs in one night. Leland had been with a bunch of them the day and night they dug a pit and roasted half a pig.

"You're telling me you hung out with those jerkos this summer?" David still didn't know if Leland was putting him on. But there he had been this morning, like one more thug in the land of thugs.

"I went along a few times. Hey, what was there to do, buddy? Sell screws in my dad's store all day long. Those guys always have beer. They've got great cars. And oh man—" He groaned and grabbed his crotch, then grinned.

"So what else aren't you telling? You horny-toad, you stuffed it up some girl, didn't you?"

"Aw no, man, but shee-it, at least with them there's pos-si*bility*. It could happen. It's not out of the question."

David cuffed Leland on the chin. "Is it like the country club, Piper? Do you have to get voted on? Do you have to qualify?"

"Fuck one of their women and you're in."

"How do you do that? Is it your idea or theirs?"

"Shit, Puckett, *I don't know yet.*"

"I gotta go, I got a date."

"Oh man, you're so lucky. That nice Glee—"

"It's not Glee."

"Why not?"

"I got an itch, that's all. It's somebody else."

"Somebody new! How do you do it, you aren't even in town."

"Somebody else, that's all I said. Piper, you watch it. Those guys, they'll cut you up to feed to their dogs."

"Man, they ain't got dogs. They just got fast cars and fast girls, and buckets of booze."

David shook his head. "Sounds like trouble to me."

Leland spoke urgently. "That's cause you don't need it. That's cause you already got what you need. You're not jacking off into a wad of toilet paper—"

"You foul asshole," David said in friendly fashion. "You've got just one thing on your mind, don't you?"

"Shit, man, what else is there?"

Saul was in his workroom finishing up a stack of repairs for the dry cleaners. The room was an oven. Saul, working in his boxers and an undershirt, had two fans going in his direction. David moved one so it would blow on him as he sat on a box. He told his father his new school schedule. His father had pins in his mouth the whole time, a convenient way to avoid comment. Mmmn, he said once or twice. He peered at the cuffs of trousers and did not look at his son.

"What's for din-din, hey Pop?" David felt intrusive. He could feel anger seeping up over him like water standing in a bar-ditch. The evening stretched out in front of him. He didn't feel up to seeing Glee. She was going to want to talk about *what's wrong.* He didn't want to argue. He didn't want to talk at all, or screw, either.

Saul took the pins out of his mouth and lined them up in a pin cushion. "Your mother got some TV dinners. We have to eat them tonight because they're supposed to be frozen and they're defrosting in the fridge. Go see what you can make of them."

"I could make a salad or something—"

"Rabbit food. Not worth the trouble. Go peel back those cardboard wonders and see what we got."

The dinners were Mexican: enchiladas with rubber cheese strings on top, a little hard dab of beans, bright rice, each serving in a section bounded by a ridge. It seemed crazy to turn on the oven, it was still hot as hell, without a sign of a break in the weather. But he did not want to eat canned soup, and he did not want to go to the store, either. He did not want to suggest going out; he couldn't bear the idea of sitting across from his father in a cafe, trying to make conversation.

He called Sally Cottle. He tried to make a little conversation about the day, but she wasn't giving him much. Finally he blurted out, "I wondered if you'd want to go to the movies Friday. There's an Elvis at the Star Palace."

"I don't think so, David."

He could not believe his ears. "You've got plans? Or—you won't go out with me? What?"

He counted to ten, waiting for her to answer. He wasn't about to back off; he had his neck out there for her to hack at with her stupid grudge.

Finally she said, "I didn't think you were serious. I saw you with Glee at lunch."

"I told you I was serious. Look, here I am."

She sighed. "Why don't you come over after supper? Tonight, about eight?"

"Sure, sure. You want to go get a Coke or something? We could drag the strip and see who's out. We could go to the Bronco and have one of those green lime passion things."

She giggled. "I can't stand their drinks."

"Whatever you want," he said expansively. His chest was hurting.

"Just come here. We can talk at my house."

He tried to make conversation with Saul. There seemed to be only school to talk about; Saul never discussed the weather. "The counselor called me in. He said I don't have enough in my schedule. He wanted me to take physics or calculus."

"Mmm," his father said. His undershirt was frayed at the edges under his arm.

The enchiladas had bubbled around the edges, but there

was a cold spot in the center of each, and the tortillas were soggy and rubbery. "I'm not a scientist, we know that, don't we?" David sounded like a salesman to himself. "I thought about adding electronics, Leland could help me with that, but I said I'd take speech. Speech can't be that hard—" He saw that Saul was annoyed, though he couldn't tell if it was the beans or the speech. "Maybe I'll be a lawyer, right? Whatever you do, you can't go wrong working on your speaking ability."

"You learn to tell people one thing and mean another," his father said. Some rice clung to his mustache.

"I don't think so. I think you learn to be clear. To be forceful, get your ideas across." He had heard speech was a snap, that was why he had signed up. He had had three hours the counselor said were "empty": study hall, library aide, and tennis practice. "How are those empty?" he had argued. "I have to be someplace, don't I?" But it was true study hall was a waste of time, he wouldn't be able to practice much during the winter months, and being an aide was an excuse to see the magazines first when they came in, and to talk to the girls working on research assignments.

"I'm not telling you learn to lie," his father was saying. "I'm saying, learn to keep your counsel. Choose what you want to say before you let your mouth run loose."

"That sounds so—self-conscious, Pop."

"You think the world wants you honest? You think what you've got is so great you can let it hang out there for the world to get to know? It's like chess, Sonny. You guess what your opponent's got in mind—"

"I'm not going to do debate. Just the class."

"I'M NOT TALKING ABOUT DEBATE, I'M TALKING ABOUT LIFE."

"All right, all right, don't get so excited."

Saul tossed his throwaway carton into the sink, splattering sauce and rice over the porcelain. "Garbage," he said.

David followed his father into the living room. Saul kicked off his shoes, picked up his copy of *Crime and Punishment*, arranged the fan on its stand and turned it on, and settled down with his feet on the ottoman. He wiggled his toes and they popped.

David stood in front of his father. "It seems really important to me to know how to say what you mean. It sounds like you're saying you need to know how to say what you *don't* mean. How to—"

Saul waved him away and found his place in his book. Without looking up, he said, "You don't get what I tell you, be my guest. Wear your heart on your sleeve. Put your head up your ass. You'll find something to do, it won't matter. Won't matter what you say, if no one's listening."

"What do you WANT!" David felt like his chest was exploding. He could not understand how they ended up in these utterly pointless arguments. "Here's a good example! You've outscored me and I don't know what to do but yell at you! I don't even know what the game is!"

Saul laughed. "What you're good at is talking to girls, Davy boy. You could be a pimp, maybe."

David felt dizzy. He was so hot. "You dirty sot," he muttered. He went out the back, and walked all the way to the hospital, to borrow his mother's car to go see Sarah. It took forty minutes. His breath came hard, but it was good for him. It took a hell of a lot of stamina to play tennis, you could never stop working on it. On the ward he stripped in the staff lavatory and wiped himself down with a dampened paper towel. "I'll come up later and stay till you're done," he told Marge. She was pleased, as if he were doing something for her. "That's nice," she murmured. "Like limo service."

"It's your car, Ma," he laughed. If they had been alone, he would have kissed her.

He sat on the Cottles' fake Early American couch, clutching a bottle of RC Cola, wondering at his own discomfort. He had gone to a lot of trouble for this! Sarah was perfectly courteous, formal in a way he thought somebody might act after a funeral, or at a job interview. She was wearing a pale blue shirtwaist dress, not what she had been wearing at school earlier. They exchanged information about their plans for the new school year. Yes, he would be playing tennis (what a question!), and yes he would be on student council again if he was re-elected next week. Yes she was in Y-Teen, and was volunteering at the hospital as a candy striper. He could not remember anything else about her.

He took a long swallow of the cold sweet drink. "I thought about you a lot," he began, and his voice trailed away. It was a lie, except for the past few days, and he could not think how to extend the lie. He wanted her to think she was special. You had to make a girl feel that way, if you wanted her to like you.

"I don't believe that for one minute." She was not smiling.

"Sarah, lots of kids date and stop dating and still stay friends. We hadn't made any promises, there was nothing like that between us."

"You might have said something."

"I felt so awkward. I didn't know why I didn't call, but weeks went by and then it felt too late." He set the drink down on the coffee table, and saw, too late, that it would make a wet ring. There were coasters on the end tables, but they were too far away. He leaned against the couch back, breathed deeply, and tried to relax. "Sometimes I think that what happens is mostly whatever hits you as you come around the corner. Have you ever thought of that?"

"Of what, David?"

"The element of chance in everything."

"No, I can't say that I have. I think more of the element of choice."

Very good, he thought. "I think you may be a more serious person than I am," he lied. "I didn't know that about you." He chuckled. "I guess that's because I'm not smart enough to figure out other people, specially girls." She had no expression whatsoever. She might have been posing for a portrait. "I think I underestimated you."

"My parents said, 'Where's that nice David Puckett, honey? Did you all have a fight?'"

"Heavens, I can't imagine fighting with you."

"You think I don't have enough spirit?" She was sitting up very straight. She had not brought in a drink for herself. His bottle of RC was sweating big droplets onto the table top.

"I think you're not the quarrelsome type."

"I have opinions. They're not always the same as other people's. The same as boys'. As yours."

"We never disagreed."

"No. I said, Oh David, tell me about your game today. I said, what color crepe will they be using for the Sweetheart Dance? I said, what did you think of that movie, that TV show? *Tell me what you think,* I said."

"It doesn't sound like a very good time, the way you tell it." He felt very deflated. At the same time, he was intrigued. Here was a girl he thought he knew, a girl he thought there wasn't much to know about. And she was a surprise. He liked a surprise, even if it scared him a little.

She had put on records. A Johnny Mathis record had finished, and the machine made a series of noises as the arm lifted and made room for the next record to fall. It was Dean Martin, probably something of her parents'.

"I always wanted to be married some day," she said. "Not right away, not right out of high school, but some day."

"Well, sure—"

"I'm not talking about you. Don't look so nervous. I'm talking about me. I have a hope chest, do you know about them? A nice cedar chest, it smells so good when you open it up. At Christmas and on my birthday, my mother and my grandmothers give me things for my hope chest. Linens, a salt and pepper set, matching book ends, towels, stuff like that. For when I get married. Shh, don't talk. It's my turn.

"I've always known I'd be a virgin when the time came. You know, girls dream about these things, about having a white gown and veil, and walking up the aisle. And I think about that first night. I don't really know how it happens. There's a big blank place in there where I can't really imagine what he says, what I say, who does what. But I know I will be able to look at this—man—my husband—and I will be able to say, there's never been anyone but you."

"What's this about, Sarah Jane?" He was so hot he felt he might ignite any minute. Desperate, he reached for his pop and took a long thick drink.

She was staring off through the picture window that looked out onto the dark street. A nearby street lamp cast a yellow haze over his mother's car in front. She looked back at him. She seemed to have awakened from a nap. She reached up to pat her hair into place, though it was in no way disarrayed. "And you could tell, couldn't you?"

"I never tried anything with you!" He was too embarrassed to say that he had been a virgin, too. What a dumb, dumb thing. Why was she saying all this?

"You knew it would never happen. It's something on my face. My father says that. Sarah, anybody can look at you and see you're a good girl. You're not one of those girls who asks for it. And you could see that, you knew I'd never—do it— with you, so you quit calling. You gave up without trying." Bitterly, she added, "Good for you."

He stood up. Then he didn't know what he wanted to do. "That's crazy. I never thought that of you."

"Oh you did," she said, staring at her feet.

"You've got me all wrong! I stopped calling you because of your family."

She looked up sharply. He could see she was insulted, though there was nothing she should mind, if he could just explain.

"You were all so happy, you see. I would come here and the three of you—you'd be smiling. You'd talk to one another so nicely, like families in the movies. You ate at a dining table, with napkins. Your mother treated me so—respectfully. It's not like that in my family, Sarah. It's not the way I live. I was—not exactly jealous—I didn't mind that you were happy. I didn't want not to be. But all the time I spent in your house, it made me unhappy. It made me feel cheated in my own life."

She was almost sneering. "That's the stupidest thing I ever heard."

"I didn't have to have a reason, did I?" he said loudly, cornered. "Kids date, and then they don't date. It's not a big deal. It's what being a teen-ager is for. I didn't have to give you a reason. It's up to me to call!"

She stood up abruptly. "I have to study now." Such a lie! "I just wanted you to know how much I minded, how cheap it made me feel."

"But you didn't do anything! I didn't do anything! Didn't you hear one thing I said?"

"If Glee Hewett gets pregnant, are you going to marry her?" She was at the front door. He hurried over to her. "Sarah, look—"

"I go out with somebody else now anyway." She was suddenly quite calm, almost pleasant. "You wouldn't notice." More like bored, wanting him to go away. "He's not popular like you."

"Me!"

"He's just a nice boy who respects me. He *likes* my parents."

"God*damn*, Sarah Jane. It wasn't your parents! It was ME."

"Of course it was," she said. "Don't cuss."

Glee's mother, Mrs. pregnant Joe Ranger, said, "She won't be too happy, David. She's sitting under the hairdryer looking like a Martian." He could hear the dryer humming in the background. Mrs. Ranger let him in.

He sat for quite a while. Glee finally came running out, barefooted, in jeans and a man's shirt. She had taken the rollers out of her hair and brushed it. She sat down on the couch next to him and he touched her hair. It was still damp. "Now you'll have to do it all over again," he said. He was touched. "I wouldn't have minded you in rollers. I know you well enough." He leaned closer, smelling the sweet shampoo smell of her hair. "Come out to the car a few minutes?"

"Sure." Glee called out to her mother and they walked through the front door. "Hey, let's go back on the patio, that'd be better," he said. He didn't like to neck in his mother's car. He would never fuck in it.

Glee took his hand and led him down the side of the house, past rosebushes and a bed of dead irises. The patio was dark, except for a little light from the kitchen window. They stood on the far end, where nobody could see them from inside. She put her arms up around his neck and they kissed. She was bare under the shirt. He pushed his hand through the space where one button was undone, and rested it gently on her breast. "God you're sweet," he murmured gratefully. An uncomplicated girl was a blessing.

They sat on the edge of the brick barbeque pit. "Don't let's argue," she whispered. He had moved his hand to come up under the shirt and feel her back. He made himself keep his hand still. "Don't be mad at me, don't be mean," she said.

"I'm crazy," he said, meaning it. "I feel crazy."

"Don't be silly." She tugged his arm to pull it around so that he would touch her in the front again.

"Is there time for us to take a drive?" he whispered. If they went all the way to the sandhills, they could lie in the soft sand, out of the car.

"Oh Davy, I wish—I wish sometime we could go some-where—we could go to a motel somewhere away from Basin—we could be together, really—"

"Shh." He slid his hand down inside her jeans and pressed it against her bony mound. "Touch me, too." She cupped him with her hand, outside his jeans. He moved his fingers lower.

"Glee-ee!" her mother trilled. "Phone!"

"Not NOW!" Glee called back.

"I'm going—" He pulled away.

"No!" She clasped him around the waist. He pushed against her, throbbing. Suddenly he didn't want the drive anyway. He wanted to ache a while. He would sit in the lot at the hospital and give himself over to it.

She said, "I miss you all the time I don't see you."

"I'm sorry I was mean. I don't know what gets into me."

"I don't care about other boys, Davy. Only you."

He pulled away again. "Give me air," he said, laughing. "Not now."

She laughed too. "I've got a class with your friend Leland. English. You know what he did today? While Mrs. Parker was checking names? He tossed this wad of plastic vomit on the floor in front of her desk. She walked around and stepped on it, looked down—God, it was funny. She just about fainted."

"We'll do something Saturday. Friday Ellis and Leland and I are going to hang out. First Friday of the year, you know—" They thought of it as a tradition.

"Promise?"

"You know we will, and you know why," he said.

Driving to the hospital he remembered Sarah's cold haughty bitchy face as she ushered him out of her house. His erection subsided. He parked and sat with his fists clenched around the steering wheel. Oh how he had misjudged her! She had misjudged him. Whose fault was it? It was hers. What was wrong with her, that she could not think past fucking and not fucking? How was that any different from what boys are accused of? Why wasn't it as easy to assume a person had pain inside, and longing, and that the complicated, meaningful feelings had nothing to do with lust?

He put his fingers to his face. He could smell Glee on his hand.

12.

"Okeydoke, you gotta get the picture. This guy, Longli was his name, he falls off this Swiss mountain, and listen, here's the good part, *he gets stuck.* He doesn't disappear down some crack in the range, he dangles out on a hunk of rock, in full sight, but out of reach. See, they climb up to try to get him and they can see him but he is suspended, like in mid-air— He's been hanging there for a year. Meanwhile there's this fellow down in the village, he owns a big telescope, what would you do? He sets it up and tunes in Stefano Longli as he swings in the winter wind. He had a lot of customers this last year." Leland grasped the edge of the table and leaned into it so far he nearly had his face in the remains of their very substantial Mexican dinner. The whole story told, he leaned back, tilted his chair, and guffawed. "If you could see the look on you turkeys' faces!"

Ellis said, "One of these days somebody is going to stuff your newspaper clippings right down your big-mouth throat, Piper."

David found it hard not to laugh, not at the poor mountain climber, but at Leland finding himself so funny.

"I always thought a public death would be the worst kind," Leland went on blithely. "Executions, say. How'd you like to be strung up in front of a crowd?"

"I don't think they do that anymore," said David.

"Yeah, but just 'spose. Or you fall down in the middle of the street, gasping for air, your hands on your throat—" He gestured aptly.

"I say if you're dead you won't care where it happened," Ellis said mildly. He munched on a broken tortilla chip. "Only Leland will care, when he reads about it in the paper!" The three of them laughed and hit one another.

"You guys want anything else to eat?" David asked, and the other two groaned. They were at Cisco's in colored town on Friday night, and they had eaten like kings for five bucks. The room smelled of beans and onions and cigarette smoke. The white family trade, from the other side of the railroad tracks, came and went early in the evening and now, after eight o'clock, the boys sat as if on an island, surrounded by empty tables. In one corner a Negro family was eating, paying the white boys no mind. The children, a boy and girl of grade school age, were dressed in starchy dress-up clothes. Along the window wall of the cafe half a dozen Mexicans sat at two tables, drinking beer and joking. Cisco, his big paunch wrapped in a white apron, came to the table. He had the easy saunter of a successful man; his fiery food, of best quality and low price, drew customers from all over Basin. In his thick accent he asked the boys, "What else can I get you? Josefina, she make you some nice sugary cinnamon chips, you eat them with coffee."

David spoke in a low conspirational whisper. "Actually, Cisco, we were thinking it was time to toast the new school year. The new football season. If you get my meaning." He pantomimed his hand around a bottle, his ready throat.

Cisco pulled his apron up and wiped his dripping brow. "You boys get me in trouble."

"Hey, you look around you, *matador*," Leland said. Cisco's claim to fame was his cousin Pepe, *banderillero* to a top Mexican bullfighter, whose posters adorned the walls. The Negro family got up to leave. Cisco said, "You hold your horses, *caballeros*," and went up to the cash register. Afterwards he disappeared for a minute into the back, and came out with three long-necked bottles of Dos Equis.

"Now that's a good Meskin!" Leland exclaimed. Cisco's expression was completely bland. "That'll be a dollar each."

"A dollar!" Leland protested. David put up his hand to end the talk. "Open 'em up, *por favor*." When they had their bottles, they held them up in the middle of the table. "To our last year, may it go fast," he said.

"To not suiting up." Ellis added, their annual toast.

"Say hey!" Leland said. "To no jerseys, no tackles, no pain."

They cheered and drank. David pulled the bottle from his mouth to add, "And no glory, alas," which caused Leland and

Ellis to make faces. David drank the rest of his beer in a gulp, and belched loudly. Leland followed suit. Ellis' burp was small and high-pitched, and they burst into raucous laughter.

Cisco gathered the bottles quickly. "You boys can't handle *cerveza*, eh?" he teased.

"You know, we're seniors now," Leland bragged.

Cisco said, "You come back when you graduate. I buy you a beer myself, the end of being boys."

"Add it up, we'll divide it by three." David told Cisco. "And add a dollar for the great service." He belched one more time and patted his chest. "Girls are nice, but they're not up to the company of men," he said grandly.

Cisco lifted his pencil off the pad where he was doing his figuring. "Women are madonnas," he said.

Leland hooted. "You lead me to 'em, buddy, and I'll worship at their shrine."

As they clambered into Leland's '52 Chevy, Ellis sniffed the air. Ellis's father had been a tenant farmer in Central Texas; Ellis was always noting the weather. He said, "Dry as ground bone still. But rain's gotta come. That drouth broke last year. It's September. Fall's in the air." They were, after all, at 3,000 feet. The night would cool fast.

Leland turned the key and revved the motor. Before he dug out from the gravel-strewn dirt in front of the cafe, he said, "What do you know, Whittey? I don't 'spose you could fry an egg on the walk anymore, but it's still summer. I smell like a mule from sweating."

"That was all those chiles, Piper," David said, pronouncing *chiles* the way it sounds in Spanish.

"I tell you, if this is the first week of school, why don't we celebrate the end of summer, and go skinny-dipping at the windmill?" Ellis suggested.

"Hot damn! Now there's an idea for picking!" Leland said, and gunned the motor.

"I'm all for it," David agreed. The sudden thought of his body in water was quite appealing. Dusk was over, night was rapidly blacking out the sky. They sped back into the main part of Basin, out the county road, and onto an old pasture they knew, where there was still a working wheel with a tank up six, seven feet high. They climbed out of the car and shed their clothes on the ground. Sometimes, with other boys, in

the showers at school, David was wracked with self-consciousness because of his skinny body, his pale skin, his
drooping sex, though there was nothing wrong with it, he
knew that. With Ellis and Leland, he felt like a little kid
before he noticed other boys were bigger. Ellis could have
been his brother, they were built so much alike, Ellis a little
bit skinnier, his arms a little longer and stronger. Leland was
tall but like a big flat board, and he always seemed to be
walking into invisible walls, gracelessly catching himself before he stumbled. The Three Sticks. They were buddies.

There wasn't a ladder, so David climbed up on Leland's
shoulders and heaved himself up to the edge. He pulled up
Leland, who stood on Ellis' hands, and together they hauled
up Ellis. With a whoop and a holler, they fell backwards into
the tank.

The tank was just big enough to float in place and maneuver a little, not big enough for strokes. They dunked one
another and snorted like seals. Ellis climbed up the rickety
little ladder to the top of the windmill and cannonballed off.
Deeply tanned from his work, he was a study in two colors,
pale as bread below his waistline. David and Leland hugged
the side of the tank to stay out of the way. Although this was a
favorite part of the sport, it was dangerous. The water was
about six feet deep, not allowing any real dives. And if there
was any breeze, the windmill moved, the wheel rotated.
David had gone out once when Jason Short got his ass
knocked right to the ground from up there, and broke his
leg in two places. With the three there tonight, the bravado
level was reasonable; they didn't have to impress one another. They just wanted to have a good time.

"Oh brr!" Leland said before he jumped. Wet, you could
feel yourself turning blue in the high prairie night. After the
shock of air on your bare skin, the water felt warm going
back in.

As if on signal, the three of them quieted and hung in the
water, bouncing and dogpaddling to keep their heads clear.
Leland, several inches taller than the other two, could manage to stand still, craning his neck high to clear the water.
David worked his way to the edge and leaned his head
against the tank, holding onto the edge behind him. He
looked up at the sky, which was now smeared with milk white
stars. "Look at that, will you?" he said, with awe in his voice.

"It's just flat-dab gorgeous, ain't it?" Leland said, ever playing the yokel. Ellis added, "That's heaven up there."

In the next few moments, in the silence, David felt suspended in the water, and then suspended again, as if the tank floated in the sky. It *is* beautiful, he thought. Somewhere far off a pump was beating like a giant heart.

He dunked his head and brought it up, shaking like a puppy. A person doesn't live under the stars, he mused, unless he's a nomad, or a mystic fool. What's the point of craning your neck to see something shining so far away it's probably dead already? Where will stars at night ever get you?

He reached out and splashed his friends as hard as he could, and after one more round of horseplay, they went home.

"Come on in," David said as Leland pulled up in the alley. "Maybe my pop's got some beer. We can chew the fat a while longer."

"I feel whipped," Leland said. "I'm going to bed."

"I can get home from here," Ellis said, and got out too. He and David thumped Leland's car and went into David's room.

"I don't feel ready to be inside," Ellis said. "Want to sleep out?"

They dug out a pup tent from Saul's storeroom and lugged it over to Ellis' where they set it up in the yard. In town, it was warmer, the air still. Besides, there wasn't room in Ellis' house for David to sleep over. Inside the tiny tent, they were quiet and still and congenial, tucked into old army-green bags with plaid flannel linings. They had been doing this since they were twelve. David had always liked to hang around the Whitteys. Ellis' mother made big pots of beans, and homemade light bread, and in the mornings there were soda biscuits and grease gravy. Everybody couldn't sit down at once; she fed the little kids first, or they ate off their laps, sitting on the floor. Mr. Whittey called his wife Mama, she called him Mr. Whittey. Ellis told David once that he could remember the first time he heard his parents whispering to one another, saying their Christian names. It had thrilled him to discover their secret.

"You mind about football?" Ellis asked. He meant not playing. Football was all Basin cared about in the fall. Every business sponsored the team, plastering walls with big posters and photographs. Everybody assumed that if you were high school age, and male, it was on your mind.

"Hell no. Football's boring." David realized that football had not even been mentioned that morning he spent at the country club. Maybe it was because the Kimbroughs had a daughter. Maybe it was that rich people could afford to have other things on their minds. David wished he could talk it over with Ellis, but he felt sheepish about having played out there and not saying anything about it up until now. It was too late. "What about you?"

They already knew what each other thought, but it was comforting to say the same things once in a while. "Not me," Ellis said. "Where I was a kid, the sport was getting in your daddy's crop. The big kids were Negroes, and we didn't play with them. Out here, it's like this annual brain disease. Football! Travis is miserable about it."

Travis was one of Ellis' little brothers. "What for? He's only fourth grade."

"Fifth. He showed up after school the second day for practice, and the coach told him he'd been cut."

"Cut!"

"Yeah. He said he's not big enough, he should find another hobby. He didn't even tell him find a sport. He said hobby. Travis told him, 'My brother's going to be state tennis champ!' and this asshole says back, 'Well, I hope that makes you feel better, son.'"

"Asshole is right. So let's get Travis a racket."

"I think swimming. I'm going to pay for him to take lessons at the Boy's Club this winter. He's not going to be very big, but he's already strong. He could swim, I think."

"You look after them, don't you?"

"Aw, it's like looking down and seeing yourself at all the stages you just went through. Ornery little kids, they are, but tough, and smart enough, good guys. I don't understand the girls so well, I guess that's Mama's business. But the boys are like pieces of me."

"You'll make a good daddy one of these days," David said, meaning it.

"Not too soon, let's hope!" Ellis laughed.

"Well—you do have to have a girl first." David scrubbed Ellis' scalp affectionately.

"So—?" Ellis said.

"Hey, what haven't you told me?"

Ellis turned and lay on his back. He sighed and tucked his arms behind his head. "Know who Betty Leyerbach is? Little blond? She's in our class."

"I don't know. I don't think so."

Ellis flipped over restlessly and propped his chin on his hands. "She's only about yea-tall, skinny as spaghetti, she wears these little circle bangs—"

"And you're dating her!"

"Yeah," Ellis said with satisfaction. "I saw her at the hiring hall one day, her dad's a dispatcher. And then I saw her at Mass and decided it was fate."

"So how far's this gone—?"

"It's not like that, David. She's sweet. She's *Catholic*."

"What do you guys do?"

"Same shit as anybody, what do you think? Go to the movies. Went to the Teen Center a couple of times. But I like to go over to her house and sit on the back step and talk, too. She's got a nice family. She never—she never even dated before. She's so shy, till you get to know her."

"That's great, Ellis. Boy, things go on when you're out of town!"

"Remember the year we got to be friends?" Ellis said. "Seventh grade. I don't know what my daddy was thinking, bringing us out here. He couldn't make it, farming. I guess he thought oil fields were full of something you could pick wild. He didn't know he'd be a donkey ever after."

"You got here just in time to watch the whole prairie dry out good." David said.

Ellis laughed. "You know last year, when it rained? Mikey, he's second grade, he said the teacher let all the kids go outside and stand in it all afternoon. They'd never seen a real rain. *They'd never seen rain.*

"Someday do you think we'll look back, Davy, and this will have been a wonderful year? Our senior year? Will we never forget it?"

"I don't think I'll ever think of it again, man. Once it's over, there's too much ahead."

"I hope so," Ellis whispered. "I mean, I hope it gets better and not just grown-up."

13.

Speech was turning out to be David's favorite class, as good as English. He wrote an original oratory on the dangers of appeasing the "sleeping bear, the Soviet Union." Mr. Turnbow said it was good enough to take to a speech tournament if he wanted. The first one would be in Abilene late in October. All David had done, really, was go through a stack of magazines half a foot high, picking out ideas he could agree with, and then arranging them to suit himself. He used a lot of stuff from the *U.S. News and World Report*. When he got up to say it, though, he believed it, and he wanted the class to believe it too. If we don't stop giving pieces of the world away to those tyrants, we won't have any world left. You can't keep evil at bay by feeding it. You have to stand up to it. Of course, he didn't say what they ought to do. He didn't want a war, that was for sure. He wasn't planning to throw himself away on some cold battlefield, like Korea had been. Ellis had had an uncle, his mother's brother, killed over there. There had been kids from Basin, too, probably joined up for the excitement, who had had their tanks blown all to hell. On the other hand, you did have to keep the Russians and the Chinese over on their side of the world. You couldn't have Communists in the Western Hemisphere. You couldn't have them inching their way right around the world.

The next assignment was to prepare a four- to six-minute interpretation of a poem or group of poems, and David knew just where to go for that, Robinson Jeffers, one of his favorites. When he read the two poems he had selected in class, Turnbow said, "I want to see you after class, Puckett."

Mr. Turnbow gave David a bright yellow copy of a play called "The Heiress." It said it was based on a novel by Henry James. David had never read any James yet, but he knew he would get around to it, in college if not before. "I want you to try out for the part of Morris Townsend," his teacher said. "I need you. I won't have a good show without a strong Morris. I know you can do it."

David had never tried out for a play—the idea of acting always seemed a bit precious to him—but as soon as he had the script in his hand he was eager to see if he could do it. Maybe it was being invited like that, the teacher seeing something in him, like a coach checking out a boy's broad back.

That night he helped his mother at the hospital ward. After supper, he told Sissy he was going to try out for a play. "You might like working on a play," he said. "Can you act?"

She giggled and said she had no idea. She was looking fine, perfectly normal; she was going to be discharged the very next day. Someone had set her hair for her, and it was wavy on each side of her part. She showed him a small leather wallet she had made, sewing through already punched holes to hold the two cut pieces together. He said it was nice, she had done a nice job, and she shoved it into his hand. "You take it," she said. He demurred, but she said, "Please, you've been nice to me, you take it."

He asked her if she was still writing in her notebook. She said, "Nothing happens here. I write things I remember, or I copy passages from the Bible." He asked her about that, and learned she was Church of Christ, and had been baptized by immersion, the same as her momma. She spoke very softly. "It was the devil trying to work his way," she said. He supposed she meant when she acted crazy out on the desert, but he did not ask to make sure. He did not think it would do her any good if someone heard her talking about the devil.

After the patients had gone to bed, except for the few who sat in the day room playing cards, David read "The Heiress." He loved the elevated language of the play. People in 1850—people who had an education—spoke carefully, with fine words and extravagant courtesy. That was Morris Townsend's forté, fine language. He said things to Catherine, the wealthy woman he was pursuing, like, "You are so gay, so sought after. It makes my way harder." He was able to turn her every doubt to his advantage, as when he said, "If you are puzzled, you are thinking of me, and that is what I want above all—that you should think of me." And of course it worked perfectly. Poor plain Catherine fell hard. David could see that Morris was a kind of villain, although the father, who saw through him and blocked the marriage by threatening to cut off his daughter's inheritance, was the true villain. It was the father who was cold and implacable and ungiving! The father who taught Catherine that she was not lovable. Perhaps it was true that Morris was willing to marry her only because she was rich, but that did not mean he would not be a good husband. It did not mean that he would not be affectionate company. There was nothing in the script to suggest that he would not be kind to her. And when, at the end, after he had returned, truly sorry, and they had made plans again, Catherine jilted him in revenge, David felt like crying in frustration. How could she be so stupid! *She would have got what she was paying for; was that so bad?* That sort of thing must have happened all the time, must still happen. Morris was a man with no resources, who was willing to trade what he did have, his own charm and intelligence, for a comfortable life. That did not seem villainous to David. And he wanted the part. Something about the deceitful, artfully soulful Morris touched him. And he could see the pleasure there would be in dressing in a fine period costume and saying those lines, appearing before all his classmates in this guise of charmer-scoundrel. They would see that he had a talent he had not used before!

He stood in front of the bathroom mirror and practiced the dialogue. He lifted his eyebrow and tilted his head just so, standing as tall as he could. He tried lowering his voice. He stared at his reflection as if it were Catherine, making his eyes say, *Trust me.* Then he went to tryouts.

Except for one girl from student council, the kids at the audition were ones that David did not really know. There were no athletes, no pep squad girls. It was not that the students were weird, exactly, it was that they were like woodwork, unremarkable members of a large student population. It was interesting to watch them read. Most of them were not especially good, but they tried hard, and several were all right. You could hear them, and you could tell they wanted to be someone else, someone different from themselves. You could tell how much they wanted to be in the play. One boy who had been in a couple of David's classes over the years, Derek-something, was an obvious choice for the father, Dr. Sloper. Derek was fat, with a nice clear voice, and you could see that in a costume, with sideburns and makeup, he would look prosperous and older. Girls seemed to have come from everywhere, pale-lily types and fat girls, but also perfectly presentable girls he just did not know. He read with several of them, twice as Dr. Sloper, a part he did not want, and after the first hour or so, as Morris, with three different girls. Although one girl looked a lot like he imagined Catherine looking, plain as oleo, she had an insipid voice, and she could not seem to stand still. David noted how distracting her purposeless movement was, and immediately resolved to stand in place, as if he owned his little part of the stage. Each time Mr. Turnbow interrupted to change the student reading Catherine, but kept David on, David felt more confident. He stopped wiggling and gulping, stopped worrying so much about how he sounded, and concentrated instead on the words, on Morris' goal, to win Catherine and her fortune.

It was getting late, after nine o'clock, when Mr. Turnbow called up Patsy Randall to read Catherine. She was not a very attractive girl, bony and broad-shouldered, with wild curly hair she didn't seem to bother styling. She might have had an okay figure, but you could not really tell under the shapeless boy's shirt she wore with jeans. She was in David's honors English class, had been last year, too, and she was a good student, always asking questions as well as answering them, but David, who had occasionally admired something she said, had not paid her any real attention. She did not have the delicacy he liked in a girl, nor the style. And she had never so much as looked his way, as far as he could remember. But when she began to read, he felt a shock of recognition, as if she were someone he did know and had forgotten, or someone he should have known, or, even, someone he had known in a dream, or another life. She made him nervous, in a pleasantly disturbing way. Her voice was wonderful, as deep as Susan Hayward's in "I Want To Live." She already had a repertoire of timid movements for the Catherine character—he guessed she had spent some time in front of her mirror, too!—and she had a compelling quality. He watched her read with a real turkey named Mark; she helped Mark along, made him look better than he was, while all the while you only really cared what she was saying. David could see what Mr. Turnbow meant about Morris' part. If the actor playing it were weak, he would not be able to use Patsy Randall, for she would dominate the relationship, and the play. He was eager to read with her, the way he had sometimes been eager to play a certain tennis player, not because he could beat him, but because he could not be sure. When he did read, he felt like a current was passing between them. She read better than ever, and he knew that she made him look good. They read the scene where Morris proposes to Catherine, and as her eyes lit up, as if what he said were real, as if it mattered, as if she loved him and he could have what he wanted, he felt a gush of pleasure and anticipation, whether as David entering his first experience as an actor, or as Morris looking forward to a gentleman's life, he did not have enough experience to tell.

Mr. Turnbow said, "Let's call it quits for the night. I'll post callbacks in the morning, for tomorrow night. If you're not cast, remember we really need you for crew, and there'll be another play in the spring. You're a great group!" He came close to where David was standing and spoke to the girl from Student Council, Betsy, who had folded up some of the chairs and stacked them in the wings. He was telling her he admired her leadership qualities, and he wanted her to think about stage managing the play. David admired Turnbow's enthusiasm and warmth, and his voice, too, which lacked all but a trace of the nasal West Texas twang, and he admired the way he took Betsy's obvious disappointment—she was not going to be cast—and turned it to his advantage and hers at the same time, giving her a different task in the show and making it seem important, too, which it probably was.

"And you two," Mr. Turnbow said as he caught David's eye. Most of the kids were gone. Patsy Randall had helped Betsy pick up scripts and turn out lights. "Patsy, David."

As soon as Mr. Turnbow came close, David felt like shouting. He could see the excitement in the teacher's eye. Mr. Turnbow said, "You have no idea how good this is going to be." He wanted David and Patsy to come by during lunch. "I have some tapes I want you to use to practice, get rid of those tight little *e*'s, put some crispness in your consonants. Can you do that, say a couple lunch hours a week for a while?"

David grinned and, not thinking, reached out and took the girl's hand and squeezed it. She smiled and squeezed back, then pulled her hand away nicely. "Whatever it takes," she told Mr. Turnbow. To David, as they went out of the building, she said, "Looks like we'll be working together, huh?"

He stopped in his tracks, and so did she. They were almost exactly the same height, but she was not a small girl. He lifted his brow and smiled again. "I'm looking forward to it a lot," he said smoothly.

"You're already him, aren't you?" she said. He could not tell if that was supposed to be a compliment or not.

The next time he saw Sissy was Friday, after the "Heiress" cast had been posted. The afternoon had cooled and turned blowy, and he and Ellis had batted balls back and forth the last hour of school, and for a while afterwards. They had grown desultory when David noticed Sissy standing off to the side, at the end of the court. "Want to do this tomorrow?" he asked Ellis, picking up two balls and walking along the edge of the concrete, where it was cracked like a dry cuticle.

"I'm going out with my daddy tomorrow," Ellis said. "We're going over by Hobbs somewhere, I don't think I'll get back till late Sunday."

"That doesn't give you much of a break."

"It gives me a check, ole buddy," Ellis said, and headed back toward the gym.

David waved at Sissy on his way in. When he came back out and started his walk home, she appeared off the grounds somewhere and came up alongside him.

"You live by me, remember?"

"Oh yeah," he said. She was carrying a couple of books and an ugly plastic pocketbook. "I thought you weren't staying there, though."

She shrugged. "It didn't work out, staying in a foster home. My parents wanted me home real bad."

They walked a few blocks in silence. David felt like he ought to be nicer, but he didn't know how. Away from the hospital, where he had tried to make her feel like she would be better soon, he had nothing to say to her. She wasn't likely to have anything going on at school.

"Come in a minute?" she asked. "I'll show you my room."

He was taken by surprise. It seemed such a pathetic request. Show you my room?

He met her mother, a grown-up Sissy with the same mousy

hair and weak face, the way Sissy would look one day, all worn out. Mrs. Dossey was in the kitchen peeling potatoes while a baby squalled and banged on a pot practically underneath her feet.

Sissy's room was done up in pink and white. She had frilly curtains, a pink flowered bedspread with a white ruffled border, and half a dozen dolls propped against pillows. It was the kind of room you invented for a girl but didn't know if any really had, a nicer room than the rest of the small house, though the furniture was shabby, and he guessed the trimmings were all from Sears. There were magazine photos of Janet Leigh and Ava Gardner taped to the mirror. Glee liked Ava Gardner, too, and James Dean and Natalie Wood. Glee's bedroom was yellow and light green, with a big mirrored dresser and a carpeted floor. Girls seemed to need stuff like this around them, to remind them they were girls.

"Go on, you can sit on the bed," Sissy said. The mattress sagged as he sank onto it. She reached into a drawer in her dresser, under some other things, and brought out the notebook he had bought her, bright blue with a kitty on the cover.

She sat down on the stool by her dresser, and began immediately to read in a small piping voice.

> There is a boy in my history class with pimples so bad on his neck it looks all blistered over. Once I had a pimple on my chest and it took a long time to come to a head. Every day I'd look at it a bunch of times, wanting it to do whatever it had to do. I felt like I had done something bad to deserve this little sore thing. It burst one night while I was asleep and made a little wet spot on my pajama top. I never had another, at least not yet. I never had any on my face. I guess I'm just lucky.

Christ! David thought. He could not think of a word to say. Sissy was looking at him happily, all pleased with herself. "I do have moles, though," she said.

He tried to think what Morris would say, not that girls in 1850 ever mentioned the body. "The hair on my chest is not much more than fuzz," he heard himself say. He took a long slow breath. "We all have our flaws and worries, don't we? We all worry about things nobody else notices."

"One more?" Sissy said, and turned a page. She looked almost perky, now that she had his attention. David thought she must be the strangest girl he ever met; actually, he was beginning to think all girls were nuts. One day he would ask her about the rabbit, and about her dad. Probably she had talked about them until she was sick of it, in the hospital. She read.

> *Mrs. Munsing, who lives next door, came here from Minnesota when she was a young woman, because of her allergies. She thought the clean high air would make her well. She got married and had children. Her son died of rheumatic fever, and a daughter died of polio. Her husband died of a heart attack when he was only 51 years old. But Mrs. Munsing, who moved here to stop sneezing, hasn't even had a cold in thirty-five years. She told my mother God picked her out especially for suffering, and made her strong so she would live long enough for a lot of it, like Job.*

"Well!" David said. "You could probably make a story out of that." He meant it too, though it was not the kind of story that interested him, and Mrs. Munsing seemed a dull sort, whatever her sad life. "It's sort of like an O.Henry story, or de Maupassant, ironic," he said, though those writers were clever, annoyingly so. Irony did not work if you said, Look, isn't this the oddest thing anyway! Irony was not Ripley's Believe It or Not, not Leland's store of amazing newspaper anecdotes. Old Bodkins had told the class once, kids your age have no sense of irony, which he thought might be true because life for Basin kids was so predictable. A sense of irony was like a highly refined sixth sense. *He* knew life was likely to turn around on a dime and show him something he hadn't been expecting. Irony was his mother journeying to New York and coming home as burdened as if she had never left. His father, child of immigrants, finding a way to live in a foreign land. Irony was his sister leaving one tyrant and marrying another. Irony always had something absurd in the heart of it, it relied on gullibility or bad luck. David preferred stories that were tragic and inevitable, where events piled up on one another like a mountain of rocks, until one last event toppled everything. Like *Anna Karenina.*

A bubble of nervous laughter erupted from Sissy. "Oh, I couldn't write a story! When I finish a notebook, I tear it up out at the trash barrel and start a new one. I wouldn't want anyone to read it."

He felt jerked back to her. "But, how can you? After you've written it all down!"

"You save yours? You write stories?"

"Sure. I mean—I haven't really finished one yet, but I write down ideas."

"I wouldn't know how to do that. I don't know anything about writing stories."

"You have to read a lot," he said. "I could lend you a book, or tell you some to read. Did you ever read *Tess of the D'Urbervilles?* By Thomas Hardy? Oh, it's a wonderful long book. They have it in the school library."

"I have to read something for English," she said. "I could read that." She put her notebook away. He got up and said he needed to get home. "Is it sad?" she asked. "I'd want it to be sad."

"Sure, it's sad," he said. "Of course it's just a story. It's nothing that really happened." He thought he ought to reassure her, so she wouldn't overreact.

As he was leaving the house, Sissy's father came up the steps in long stride, his jeans and boots filthy with dust. He had a toothpick in his mouth. Mr. Basin Low Life, David thought. What did he ever do to her? That's what he wanted to ask her. He wondered if his sister had told Pete Kelton all the ways Saul had mistreated her. He was sarcastic, she could say. Would that rouse sympathy from Kelton?

He ran the last block home as fast as he could, wanting his chest to feel the sprint. He burst into the house and found his father in the kitchen stirring something at the stove. That might mean Saul was in a good mood.

"Hey Dad!" he shouted. "I'm in a play! I got the best part!"

His father turned and licked the spoon before he spoke. He said, "Now won't you be good at that?"

14.

He ate dinner—a stew, with tough undercooked chunks of beef and soggy carrots—and excused himself. His father said David had to go around the house and close all the windows before he "took off somewhere;" it was going to rain. David banged each window shut, satisfied at the sharp sounds. The window in the unused bedroom had been left open for a long while, and dust was piled like a dune on the sill. The whole room had a musty smell. He felt like he would explode if he did not get out of the house. As soon as he stepped out, in shorts and a sweatshirt, he saw that the weather was changing fast. The crackly air made the hair on his arms stand up. He felt a wave of moodiness surge through him. He set off at a steady lope out of his neighborhood, across the main street, and off to the east part of town that had sprung up with the oil boom. Houses and trailers seemed to have been tossed on the caliche plain like dice on a table. The ground was so hard, so soil-less, they had only to pave it with a huge sheet of asphalt that ran up against the curbs, gutterless. For dozens and dozens of blocks in any direction, houses sat on a waste-land. There were no trees, only the scruffiest of bushes, sometimes a sad attempt at a yard, usually gone to stickers. Here and there, semis and oilfield equipment were parked on the residential streets. He passed a yard closed in with cyclone fencing; several Dobermans flung themselves at him, clanging against the fence, growling and barking ferociously.

The wind was gusting and the sky was full of dark clouds. The air had a funny electric smell, something besides the dust that was picked up and blasted in his face at intervals. He ran harder. He ran to dare his chest to hold his heart.

Glee was having a slumber party for the pep squad girls. He turned and ran back across town to her house, slowing down the last couple of blocks, until, as he approached, he was walking heavily, his hands on his hips, bending over to gulp air. He stopped under a sycamore across the street, standing where the sidewalk would have been if there had been one. There were lights on in every room of her house, and he could hear the McGuire Sisters singing "Sugartime." The curtains had not been drawn, and he saw girls moving around in the living room. Two of them were dancing together. A gust of wind came up and blew leaves around his feet; he saw the curtains shudder in the big living room picture window.

Suddenly the front door opened and girls poured onto the walk. He realized they had come out to look at the sky, which was black and dramatic. What had been on the ground—leaves, dust, bits of paper—was now in the air, caught in the odd sporadic gusting, and the air itself had a quality of it, a smell and a feeling, that made him sense danger in the offing, the air you expected in certain scenes of very dramatic movies, just before the heroine's lover's plane was downed over the Atlantic. It was a condition of the plains that came in the fall, and even more frequently, more dramatically, in the gusty spring, when it was not so cold as to drive you inside. Sometimes it was like this before a great dust storm, sometimes before a rain.

The girls were dancing around in the yard like witches, waving their arms and twirling. He was startled by huge drops falling on his face and arms, and he saw that that was what had brought them out, the beginning of rain, that and the wind. They had heard it, or smelled it, before he saw what was happening, although he was out in it.

One of the girls was pointing at him, and then they all turned his way, one by one, laughing and peering out, their heads stuck forward like geese. Glee was one of the last to turn; girls gathered around her. She broke from them and started walking across the yard and into the street, holding her hair back from her forehead with her hand. She was in shorty pajamas. They were all in pajamas or long tee-shirts. "Davy?" she called. "Is that you, Davey?"

He ran, hard as he could, straight into the wet wind. He had just turned onto his own street when the sky seemed to open and great sheets of water cascaded onto the street and onto and over him.

Glee called, whispering into the phone. "Why did you run away? Why were you there? *What were you doing?*"

He held the phone and could not think how to answer. He

saw himself as she had seen him, a stranger looking onto her party, a voyeur, or worse. "I don't know what you're talking about," he told her.

"Everybody SAW you!"

"Tomorrow, Glee," he said wearily. The rain was pounding on the roof, he could hardly hear her. He wanted to crawl into bed and pull a quilt over his head. So he did.

It rained all night without letting up, and through the next morning. It was early afternoon when it eased to a lighter rain, and late afternoon before it stopped.

Around three o'clock, Leland came in his father's pickup with the big wheels, splashing through water inches deep. They went by Glee's. The water had covered her lawn and lapped against her first step. David waded up to her door. The other girls were gone; her stepfather had taken them all home the night before, soon after the rain had begun. David carried her out to the truck. She was delighted. She was still puzzled; when she said, "I still want to know—" he put his hand lightly on her mouth and said, "Shush," and she did. As soon as they were in the truck—he scooted to the middle, himself—he turned to put his hands on her neck, and kissed her tenderly. "I am flooded with love for you, my sweet," he said in a throaty, melodramatic voice. She stared at him for an instant, then burst into giddy laughter. "You're so silly!" she said, "You're so silly!"

All over town, cars and trucks were cruising through the shallow water. Drivers leaned out and yelled at one another cheerily. There was a festive air, as if the cars were heading somewhere for a parade or a rodeo. Some cars were stranded, unable to push through. People's yards lay under water. Little kids were everywhere, splashing and yelling in the light rain; some had climbed up on car hoods, stretching themselves tall for a better look, as if they stood on a high knoll. David saw a big red collie swimming down a stretch of low culvert. It was warm. When they crossed the county road and headed east, into the newer, stark section of town, the flooding worsened. There was no place for the water to go, and so it had simply risen, on many streets, right into people's houses. Leland parked and asked if they wanted to get out and go see worse.

"What does that mean?" Glee asked in a squeamish little-girl voice.

"The next block over is Chesterfield, where my cousin lives. He says neighbors have boats out."

Glee made a face, but crawled down out of the truck. They sloshed across someone's yard and around the block. Glee's bangs flattened on her forehead in the misty rain. The street where Leland's cousin lived converged with another street in a low-lying intersection. The water had filled the space, making a considerable pool that lapped up over the four corner lots, toward the houses themselves. There were people standing knee deep in water, gesticulating and shouting at one another, and children splashing. There were several little fishing boats out in the middle.

David went back to Glee's house with her and spent the rest of the afternoon lying on her bed while she played records and jabbered about school and her friends and the games that were coming up. Of course Saturday's home game against Amarillo was cancelled because of the flooding. "So what should we do?" Glee asked him. "With the evening?"

He crooked his finger to beckon her to the bed. She glanced at the door, which was closed but did not lock. Her face flickered with a smile; she tiptoed across to him and sat on the edge of the bed. He pulled her arm so that she fell across him. "They won't come in, will they?" he asked.

"I don't think so, but we can't do anything here, Davy, I couldn't!"

He laughed at her and rubbed her breast. "Just kissing, Hewett," he said. She was warm and soft and uncomplicated. He felt grateful for the flood and the long quiet evening. "Until something comes on TV."

"I'll tell Mom you're staying for supper, okay?" she said happily. She brushed his hair with her fingers. "You look lazy, David, didn't you sleep in all that horrid rain?"

"I couldn't sleep," he said. "I was thinking about you."

Her mother insisted that he stay the night. She put quilts and pillows out for him on the couch, and she and her husband went to bed early. Glee and David sat bundled on the couch and watched an old movie about mummies escaped from an Egyptian tomb. Very stealthily, they made love. He did everything in slow motion, murmuring in her ear. "Do you think I'm different?" he asked. "You're the best," she whispered back. "Ohhh," she said softly. He didn't know when she left him. By then the movie was over, and he had fallen asleep.

When he got home Sunday, his mother was in the kitchen in her wrap, drinking coffee and reading the Sunday paper. "Leland called," she said. "He wants you to call him. It's about this drowning—" She tapped the paper. He sat down and read the article. A three-year-old boy had drowned on Chesterfield, about five in the afternoon on Saturday. He had waded into the pool the flood had created at the intersection of Chesterfield and Clermont, right where they had been in their sightseeing.

"Oh man, we missed it!" Leland said when David called.

"I don't see how it happened," David said. "There were people standing all over the place."

"I know, I know. My cousin was there, too. This little kid, he just walks right to the middle, to the deepest part, and without a splash, he disappears!"

"Didn't they see him going in?"

"Sure, they saw him, but they thought when he got to the deep part he'd turn around and come back out."

"He was three years old!"

"I *know*. They didn't know how deep it was, maybe. They didn't think that a little kid like that could get—*lost under water, on a city street!*"

"Somebody should have seen. Somebody should have gone in. Jesus Christ, they all stood around and watched him drown! A little kid!"

"Aw shit, Puckett, you can say that, you weren't there. You can say what you would do and wouldn't do, you're so smart."

"I wouldn't have just stood by, I can tell you that."

"You don't know, you weren't there. You wait till somebody's in trouble in front of you and see what you'll do. That's the only way you'll find out. Wait and see how wet you want to get."

15.

"I'll never see you!" Glee protested when David told her what his rehearsal schedule would be. It wasn't really true. The first week they rehearsed after school, and he went over to Glee's a couple of nights to do homework. When they moved into night rehearsals, it was only Sunday through Thursday, so he had his weekends, just like any other time. It was only at the end that it would take all his time. Besides, when he explained to her what his part was, she changed her tune. She liked the idea that he was the star, "A star," he corrected her. "Hardly the word anybody would use. There are three of us. You say, 'lead,' not 'star.'" She told everyone. Her friends came up to him in the hall and said they were dying to see him in a play. Glee was only jealous of his time, not of the girls on the set. She knew Patsy Randall was no competition, and the other girls, David told her, were all sad sacks, except for Betsy, the Student Council girl who was stage manager. He thought Betsy was keeping tabs on him, but there wasn't anything to tell.

He didn't have time to go up to the hospital, and his mother complained, but if he borrowed her car he could spend the last hour of her shift up there, and if he was home, he put a kettle on for tea, or heated a can of tomato soup when she was due. One night he brought home a caramel from the prop table and sliced it into six pieces and arranged them artfully on a saucer. He set the saucer on a paper napkin on the table. Marge loved it. "Silly boy," she said. She played with the pieces of candy, moving them slightly on the saucer. "Go on, eat one," he told her. She never did anything for a lark. She never did anything for herself. She laughed and flipped a tiny slice over, like an egg on a skillet. "You know I don't eat sweets," she said.

"Just this once," he told her. He talked her into it. She put a slice on her tongue and sat while it melted, looking off in the direction of the stove. She sucked at the juices the candy made, smiled at him, and got up to get her whiskey.

He wondered why there were caramels on the prop table. Every once in a while he would see someone carefully peeling a piece. Some kids popped caramels into their mouths whole and chewed furiously. Some nibbled like rats. He never took one; they were too sticky for his taste.

He sat on a chair in the wings with his English text on his lap, telling himself he ought to use the time to study. But the scene on stage was between Catherine and Dr. Sloper, and he could not stop watching Patsy as Catherine. She was wearing a long muslin practice skirt with a dirty ruffled hem, and her hair was caught up in a rubber band, pieces escaping at the neckline. When Mr. Turnbow stopped the scene to talk something over, she chewed on her lip, or sucked her cheek in. She wore no makeup, and under the stage lights she looked pale. Her shoulders were like slats under the man's tee-shirt she wore, but he could not stop watching her. She stood very still—when she moved, there was some reason—but her face was so expressive. Her cheekbones seemed to tremble as her father rebuked her. Once she looked over and saw David watching her. Their eyes fixed, quite clearly, for an instant. She did not acknowledge him at all, she went back to her business, but he felt as if she had touched him inside his shirt, or on the back of his neck. That was what she did on stage, she got to you.

Mr. T. called a five-minute break. David went outside. He walked briskly away from the auditorium, to the edge of the schoolyard light, breathing deeply. He put his hands on his hips and threw his head back. The next scene was between him and the father. He had to defend himself with just the right blend of confidence, deference, and, somewhere, a quiver of doubt. This man could take away what he wanted, his bulk and authority could be a wall Morris could not get around. David did not know where the doubt ought to show. He didn't know how to ask Mr. T. about it, maybe not in the scene, maybe at the end, privately. He did not want to seem too cerebral; he did not want to seem to think himself too important.

He stood in the shadow and practiced raising his eyebrow,

practiced smiling so that anyone would say he was being respectful, but so Sloper would still hate him for his cockiness. Oh, it was subtle, all right, and you had to use all you had to project subtlety from the stage. The trick was to be honest and true, while all the time using the smooth speech and the careful gesture of the deliberate gentleman. The play was a world of artifice, he had to be a master of it. Each movement, each inflection of his character, he believed, came out of deliberation or carefully built habit. He had never realized how much power there was in really knowing yourself. He thought there were certain boys who had an instinct for creating themselves—he thought of his friend Burt Lasky, who was handsome and insouciant—but in the end, those who produced themselves deliberately would have more control. That was what he was learning from drama. He wished he could discuss it with someone. He told Glee the play was fun, he told her little anecdotes about rehearsals, but he could not say, "I'm discovering myself, little by little."

When he walked back in the stage door he was met by a great blast of laughter. He heard Betsy's silly giggle, Don Witham's snorty laugh. For one terrible moment he thought they were all laughing at him, but it was only an accident of timing. They were laughing at Derek, who played Sloper. Derek was chewing as fast and hard as he could while everyone stood around and watched him. David was baffled.

Patsy slipped over by him. "It's a tradition. A joke. The set people put out those caramels, and then they wait for one of the actors to have a mouthful when he's called on stage. It always works eventually. You're caught so off guard you can't think. Derek could have just spit it out, but look at him, trying to get it down." David shook his head and tried to look amused. Mr. T. called out, "Remember the caramels go when we start dress week, you clowns!" He was an easy guy. Derek took a big gulp and waved his arms. "Ready," he said, and laughed loudly.

"Ho, ho," Patsy said.

Sissy caught up with him in the alley after school. He slowed down for her. At the back of her house they leaned against the rickety fence and talked a few minutes. She said she had checked out *Tess of the D'Urbervilles* from the school library. She said she could see things would have to get bad for Tess, because she was a sinner. David did not try to argue the point. Sissy was perfectly serious. He thought it might do her good to plow through someone else's sad story.

Another afternoon they took a long way around, it was such a perfect, balmy fall day. In a yard not far from her house they saw an abandoned project, a fall-out shelter. He said, "Someone started into that with a lot of trouble, they might as well finish it." He was thinking, in case of tornadoes, although Basin was never in the path. Sissy said, "You can't hide from Armagedon, can you? Besides, who'd be left if everybody else was dead?" She could give him the willies. When he told Leland about Armagedon, Leland said, "Whooey, that girl needs cheering up." David suggested that Leland ask her out. Leland hooted at the notion. "Don't you know she adores you, Fuckett? Because you're so understanding." David wrote some notes so he wouldn't forget her strange remarks. He tried to imagine Leland and Sissy making love. He was sure they were both virgins. He would have liked to write a story about them. He thought it would be comic.

One night at rehearsal, waiting for a scene, he sat down two rows behind Patsy with his civics book. She was reading a textbook. He noticed how pale the skin on her neck was. She laid down the book and picked up a library book. He could see that it was Robinson Jeffers,' *Roan Stallion.* He had checked the very same book out the year before, from county. They did not have Jeffers at school. He remembered that after he read it, he walked for miles in the dark, he simply could not recover from the drama of the long narrative poem.

There was a scene in progress on the stage. He moved quietly down to Patsy, sat, and leaned close to whisper. "I'll give you a ride home if you want, and you can tell me what you think of a woman who falls in love with a horse." He did not think she could fail to be surprised, maybe as excited as he felt; he had not known there was another human being in this county who knew Jeffers, let alone a high school girl. Patsy held her finger in the book, and whispered back. "I don't want to talk about it. It would ruin it to try to understand it, like school."

He felt humiliated. He popped up and jumped over the seat, making a racket, and went back to his civics book, his face burning. Patsy turned around in a few moments and hissed at him. He looked up. She put her fist to her chest and pounded over her heart, smiling at him. It was all very stagy, and too late. Jeffers did not make his heart pound; he made his head thick with ideas.

As rehearsal was breaking up, she touched his arm and asked if she could still have the ride. He did not know how to refuse. It was gusty and cold. In the car she said she walked everywhere, a mile and a half back and forth to school. She was relaxed and friendly, as if she had not just put him down and then made fun of him. He just drove, but it stirred him when she said, right after she told him where to turn, "I don't think a day goes by that I don't think of that line of Jeffers', 'I would sooner be a worm in a rotten apple than a son of man.'"

David remembered the line. It was in a poem about men stoning a mammal in a pit. "I read he lives in a tower. He climbs the steps every morning and sits above the ocean to write."

"I guess that proves you don't have to live a dramatic life to write," she said.

"Oh, but wouldn't it be more fun to have things happen!" he said earnestly.

"Maybe reflection is for old poets."

He liked her better now.

She lived in a seedy tourist court on the edge of town, a rundown motel that rented studios by the month to oilfield workers. She invited him inside, where there was a small room, combining kitchen and sitting room, with a sofa covered in a faded yellow chenille spread, a broken down arm chair, and a card table with two straight-back chairs. He saw a tiny hall with two doors. The room had a shabby air, but it was clean. Patsy opened a window a few inches and told him to sit down. "I'll see if I have some pop." She opened the fridge. "Aha. Want to split the last beer?" He said he wouldn't mind. She poured the beer into two glasses as he watched from a chair. He rubbed the prickly fat arms of the chair with his thumbs. He liked it that she poured the same amount into both glasses; Glee would have given him two-thirds of the beer.

Patsy curled up on the sofa, her legs tucked, a couple of pillows behind her back. She pulled the rubber band out of her hair, wincing, and her hair flew out around her face. She stretched one arm up high above her head until something popped. "It gets me in the neck, all that concentrating," she said.

"Yeah, I know what you mean," he said. He leaned forward, his elbows on his knees. "Is it just you and your dad?" She had already said, coming home, that her dad was a night watchman for a cement company, and did maintenance for the motel. She did lots of chores, cleaning up the rooms weekly, or when somebody moved out.

"I have to make him supper before he goes," she said. "If I didn't, he'd eat sardines and crackers. I don't know what he'll do when I leave."

He took his glass over and set it in the sink. It made a sharp sound, though he was careful. He turned and leaned against the counter. "Where is it you're going, Patsy?" He noticed the room's odd neutral air. There were no photographs, no personal items lying around, except for her books and purse on the floor near the sofa.

"I'm going to be an actress," she said calmly. She had turned on a lamp and as the light struck her face, it darkened the hollows under her cheekbones. "I'll have to move somewhere I can work and go to night school. We've talked and talked about it. There's nothing in Basin. Daddy understands."

"There's nothing here," David said. He realized there were many things he wanted to tell her, or ask her, but they were jumbled up in hot tension, he did not know where to begin.

"That's why my mother left," she said. "I didn't understand for a long time, but now I do. She couldn't say, This is it, my life, this is enough. She had dreams. Maybe she didn't know when she married Daddy, when she had me. She wasn't grown up yet." She sighed. "That's my story, David. My mother left, when I was thirteen." She spoke flatly, staring at him, almost like there was a dare in the telling.

David sat back down in the chair. He leaned into the sprung cushion and stretched his legs out in front of him. He thought if he had another beer, and then a long nap on the couch where Patsy was sitting, he could get up and tell her everything. He did not care about her mother, but he wanted to hear her voice. "Where did she go?"

"She went to LA with her dentist."

He shifted in his chair. A lump was digging into his right hip. LA.

Patsy's mother said she would send for her. For a year, into a second year, Patsy received postcards: orange groves, Hollywood hotels, movie stars' homes. Then, nothing.

"That's tough," David said.

"I worry she's a waitress, living in a crummy room." She smiled and tossed her hair. "Who knows? She picked it."

"You want to go out there?"

"LA?"

"The movies."

"No, I want to work on the stage. I want live theatre." She was wearing jeans and a navy sweatshirt chopped off at the elbows.

He thought he'd like to hear her read from *Roan Stallion*.

She got up and washed the glasses and some other dishes at the sink. She spoke over running water. "Next time you tell me what you want to be, David. Right now, I'm feeling foolish. Like I said too much."

"You didn't."

"I hope I'm not kidding myself. I'd rather be dead than stay in Basin."

David moved across the room. He stood a few feet from her. She turned the water off. "Nobody's a fool for wanting to be somebody!" he said. The hairs were standing up on his arms. "You're not counting on a fairy godmother. You're counting on working hard."

She turned around, her hands dripping suds, and smiled at him. "Don't forget luck. That's what I'm counting on. That's the part you pray for. In the end, that's all poor people can count on. One-third work, and two-thirds luck. And that's scary, 'cause if you were lucky, wouldn't you be one of the rich ones?"

16.

He was sorry to be where he was, in the back seat of Burt Lasky's father's Olds. There were four of them, parked somewhere out of town, staring off into a black sky with the tiniest sliver of moon. Burt was in the front seat with Glenda Faye Budge, David was in the back with Glee. The car smelled of whiskey. Burt had a silver flask, and they had talked the girls into taking a couple of sips.

He knew Glee was happy to double-date with Burt and Glenda Faye. Burt belonged to nothing, did nobody favors, but he was tall and well-built (he played tennis, and swam), and rich. He never went with one girl for very many times, without interspersing other girls, but it didn't seem to matter. The girls who went out with him were good-looking, popular girls. They liked Burt to escort them to dances and other public events. He always looked good next to their pretty dresses.

Glenda Faye's father was a lawyer, the kind that made the contracts between oil companies and everyone else. She usually dated football players, or went out with rich boys who were friends, the way rich kids were, from hanging out at the club together since they were little. Glenda Faye had that air of inaccessibility that bordered on snobbery but was too courteous, too gracious, to be downright hateful. David could not think of a time she had ever spoken to him. She was like Beth Kimbrough. She was one of those girls. They were probably girlfriends.

Now, though, she was in the front seat with her pale pink cashmere cardigan unbuttoned and barely hanging off her shoulders, and her matching pink straight skirt hiked up around her hips. She was rustling and shifting and occasionally making odd noises, while Burt, silent and careful, moved his hands wherever he wanted them to be.

Glee cast flurtive glances to the front, but tried to keep her eyes on David. She was growing uneasy at his lack of enthusiasm. David thought she wanted to be distracted. It seemed increasingly likely that the couple in the front seat would soon be lying on that seat, and David, though initially surprised, was now fairly certain that Glenda Faye was not turning out to be a cool and classy girl after all. Maybe that made Glee feel better. Didn't a girl want to be two things at once, two impossible things, a virgin who *never had,* who was saving it as the supreme gift, and at the same time, a girl who could twirl a boy around her finger, because she was so sexy, *because she knew what she was doing?*

He reached across Glee and opened the door. If she had not had her legs up on the seat, and his hand firmly on her arm, she would have fallen straight out. "What?" she protested. He told her to get out. He slid out and leaned back in the half-opened door. "Ten minutes, Lasky," he said. "I mean, ten minutes, that's it."

"You're crazy!" Glee said. He steered her away from the back of the car. She stumbled in the weeds. It was a dark night. In a moment, when he stopped, she wrapped her arms around his chest. "What's going on?"

"I'm not going to sit in there and listen to Lasky fuck Glenda Faye," he said curtly.

"Oh stop," she said. "They weren't. Glenda Faye wouldn't." She didn't sound convinced. She ran her hands down his body. "This is weird," she said, like she was deciding to enjoy it. "Nobody can hear us, that's for sure."

He pulled away. "I'm not in the mood."

"You are such a big grouch!" she cried.

He jammed his hands into his pockets. "Be quiet," he said. "Listen to the night."

"Oh yea, now there's an exciting adventure. Listen to the oilwells."

"Pump jacks."

"What*ever.*" She moved close to him again, but kept her hands to herself. "It's really spooky, Davy, what if he drove off and left us?"

"I'd kill him."

They both stared back at the car, but it was only a vague shape in the dark. He was thinking about the afternoon. Burt came by to take him for a ride in his new car, a little red

Triumph. They killed a six-pack, maybe not far from where they were right now. They sat in the gusting wind and Lasky told him how he was going to go to the University of Texas and find a Jewish girl.

"You care about that shit?" David asked.

"You only call it that because you're not really Jewish." It was one of Lasky's old themes. It used to be the Laskys tried and tried to get David over to their house for holidays, for Friday nights, but when it became really clear, when the year of bar mitzvahs passed and nothing happened, when they started high school, all that stopped, and Burt had to say, Of course your mother's not Jewish, you're not either, really. It was one more way for Burt Lasky to be superior. Saul wouldn't have anything to do with Lasky. He called him, "that German Jew." (Only Chasen the junkman was proletarian enough for Saul!) But David and Burt had hung out together off and on in junior high. They had played tennis the first couple years of high school, David had gone over to the Laskys' to swim. They had something in common, for all their differences. Lasky wasn't really in. He felt better next to David; that was the whole secret of their friendship.

"I don't know who I'm going to marry," David told Burt that afternoon. "I don't even know where I'm going to go to school, let alone what I'll be." Dr. Lasky was an oral surgeon; it was certain Burt would go to dental school, move back home, set up with his father. It was boring as hell, thinking about it, and it wasn't even David's life.

When they went back to the car, Glenda Faye was collected again. She and Glee giggled and gossiped all the way to town. Glee told what she knew about poor pregnant Shirlee Ames, and Glenda reviewed Carl Stuckey's every movement since Shirley left town. David and Burt did not attempt conversation, though once Burt looked back over his shoulders at David, with a smirk.

As they came onto County Road, David leaned up and asked Burt to drop Glee off at her house. He said he didn't know if he'd have a car, which was a lie, and Glee knew it. She didn't say anything, only glared at him. Burt and Glenda waited while David walked Glee to her door. "They put me in a bad mood," he apologized. It wasn't Glee's fault, after all.

"I'll say," Glee said, and slammed her door in his face. He

liked her little fit of spunkiness, but she'd be really pissed if he didn't call her yet tonight.

"Now me," he said, when he got back in the car.

As soon as Burt dropped him off, he took his father's car. There was a lamp on in the living room, his father was probably drinking, his mother would be home any minute. He didn't even go in first. He drove to Patsy's, parked a couple of units away from hers, and walked over. There were lights on, a radio playing. What if it was her father's night off? What would the guy think of him arriving at this hour? What would Patsy think?

He would find out.

He knocked lightly and called out, "It's David Puckett."

She opened right away. She was wearing jeans and a man's baggy cotton sweater. Something by Buddy Holly was playing on the radio. She grinned. "Sorry, the grill's closed."

"I know it's late. I know it's crazy. I had a date and I took her home because I wanted to see you." The song stopped, the DJ started blabbing, there was a screen door between them still. "I'm sorry, I shouldn't have." There was a delicious smell in the air, from inside the room.

"I'm writing. I mean, I just stopped. I was making a bacon sandwich. Are you hungry?"

He dared to reach for the door. "I thought the grill was closed."

"Come in."

There were papers all over the card table. She made them sandwiches, spreading the bacon a little thin to make two, and filling up space with layers of lettuce leaves. She took a big metal bowl off the counter and swept her papers into it, then sat down with him. She gave him a Seven-Up, and herself a glass of water.

"You knew I wouldn't have a date?" she asked.

"I didn't know. I didn't think much. I thought I'd see what it looked like over here."

"I'm not dating anybody now. With the play, and school—I'm taking trig, chemistry—"

"Why?"

"Why not? To prove I can."

"I hate math and science," he said. "I like English."

"I know. Mrs. Schwelthelm's good, isn't she?"

"That and speech, that's all I can stand. My other teachers are brain-dead."

She laughed, making noises through her nose. They finished their sandwiches in silence. When she had cleared the table, he asked her when she'd been writing.

"Listen, I—" He would swear she was blushing. "Nothing you'd be interested in."

"But I would. I write."

"You do?"

"I keep a notebook. More accurately, I want to write. I have these ideas for stories, but I haven't put any of them together. I can't seem to make myself sit down and do it."

"You have to make yourself! It helps if you set a time. You say, like a date, like now. Saturday night, after I do the dishes, I'll write. It's that important. You set time aside for it."

"Show me something?"

"I dunno."

"Read me something."

She rummaged through the bowl and came up with a half-piece of paper. "Okay," she said. "But I can't look at you." She turned halfway away from him. "Okay," she said again, and read:

Cherry blossoms cannot bloom.
nor sweet waters fill the earth
till you return to the warm hollow
of my arms.

She turned back. "Really, I can't. I don't know you well enough. It's embarrassing."

"It makes me want to read everything."

She looked at him, laying the paper down on the table. "You know Emily Dickinson?" she said.

"Sure. 'I'm nobody, who are you?'"

"She wrote, and wrote, all her life, and never showed anybody."

"She was a strange lady."

"A poet."

"Usually poets want to be read."

"I'm not ready."

"What's it like? How do you get the ideas? That poem— that's a love poem. That's a poem after you love somebody."

She turned her head. "A lot of writing is pure imagination. Or you use one experience to feel another, like in acting."

"And language. It's like one of those Japanese poems."

"Sort of. I didn't follow rules."

"If you wrote that tonight, you had a lot better time than I did."

"Oh yeah!" She smiled. "Weren't you out with the cheerleader?"

Everybody knew his business. "I had a double date. The other couple was very hot."

"I hate dates. I hate getting dressed and getting picked up and finding out where I'm going. I hate talking about school and other kids—"

He reached out to touch her hand. "It doesn't have to be like that. If it's somebody you like. You just—get together."

She snorted. "Is that what you do?"

He got up. Glee was going to be in Snyder for a game next Friday. She'd be mad that he didn't go on the booster bus, but he could plead exhaustion, he could say he had to help his mother. "Like I could come by Friday night? We could go have a hamburger, and then you could show me some more poems."

"What about your girlfriend?"

"People are always saying that to me!" He banged his hand on the flimsy table. "Sorry," he said. Quietly, leaning toward her, he added, "The whole idea is not to do it the other way. We're going to be friends, Patsy. We're not going to talk about school and other kids."

"We're not really going to go out at all, are we?"

He didn't know what she meant, what she wanted. "I'll come over Friday, six-thirty, seven, okay? We'll see what happens. Don't dress up. Don't think about it."

On the radio, it was time for a Golden Oldie. The Platters sang, "The Great Pretender."

"Listen," she said at the door. "Don't tell Mr. Turnbow I said this. But when you get into costume? Play with it. Pick little bits of lint off of it. Straighten the lapel, that sort of thing. Not a lot, but when you think he's a little nervous."

"I could try that," he said. You did wonder what to do with your hands.

"And when you come over, it's your turn. Show and Tell. I can't be friends with you if I don't know who you are."

She was working on a poem that started out, Morals are

meager comfort for lame dreams—He wasn't sure what she meant, he thought she was talking about being good when you felt like being bad, but he didn't want to ask, it wasn't important to understand completely. That Friday night, he told her about the woman who loved a much younger man, out of her grief. It took him nearly ten minutes to tell it, all sorts of things came to him as he talked. He thought about how Sissy was always popping up and following him, and it made him think, this woman could see him playing tennis. She could come back, day after day, while he practiced, and then one day she would say something. He would find her beautiful at first, but she was older, he would want it to stop. That's when the woman would kill herself. "For God's sake, write it down!" Patsy said. He told her he was Jewish. He told her about his father leaving them for five years. He thought they had that in common, though Saul came back. He touched her hands, he touched her arm, once he brushed her hair off her forehead. He didn't kiss her. He didn't want to cross the line. He felt so close to her. Driving home, he thought: There is a kind of sex that takes place all in the head.

He wondered if Patsy could be his muse. Maybe that was what he'd needed all along! The idea made him smile. When he got home, he turned on his radio and sang along. He took out his notebook and drew two lines of little posies. God, he had so many ideas, talking to her.

Of course that was all he had done so far, talk.

17.

David and Glee went to a dance at the Teen Center. Pete Kelton was the disc jockey, "slinging platters for your entertain-uh-ment!" The place was packed. It was cold, the movies downtown were for old people this week ("Elephant Walk!"), this was the first dance of the year with a DJ instead of the jukebox or radio for music. It was the sort of occasion Glee especially liked. She was nicely dressed, in a short blue flannel skirt and a fuzzy white sweater. All evening she could run up to friends to get and give hugs, exchange silly remarks, and, generally, show off. She kept a steady tug on David's arm, steering him from one cluster of kids to another. He didn't have a lot to say; the play was going into dress rehearsal, so he could claim to be busy, he could encourage everyone to come. He had missed as many football games as he had gone to—Glee tormented him with complaints about his lack of interest in his own school, besides disinterest in seeing her butt twirling on the edge of the field—but he could comment on how the team was doing—very well—and wonder who would get nominated for All-State, and where the quarterback might go to college.

It was too warm in the huge room, and the drinks were sticky, in clammy plastic cups, most of the ice melted, the carbonation spent. He wanted to have a good time—why else had he come?—but he felt foolish dancing to the beat of the hard drums, or the groans of Ray Charles. He only felt competent when they danced slow tunes, when he could hold Glee close and make her happy, saying things down onto her neck, like, you smell good tonight, I like your hair, you're the prettiest.

Kelton was doing a favorite act of his. He pretended to be the "slippery killer," who drops knives and falls on victims. He stuttered and flailed his arms, he laughed at his own jokes. The kids called out to him, "Killer Kelton!" and then turned away, so he would go back to playing Paul Anka and Sam Cooke. Nobody could look at him very long. He was skinny to the point of emaciation, with a high roll of slick black hair. He wore tight pants and a shiny shirt open low, with a gold chain. His voice was too big for his body, round and loud and deep, bearable over the air, but embarrassing when you connected his sound and his look. Girls who had come alone to the dance found their way to the table where he was working, and stood with their arms folded, or leaned against the table, waiting for him to put a record on and lean over to ask their names, and what's their games, and whatever other BS came out of his big mouth.

David did not miss his sister; he had never felt any particular attachment to her, they were not an affectionate family, they had not grown up "doing things together." Yet, looking at her husband Kelton, he could not help thinking that if she were what she ought to be, what she really was—a teen-age girl—she might be at this dance, maybe with a date, or maybe with a girlfriend, hanging out. She might even be waiting for a chance to talk to Kelton, their "Red Hot Host, Your Pal and Music Master," instead of sitting at home by herself twiddling her thumbs. But she had done all that, early on. Wasn't that how she'd got herself into a foolish marriage? She had entered a contest to make up menus for some crazy creature Kelton had invented (fried fly wings, frog filets, disgusting nonsense), and he called to say she'd won, she could come down and pick out twenty records. Of course the records were rejects, every one, and Joyce Ellen didn't even have a record player, but it was Pete Kelton all along she'd wanted as her prize, and whatever they had done, going through records, it has been a fairly straight march—six, eight months?—to elopement and him at the Teen Center preening, while she watched TV at home.

At ten there was a grand roll of drums and an announcement: the Cooper-Railey Muffler Shop was providing hot dogs for everybody. Donations would go toward the Teen Center activities fund, because, said Earl Railey, son of the real Railey, and only two years out of high school himself, "The dawgs are on us!" Early Railey looked eighteen going on thirty. His pants hung in the seat, and his shoes were scuffed. He was married, and his wife was pregnant. She was behind a table, stuffing sausages in buns.

Glee wrinkled her nose at the sight of the food, but David was suddenly voraciously hungry. He loaded up on mustard and pickles and onions and relish, and had a big mouthful when he looked up and saw Beth Ann Kimbrough coming in the door. He felt like Derek the night he ate the caramel; no matter how hard he chewed, he'd never get through the load in his mouth. Beth Ann was with Warren somebody, who had graduated the year before and gone to TCU. A tall boy, he was wearing a sports jacket and looking amused to be home among the babies. She was wearing a dress with a skirt that floated around her knees. They had been elsewhere, maybe to the country club, to dinner. She was a princess, visiting the serfs.

A Johnny Mathis song came on, and she danced with Warren. There were only half a dozen couples on the floor. Everybody was eating, or talking to someone who was eating. Beth Ann and her dated looked like they were dancing in a glass bubble, nobody could touch them. Her skirt fluttered when they turned. When the song was over, she clapped her hands lightly, and looked once around the room before departing. She saw David. She raised her hand to wave at him with her fingers. He swallowed, he still tasted hot dog, his throat burned.

The next day he went over to Glee's to study. After an hour he suggested they take a ride. It was a clear, sunny day, with the sharp bite of late fall in the air. The sky went on forever. She wanted to talk about Homecoming; she was buying a new formal. He wondered who would take Beth Kimbrough. He wondered if Lasky had asked a girl, or some girl had asked him. He thought about his white jacket—his father had picked it up for him in Lubbock at a buyers' closeout—and wondered if the yellow streak at the bottom on the back actually showed. The lights would be low. He resolved right then to make it a special evening for Glee. He'd take her to the Alamo Hotel for dinner. He would enjoy that, remembering the banquets he'd bussed his freshman and sophomore years. And maybe, once he was at the dance, he would have a good time. Everybody would be looking good. It was one of the rituals of high school life. At least he wasn't one of the ones left out.

"So which do you think?" she was asking. "Pink or pale green, I think those are my last two choices." He thought she would look silly in pink, with her dark skin. "Green," I think, he said. "Sure, green would look good. There'll be lots of pink, you don't want that." She leaned back, satisfied. She and her mother were going down to buy the dress the next day. Now David would know the color, when he chose her corsage.

He started trying to tell Glee about suburbs. They were studying them in his sociology class, which was to say that the teacher had shown them a film and given them an article to read, typed out from *Time*. It had to do with freeways. If you could get in and out of the city, you didn't have to live in it. He had to write a little essay, would you want to live in a suburb, or wouldn't you. Glee smiled and bobbed her head. "That's nice," she said. She had never been to Dallas or Houston; she didn't know what a real city was. She wasn't any different from most Basin kids. Where would *he* ever have been, if it hadn't been for tennis tournaments? It was something, to have a father from New York City, and never the mention of a visit, never the chance to see relatives, or the Empire State Building, or a real library.

"If you lived in a suburb—if you were a wife, see, with a baby, and your husband worked in the city—you'd be there all day, with the other wives. You'd drive to the supermarket and the cleaners and all, but most of the time you'd be inside your house. So the houses are nice, they make them big."

He had an idea. He had seen banners for a new housing development, Sherwood Estates, he told Glee. (A little forest, in Basin, Texas? he wondered. Maybe a bush, at the corner near the model house.) "These places are like that, it's just that we're not a city, so it's not a suburb. Let's drive out there."

Glee wasn't paying any attention to his explanation. She was along for the ride. Where they went didn't really matter. She never looked past the end of her nose. He knew there was a larger world out there, and she didn't care. He felt poised to enter that world, to break away from this one, and she only wanted to move up out of high school into the next stage.

How could anyone want to live in a suburb? Barbecues and

TV, fucking after the kids went to bed. He got the picture, little that they discussed it in class. He wanted to live in a city, right in it. He could see himself in a tiny apartment, maybe a dirty building, but he'd paint the apartment white. All he would need would be a bed and a table and chair. He would sit at the table at night, and write a novel about teen-agers, he would tell the world what they were really like, and get famous. He would get rich and go to Hollywood, like Fitzgerald. Only, who cares about teen-agers? And what did he know? And look what happened to Fitzgerald when he got to Hollywood.

The development consisted of a dozen houses tidily arranged on an utterly flat and desolate plate of land east of town. There was no bush in Sherwood Estates, nor a tree, nor a flower. There were poles, with lengths of plastic streamers hung around the model house, and driveways gouged out of caliche. The yards looked like slabs of stone. The houses were in various pastel hues: aqua, pink, sand, mint, yellow. There was one floor plan, and its reverse; the houses sat side by side, their garages only six feet apart, and yards ten feet wide on the outside.

The salesman was standing in the driveway talking to a couple that had come out just as David and Glee arrived. They went inside, alone in the place. David had never been in a tract house before. There was something spooky and yet wonderful about it. Everything was perfect. The kitchen had a large center bar, tiled in turquoise and yellow, with pine cabinets and yellow walls. The living-room was painted a neutral, sandy color, and the blond wood furniture was upholstered in turquoise and light brown. Huge lamps sat at each end of the couch. The drapes were beige with flecks of gold and aqua; they were pulled back to let in the bright light. Glee squatted and patted the carpet. "God, it's so *nice*," she moaned. She rushed around the kitchen, opening the refrigerator door, peeking in the empty cabinets. A bowl of plastic flowers sat on the yellow formica table. Glee ran her fingers over an ugly pink rose.

She led the way into the bathroom. The shower was huge, like a bright yellow cave. Glee stepped next to David and he put his arms around her. "I bet there would be lots of hot water," he said. He couldn't help thinking how nice it would be. Glee was nearly whimpering. "I hope I have a nice house like this some time," she said. "I'd cook dinner every night. I'd keep it clean."

"That sounds boring," he said softly. She was wiggling, moving in as close as she could get. He realized that he was as eager as she was. He stepped out of the shower, locked the bathroom door, and stepped back in. She had already pulled off her panties.

"You kids in here?" they heard the salesman calling. Glee was giggly and nervous, and happy. David leaned back against the cold shower tile; he turned his face to let his cheek cool for a moment. He closed his eyes.

"Always someone dropping in," Glee whispered. She was tugging and rearranging herself, laughing. He stepped out of the shower. Her eyes were shining. For a moment he felt sealed in the fancy model bathroom, trapped in Glee's fantasy.

18.

He often found himself staring at Patsy. She was a puzzle he wanted to unlock. She intrigued him; on stage, she mesmerized him. She might listen to the director intently, leaning slightly into the pool of light, and the act of listening was suddenly fascinating. She spoke with such clarity and resonance, you could hear her perfectly anywhere in the theatre. He asked her about her voice; he knew his own was weaker, that he strained to match her. It's all in the breath, she told him. She showed him how you have to breathe from deep in the cavity of your body, how your diaphragm is a floor. She put her warm hands flat against his ribs. He caught on fast. She said, "Of course you would, any athlete has learned something about breathing!" The strain in his throat went away. He could hear the difference, and so could Mr. Turnbow. "You've relaxed, David," he said. "You've started really acting."

The acting had seemed easy at the beginning, like playing dress-up. It was only as he got better—Patsy told him so many things—that he saw how much work it was to get it right. He learned lines easily, he learned how to turn, stand, walk across stage. He learned to keep his body "open," for the audience to see. Derek was a big Dr. Sloper, and David enjoyed the feeling of taking him on, standing up to him. He thought their scenes worked fine. Derek had a big voice and lacked subtlety, so David tried to be especially smooth in his scenes with him. With Patsy, something else was happening. There was a fine wire between them, a tension he could almost reach out to touch in the air. She could have taken every scene from him, but what mattered was that they were a team. What they made together made the play work. "Lucky me," she told him. "I thought Mr. T. would cast Jerry

McCain, Morris straight off the ranch." He realized she considered it her play.

He took her home after rehearsal each night and stayed a little while. They talked about their scenes. She told him about parts she wanted to play some day: Nora in "A Doll's House," Antigone, Lady Bracknell in "Earnest," Gittel in "Two for the Seesaw." They talked about what it would be like to move to New York. You would be poor, you would have to find work as a waiter or a clerk or who knows what, but you would be in the heart of the heart of the world, where everything was happening, where there was everything to learn. She thought about going there and taking acting classes on Bank Street (he wondered how she knew about these things); she said, "You could, too, you're talented," but it was unimaginable. He said he wanted to go to college, and as he said it he wanted it more than anything. College was how you climbed up out of the hole your parents were in. It put you in the running.

"Do you need college?" she asked.

He began to think of the future more clearly. "Maybe," he said, and his voice shook, trying out the idea, "I should study literature, and go on to graduate school. If I want to write, wouldn't I learn from the masters?"

"You'd learn old things!" she said. "Things you could learn reading on your own." She seemed to find the idea disappointing and unimaginative, but he was caught up in the notion. He saw himself at a podium, talking about Keats. He would have a tiny office with a window looking out on green lawns. "Maybe I could be a college professor." How many times had he said "maybe" in the last five minutes? She made him want things more than ever, but she made him wonder if what he wanted was the right thing. She acted so sure of herself, though her plans were more ghostly than his own. Get out of town: was that a career?

"In a tweed jacket, with a pipe? You'd look good like that," she said. He could not tell what the tone meant. Was she making fun of him? Was she seeing his vision?

He never stayed long. They were exhausted after rehearsal, and often there was schoolwork still to do. He met her father, a congenial man who did not have much to say.

The night of the first dress rehearsal, the scenes with Patsy were magic. She wore her hair pulled up high and tight on her head, and wisps escaped around her face. The sight of those cranky red hairs made him realize how vulnerable she was—Catherine, the spinster heiress, the object of his suit— and at one moment he lifted his hand to touch her face. He almost touched her, and did not, and he saw that she sensed both his impulse and his withdrawal, and suffered for his failure to follow through. He felt such power over her.

Between acts, they took a break. He stood at the back of the stage, where the door was propped open a couple of feet. Wearing a stiff collar and jacket, he felt hot and confined, and his chest ached. He leaned against the wall and tried not to think, tried to relax his chest.

Patsy appeared next to him. "She thinks she will die if she does not have Morris," she whispered. He thought she was excited. Although she was dressed exactly the same, she looked like Patsy and not Catherine. Catherine was timid and careful in her speech; Patsy was reckless, outspoken.

He took her hand and pulled her outside the door. It was a blustery cold night. He had never wanted to kiss a girl so much. She leaned against the building. Her chin was high, the faintest trace of a smile on her lips. He did not want to rush. He had always known that there would be tremendous pleasure in this moment, between the intention and the act.

Her lips were stiff. He kissed her gently, and put his hand on her cheek. "You're cold," he said.

"I'm scared of you," she answered, and put her face hard into his shoulder.

She said it was her father's night off, and she could call for a ride. "Of course you won't," he said. The wind had died. He drove around to the other side of the tennis courts and parked beside a giant elm. "Are you cold now?" he asked. His father's station wagon had a faulty heater. It took ten minutes to warm up, then it roasted you. There hadn't been time for it to work very well.

"A little." She sat rather primly, her legs together, her hands in her lap.

"Come here." He took one hand and tugged her toward him. "You're like a board." He felt her stiffen more. "What's wrong with you?"

"I'm surprised."

It seemed so natural to be with her, it seemed inevitable.

"You haven't wanted to kiss me?" All those nights, looking at one another across that crummy little room, talking pie in the sky.

"We were friends."

"We *are* friends! Patsy—" *He* was surprised. She seemed so bold, yet here she was skittish and silly. "We are friends," he said again, his voice low. He thought his voice sounded nice. He tried to think of other things to say. He felt her relax a little; he could see her shoulders lower, the tension in her face ease.

"I feel so stupid," she said. "Like we've gone off-book and I don't know my lines."

"Ad-lib," he said. When he kissed her, she kissed him back. Her awkwardness, her reticence, thrilled him. Sex wasn't supposed to be an easy game, it was supposed to mean something. Gently, he touched her face and neck and arms. Her arms were still at her side. She trembled.

"Oh Patsy," he gushed, overcome by his desire for her. He drew her onto him and leaned back against the car door. He stuck his legs out on the seat so that he could feel her long body on his own.

"I don't know what to do."

"Just feel," he whispered back. It took a long time to rearrange their bodies, small, gradual moves, until she was beneath him.

It was as he had imagined, this long act of love. She was passive, but slowly she responded to his touch. He felt her bloom inside his embrace. He reached up inside her shirt to caress her breasts, but it was too cold to undress. They both wore jeans, a terrible awkwardness, but she did whatever his hands told her to do. She brought her knees up when he tapped them with his fingers.

He took so much time, he was so tender. But when he moved his penis against her, she began to whimper, and when he pressed into her—there was resistance—she cried out and pulled away. "I'm not ready!" she said. "I'm sorry, David, I can't, I can't."

"Shh," he soothed. He stroked her, then touched her again, restraining himself from the incredible urge to push into her. It was such a cruelty, to feel himself at her door, and to be shoved away like an interloper. What had she thought they were doing?

He pressed, murmuring her name; if she would just relax, if he could just get inside her, he knew she would love him, she would be glad. She was the girl who wanted to live life!

"You have to stop!" she said, pulling her legs, knocking him aside. "I tell you, not now!"

"What do you mean, not now!" He was up on his knees, his own pants ridiculous around his ankles, his penis swollen, pulsing, pointing right at her.

She burst into a ridiculous nervous giggle. "It's looking at me!" she laughed.

He wanted to slap her. He grabbed at his trousers, yanked the car door, scrambled outside. He dressed, aching horribly, and pounded his fist against the hood of the car. He knew it would frighten her, he wanted her to be frightened. She was a fake, a girl who liked to appear so strong and sure of himself, and she was what you would expect from—from a freshman! From a girl like Sissy!

She got out of the car on her side and ran around to him. He flung off her touch. "God, I'm sorry!" she said. "It's the car, I think. The cold. I wasn't expecting—" She kept moving, she wouldn't let him not look at her. She looked like she was dancing on hot rocks. "We weren't ready, I can't get pregnant—"

"I'm not stupid!" he yelled. "I had what we needed, I wanted to feel you first."

"Getting pregnant would be the worst thing that could happen to me."

"You weren't afraid of getting pregnant," he said. "You were afraid of making love."

"It hurt. I'm cold, I couldn't relax."

He shook her off.

"Listen!" she said, her voice stronger. "I didn't want to make love in your car! I have a right to decide."

"Then you shouldn't have let me start. Don't you know anything? Don't you know what that does to a man?"

She reached inside his car for her jacket. She held it up against her, as if he might take it away. "A man? I don't think that's what you are, David," she said, and marched off across the tennis courts.

He could not sleep. He had been such a fool, swept along in some romantic fantasy. Why? Because she scribbled foolish poems and talked abut big cities! Because she had a little more experience than he did, acting. Because he was bored with Glee, and Patsy was there, like something you stumbled across in the alley. She was there.

He ground his teeth and cursed her. She was a smart-aleck, a coward, a cock-tease. She wasn't even pretty. And he, he was a fool with a prick for a brain. He tossed half the night, falling asleep so late it was midmorning when he woke, and nearly noon when he got to school. The attendance counselor hardly looked up; David always went to school, like a sheep with a herd.

He had nearly made a terrible mistake, one that would have embroiled him with a girl who cleaned motel rooms and built fantasies about being an actress, one that would have brought all hell down on his head from Glee, a perfectly nice girl, and scorn from Leland, who thought being in a play had made David a little crazy. He had been under a spell, the spell of the play. He had nearly come too close to a girl who was not in any way the kind of girl he wanted, a girl with nothing going for her except enough talent to look good on a Basin High stage. He felt enormous relief, reconsidering the night's disaster. He was glad not to have made such a giant step in the wrong direction.

It was easier than he had dreaded, there was only the week to get through, and, strangely, what had happened between David and Patsy did not seem to matter at all when they were on stage. If anything, the electricity between them was better. Off-stage, they did not exchange a word. The play was a great success. He took Glee to the cast party at Mr. Turnbow's house, but it was boring, and they only stayed a little while.

The following Saturday morning, some of the student council kids gathered on the football field. There was one last task before the game: the goal post needed to be wrapped in crepe paper. They stared up at the post in awe. It was so high.

Beth Ann Kimbrough said, "Last year Bobby Adams shinnied up the pole." They all looked at her. You're kidding, somebody said.

There were only girls there, and David, and one sophomore boy wearing glasses with a safety cord. Circumstances made David a knight. Adrenalin gushed through him like a cascade. Here was something he could do, something the whole world would see, and all it took was a little nerve. Nothing could have stopped him from ascending that height, though his heart pounded in his chest so hard he thought they must hear it on the ground, where they all stood, mouths gaping, as he worked his way up, trailing green and white paper. He had to do the climb twice. When he came down, his legs were shaking so hard he thought he might fall over. "Our hero!" one of the girls said, laughing in a nice way. He turned and looked for Beth Ann. She was smiling. A trick of the light made her seem to glow.

When Glee heard what he had done, she was so thrilled she said she would do anything for him, anything at all. She giggled and twittered, in case he didn't know what she meant. He said he had in mind something girls didn't like to do, or so he had heard. "You don't have to if you don't like it," he said. He thought it would hurt her feelings if he did not come up with something. They had been together nine months, like a baby in the womb. "I could try," Glee said. She wore her green dress to the dance, and the white orchid he had bought for her. She only ate a shrimp salad at dinner. She was so pretty, so nice to him. If she was giddy, wasn't it only that she was young? She was generous and honest; everybody liked her. It was a perfect Homecoming night. Basin High won by one point. Glee tried what he wanted, and did not mind. He liked her a lot, he had been crazy, all that was over now.

19.

David could not blame his father for refusing to go to Monahans for Thanksgiving dinner. He did not want to go, either. There was no place to escape in Aunt Cheryl's house. She, Uncle Billy, and cousin Lenore seemed to divide it up, so that you never were out of sight. They would ask Saul ridiculous questions about his relatives back in New York. Uncle Billy would try to talk "bidness" with him, though there was no meeting ground between a tailor and an oil field worker. Saul would give the food funny looks; he would go outside and take long walks around the neighborhood, so that people would call the house to see if he belonged there, like a lost dog. It had been years since these things had happened, but they were clear as fresh photos, and nothing would make Saul go. Yet Marge could not entirely enjoy her rare holiday from the hospital. To leave Saul behind violated her sense of family, her fantasy of togetherness. It embarrassed her.

Marge got up at dawn to make a Red Velvet cake to take to her sister's, and an apple pie to leave for Saul. She made the pie with sour cream, as he liked it, although she had had to go to two grocery stores to find the cream, and the pie came out looking muddy. She made a huge breakfast of scrambled eggs with fried potatoes and onions, biscuits, and stewed prunes, and they managed, the three of them, to eat it all, without arguing, without saying much of anything. They were all dressed at the table; that was unusual, too.

David and his mother left Saul behind, with a steak in the refrigerator, a green Jello salad, and the odd apple pie. Saul refused to say what he would do all day. He turned his back on them before they were out the door. Next they picked up Joyce Ellen, who was wearing a blue cotton skirt and blouse. "You look cold, honey," Marge said. Joyce Ellen, squirming in the back seat, said she was *all right*. "You've got to come over and get the rest of your sweaters," Marge insisted. Joyce Ellen turned to the window and leaned into her fist. David drove.

Marge lasted until they were out of town, then turned to her daughter, her arms over the back of the seat. "I know you've got a wool pleated skirt over there, why didn't you wear that?" Joyce Ellen was sniffling. In a moment Marge turned back, straightened her own old wool skirt, and stared forward stoically.

They were not in Aunt Cheryl's house two minutes before she had gone to a back closet and brought Joyce Ellen a white cardigan. Joyce Ellen did not protest. She put the sweater on and sat in the living room, in an armchair where no one could sit beside her, looking at a parade on television with their younger cousin Brian, a boy of eight who never closed his mouth all the way.

Jiminy Jesus, David thought, wondering how he would get through the day. He carried in the cake, and set it on the counter alongside a mincemeat pie. The house was redolent with delicious smells. It helped to anticipate the food, all of them at the table with the leaf out, cloth napkins, Uncle Billy brandishing his carving knife. Marge and Cheryl were the core the rest of them grew from. New York was very far away; this was the family David had.

Cheryl and Marge were huddled in the kitchen. Cheryl wasted no time asking after Saul sympathetically, as if her brother-in-law were impaired. It was too early in the day for Marge to crumple; she said something evasive about Saul working too hard, the tonic of a day to sleep and lounge, the cold he had been fighting and did not want to spread. David had to get out of earshot. The only thing he could think of to do was join his sister in the living room.

Brian had gone out the sliding glass door and was on the patio, bouncing a golf ball. Joyce Ellen had fallen asleep; she was snoring lightly, her legs stretched out and her blue skirt high on her knees, one hand clutching the front of her borrowed cardigan, the other flung over an arm of the chair. Behind her in the corner was their aunt's deep basin for hairwashing; the vinyl chair with its high curved back had been put away. David sat on the couch nearby and watched his sister sleep. Once, when he was in fourth or fifth grade,

he tried to bash her head in with an iron, but it was so
unexpectedly heavy that when he lunged, he fell straight
over and broke his own nose.

He heard his uncle banging around in the garage; there
was all the time to get through until the women put the food
on the table. Cousin Leona appeared out of the back of the
house. She was sixteen, but already she had the dumpy
backside of a matron. She was always ingenuously friendly, as
if she could not tell David thought her moronic, and today
she came at him in a particularly confident prance. She sat on
the other end of the couch and asked, in a high cheerful
voice, "Who do you like better, Debbie Reynolds or Doris
Day?" He mumbled that he didn't really like either one of
them. Leona, immune to his discouragement, next asked his
preference between Rock Hudson and Tony Curtis. Kindly,
he offered an answer this time. Tony Curtis made more
interesting movies, he said. Leona was putting off a faintly
sulfurous odor. She was fiddling with the skirt of her cor-
duroy jumper, her shoulders twitching, as if she had too
much going on to sit for long. David took a long breath and
said, "What are you doing in school these days, Leona?" He
was sure she was one of those girls teachers liked, bright-eyed
and quiet, never asking a question, but keeping her eyes on
the front of the room.

"Oh pooh, school," Leona said. She was wearing a heart
locket on a gold chain, and reached up to fondle it. "We
might go into Basin Saturday, to the movies," she said.

"Your school?"

She laughed. "Course not! Kids from my church group.
My daddy said I could go if there was a bunch of us."

"Safety in numbers." She would not need much protection,
he thought, then thought again. Girls like Leona were stupid
and eager, a dangerous combination. Sometimes they were
the easy ones, he had heard. She took on a sly expression.
"I'll sit in the back seat, don't you think we can fit in four?"

"Depends on the car."

"Oh yeah." He realized that the smell came from her hair.
Two curls curved on each side of her forehead, like double
parentheses, and a tight roll of hair hugged her jawline and
wrapped itself around the back of her neck.

The sisters began bringing in covered dishes. Marge spotted Joyce Ellen, stuporous in the chair, and rushed over to

her. She squatted beside the chair and took her daughter's hand. "Sweetie, it's time for dinner, wake up now," she said softly, then repeated the same words, more insistently. Joyce Ellen did not move. Marge looked up to see Cheryl staring at them. Leona said loudly, "Is she sick or something?" and David said, "I'll get Uncle Billy and Brian." He came back in time to see his mother leading his sister off down the hall. The rest of them stood around a few minutes, waiting. Billy said heartily, "Basin has had a fine season," as if they had been talking football all along. David, wanting this to be over, could only bring himself to grunt. He was hungry again, though he could still taste onions from breakfast.

Joyce Ellen reappeared, wan but washed and combed, with a weak smile. "I read so late last night," she explained. "I didn't get enough sleep." Cheryl pursed her lips. "I'm reading *The Robe*," Joyce Ellen added.

Uncle Billy swiped his knife back and forth on a long stone, flourished it above his place, and began to carve. While he sliced, they passed serving dishes around silently. David piled food on his plate.

Everyone complimented the cooking. Aunt Cheryl did produce a golden brown turkey, her candied sweet potatoes had crusty peaks, the meal could have been photographed for a women's magazine. Cheryl let them all enjoy some of it before turning her gaze onto Joyce Ellen.

"So Joyce Ellen, dear, when are we going to meet this mysterious husband of yours?"

Joyce Ellen sputtered and had to take a drink of water.

"It's too awful, to work on Thanksgiving."

"Mama, they don't turn radio off on holidays!" Leona said. Her mother gave her a smile. "No, I suppose not."

Joyce Ellen put her fork down and patted her mouth with her napkin. They were still looking at her. "He's in Dallas," she said in a small voice. "The station made him go."

David and his mother exchanged a look. He suspected his mother knew about this, but she was warning him to show no surprise, to ask no questions—unnecessary admonitions, for he did not care where Kelton spent turkey day.

"That seems very strange to me," Cheryl commented, and then, clucking, ran off to replenish the gravy boat. Joyce Ellen, nearly tearful, looked to her mother for support. They were separated, seated across the table and at opposite ends.

Suddenly this seemed deliberate, and malicious, to David. "You must sit near me," Cheryl had said to her niece. The only other empty spot for his mother was between Brian and Billy, at the far corner. They should have been next to one another, their hands able to touch under the tablecloth. Something twinged in David, recognizing the bond his mother and sister had. It was something about females, something weak, that made them cling.

Joyce Ellen leapt up and ran down the hall. They could hear her retching. Her mother ran after her.

Cheryl asked David if he could eat another slice of turkey. He said he could, he'd like dark meat this time. Uncle Billy slopped gravy over a torn up roll on his own plate. Leona cut up a slice of jelled cranberry into tiny, disintegrating pieces. Brian's elbow, on which he was leaning, slipped, and he crashed into his own plate and turned over his nearly empty water glass. Without getting up, Cheryl produced a towel from somewhere—under her chair? in her lap?—and wiped her son's face, then sopped up the water on the table. David was surprised that she did not scold her son. Maybe she was still upset about her niece getting sick over her Thanksgiving dinner.

Marge came back alone. "I put her on your bed, Leona, I hope that's all right."

Leona giggled.

Marge sat down. "Could I have a cup of coffee now, Cheryl? I feel shaky."

Cheryl said, as she rose, "I should think so."

David ate three servings of turkey, corn, creamed onions, dressing, pickled cabbage, candied yams. When dessert was brought out, he had a slice of mince pie, a piece of Leona's marshmallow fudge, and some of his mother's Red Velvet cake. He felt a little sick, and very sleepy. Leona was persuaded by her mother to play "Moonlight Sonata" for them on the piano. She held her lower lip tightly in her teeth the entire time. Then David was subjected to a ritual grilling: what courses was he taking, what clubs was he in, was he playing tennis again? A simpering Leona asked. "Do you have a gi-irrlfriend?" Her mother looked cross, and Marge said, "It's a time we got back on the road, Joyce Ellen's exhausted." She popped up like toast.

"Do you think it's flu?" Cheryl touched Joyce's forehead with her big pink hand. "Something she got from her father?"

Joyce Ellen blurted, "I'm pregnant, I'm not sick."

"Ohh!" Leona cried. "Ohh, a baby!"

Cheryl softened immediately. "Why didn't you say, dear?"

Joyce Ellen looked truly miserable.

"How can you stand to be away from your baby's daddy?!" Leona said. "Oh, I'd want to be with my husband, if I was pregnant."

Joyce Ellen said, "I just found out. I haven't even told Pete yet. I just found out."

Cheryl was on her feet. "I'll get your cake pan," she said. "Joyce Ellen, you take that sweater, it's chilly as can be out there. You don't want to get a cold now."

"If I was pregnant, I'd get on a bus and go to Dallas and tell him right away!" Leona exclaimed. "I'd go to the moon, if I had to. I'd drink champagne to celebrate."

"Leona!" her father scolded.

"You don't know anything!" Joyce Ellen cried. Leona's eyes widened. Joyce Ellen burst into tears. "I'm *tired*," she said.

David heard Cheryl tell Marge, "I wish you lived over here. I could be more help." David was glad to see she had piled leftovers in a tin pan for them to carry home.

"But she's over there," Marge pointed out. Cheryl nodded. She understood.

When they stopped at Joyce Ellen's house, David waited in the car while Marge helped Joyce Ellen in. She took her purse with her, so David knew she was going to give Joyce Ellen money. He could not think why that would be necessary. The Keltons lived in a modest duplex, what did his sister need the money for? Why was Kelton in Dallas? He didn't think anybody had explained anything. His sister was going to have a baby, though. That would give his mother something to do for the next sixteen years. One more thing for Joyce Ellen and Marge to do, one more thing to leave Saul and David out.

Saul was drunk on the couch. The television was blaring, the steak charred in the broiler, the Jello dumped in the sink. A loud argument began so suddenly David was not aware who yelled first, or what the yelling was about. Saul was a pig, Marge cared more about her sister's family than her own, and on and on. David put the leftovers in the refrigerator, the cake on the table, then went to his room and turned on the radio loud. He got out his notebook, stared at it a long while, and finally wrote: Girls have secret lives boys can never understand. He called Leland. There were relatives at the house, but Leland would come over. David could still hear his mother screaming. "I don't think so," he said. Leland was annoyed. "I'll come over there in the morning," David said, and hung up abruptly.

The screaming went on and on. Something was thrown, the walls shuddered. David went back into the house and tugged at his mother. Saul was on the couch, his knees up, his arms thrown about as if loosely connected. It was a relief to see that he was too far gone to be menacing. "Can't you see he's drunk, Ma?" David pleaded. "What's the use of talking? Let him be!" He turned off the television. "I'll make coffee," he said. "Come in the kitchen, please." His father stomped into the bedroom and slammed the door. His mother sat down in the kitchen and began to weep. Her eyes were so puffy they looked about to close. "It was a long day." David said lamely.

"When you have the first baby you've put chains around your neck. Children are your own special homemade prison."

"You can't mean that, Ma. Look at us, Joyce Ellen and me. We love you. Joyce Ellen can't get through a week without you."

"She can't, she can't!" his mother wept. "That's what I mean!"

David patted her shoulder and stepped back to the stove to watch the coffee. His mother went on. "You'll be gone soon, you know you're dying to get out of here, you hate this house, you know you do."

"Ma, I only hate it when you fight, I don't know what to do, I want you and Pop to get along—"

"I wouldn't do it over some other way," his mother said. "I wouldn't not have had you, Davy. But you'll be gone, and what'll I have then? A bitter man, a job with crazy people, a roof that's going to fall in." With her fists in her hair, she looked like she might pull it out.

David turned his back to her and stared at the pot as the

coffee began to perk. He would never marry except for love. He would not live a boring life. He would not be his father, would not be his mother's son. His mother was right, he would go away. He thought of Patsy, and his heart clutched.

He poured the coffee, and cut himself a piece of cake.

20.

He had just closed his locker when he saw Glee running down the hall. She was moving so fast and heedlessly, she knocked some poor girl aside and sent books flying. "Oh, sorry!" she shrieked, still running.

She was out of breath, her face red. "It's so exciting!" she said to him. "You won't believe it."

"Try me," he sighed. She wound her arm around his and steered him in the wrong direction. "I've got civics—that way."

"Walk me to English," she said. She was bouncing as she walked. "Ohhh!" she squealed.

The bell rang. They were outside her classroom. "Now you've got me in trouble," he said, although he doubted his stupid civics teacher would notice, or care.

"Nobody's going to get you in trouble, David Puckett." She was still relishing what she knew that he did not.

"Glee, I'm late, you're going to be tardy in another minute, will you just tell me what's on in your pea-brain so I can get to class?"

She jumped a step and kissed him on the cheek. "You know Sandy and I are practically best friends, and she's on yearbook."

He could not keep track of her best girlfriends.

"I saw her going down to the office with the announcements."

"I'm leaving."

She held his elbow. "Just *wait*." She peeked inside her classroom and waved at Mr. Rigsby. "I'm here," she called. Rigsby gave her a glancing look and turned to write on the board. "What are you doing, Hewett?" somebody called from within the class.

The principal came on the intercom. "I know you've all

been waiting for the results of the yearbook elections," he said, "so if you'll all settle down I'll read them to you right now." Glee was grinning so big it looked like her face would crack.

In a moment he understood why. She was the runner-up for Senior Class Favorite. He was pleased for her. He gave her a big smacking kiss on the mouth. Somebody in the class whistled. "That's not all," she said.

Beth Ann Kimbrough was Most Beautiful. This was no surprise. "I've got to *go*," he told Glee. Then he heard his own name. "What did he say?"

Glee kissed him this time. "You were elected Most Likely to Succeed." She threw her arms around him. "I'm so proud of you! I'm so happy!"

Over her shoulder he saw that half the English class was watching. He gave them a wave and backed away. "That's crazy!" he said. "Succeed at what?"

When he went to his locker at the end of the day there was a folded piece of notebook paper taped to it. "At what?" the paper said. He stared at the handwriting. It seemed familiar.

At what, that was the very question.

The next day he saw Beth Ann at student council. They congratulated one another rather formally. Talking to her brought a lump to his throat. She never said anything in council, unless it was to answer a question. She sat to his right, and back of him, so that he could not see her. It took a lot of self-control to keep from turning. She was so beautiful and elegant.

"I work on yearbook staff during your library hour," she told him as the meeting was breaking up. "Come by if you can."

When she saw him later at the door of the yearbook office, she got up and came out into the hall. "I voted for you."

He did not understand how it happened. "There are kids you know will have their own businesses. Kids who'll go to law school, med school."

"Everybody knows you'll go away and come back important."

He laughed. "Everybody but me, I guess."

"It takes something special. Something different."

He felt brave and silly. "I voted for you, too."

"My mother says when somebody tells you you're beautiful they might as well come out and say the rest of it: that you're not very smart."

"I don't think that!"

"Nobody thinks a girl can be both. My mother was Miss Texas, you know."

"You look like her."

Now she smiled. "My mother's the smartest woman I know. She married my daddy."

"I better get back to the library."

"Come in a minute. You've got to see what I'm working on." She was collating the senior goal statements, to go under their photographs. "Look," she said. "So far four kids want to be missionaries in Africa. One wants to go to Red China. There must be twenty who want to do God's will."

"I guess that's not too surprising around here."

"I haven't got to yours."

"I didn't put one down. Did you?"

"I said I wanted to live up to my parents' example."

"That's nice."

"If you think of something, you can still put it in."

He was looking at her desk. Tyrone Knight wanted to be one of America's finest embalmers. "Look at that," he said.

She laughed lightly. "I like the serious ones best." He said he had to go. She touched his hand. "Congratulations to your girlfriend, too, David. She's such a sweet sweet girl."

He blurted, before he thought about it, "We might be breaking up."

That night Glee called him at home. "You never learn," he told her. "WHAT IS WRONG WITH YOU?" she shouted. "Sometimes you are one hundred percent awful. You go around expecting things of people but you don't say what. You act like I'm a dog peeing on your leg sometimes. Everybody in our class likes me a lot but you!" She slammed down the phone. He called her back. "My dad's not home, I haven't got a car," he said. "If you would drive we could go to Dewey's a while." Everybody would be out. They would honk and wave. She had already calmed down. "I'm going with my girlfriends," she said. "I'm just headed out the door."

He had the car. A little after five, he went down to the

clothing store to pick up his father. Saul had suggested that they go have barbecue that night.

He spent a few minutes admiring the good clothes. He loved the feel of fine fabric between his fingers. The manager, Chuck Bradley, came up behind him. "You're looking good, David," he said. "How's every little thing treating you?"

David shook Bradley's hand. "Things are swell, sir."

"Sir, huh! I like your style, David. I could use you at Christmas, you know. Why don't you come down Saturday, let me start breaking you in."

He did not have enough money for a car, he would need money if he went away to school, but the thought of selling men's pants made his stomach clench. "I'd be grateful for the opportunity, sir," he said. He wasn't sure what his father would think.

"I'll give you a discount on clothes, too," Bradley said, "We put a good suit on you, you'll bowl over the customers. I could make a real salesman out of you, you finish school this year. Retail men's wear's a place to build a future."

Sick at the very thought, David nodded, to let Bradley know he had a customer behind him.

He walked toward the fitting rooms to look for his father. He saw Hayden Kimbrough come out of one of the little rooms, his pants tacked at the bottom, followed by Saul with pins in his mouth. They arranged themselves in front of the three-way mirror. Kimbrough tugged at the inseam below his crotch and studied his reflection. He said something, and Saul nodded. David, standing behind a rack of sport coats, watched as Saul knelt in front of Kimbrough's legs to adjust the seam.

21.

David saw how his life ran along with the pieces laid out like thread on a table top, pieces and pieces of parallel thread, never touching. As soon as he thought of it that way—Glee a thread, his parents a thread, his friendship with Leland, and so on, all the pieces, separate, never touching—he realized it was bound to change. Life was never so neat as to save you trouble when you started complicating it, and he saw that that was what he had been doing, maybe what he was doing just by getting up in the morning and putting in another day. He wanted a complicated life, he realized that, too. He wanted parts of it to butt other parts, and in this way the trivial things, the sad things, could be pushed aside, and better things could take over. Only what were these "things?" He could not find the words he knew were inside him, words like love and music and pain and work.

The only person he could think of who might understand what he was thinking was Patsy Randall. He thought of going to see her and saying, "It would help a lot if I could see the future like a play on CBS. What doors am I going in and out of? What chair am I sitting in? Who's in the room with me?" They could invent possibilities. Sometimes he thought about what had happened that last night between them, and he remembered the things they said to one another, that she was a coward, that he was no man. It did not seem right that they had hurt one another like that, not over sex. He had wanted to be close to her, that was what it had been about. He had been caught up in the drama of the play. He remembered his anger, too, but she had been scared and confused, and he felt sorry that he had not known what to do. He knew an older man would have. Other times, when he thought about her, and about their misunderstanding, it was all quite vague, and he hoped she remembered it that way, as cloud-breath on a cold night.

He saw her downtown a few days after Christmas vacation began. On a break from the clothing store, he had gone into the jeweler's two doors up the street, to look for a Christmas gift for Glee. He wanted his gift to be in a jeweler's box and not from a department store, but he did not want to spend very much money. He had fifteen minutes to look; he thought he would come every day until he decided on something appropriate.

"There are these little pewter hearts," someone said. He looked up and saw that it was Patsy behind the counter. "Hi, David. And gold lockets, but mostly girls in junior high like those. And a single pearl, on a chain. Of course, it's imitation." He flushed red. He stood up straight.

"I'm just looking." He disliked her confidence, her knowing exactly what (who!) he was there for.

"Sure," she said, and walked away.

He left the store bristling with irritation, but he went back the next day and let her show him everything she had suggested, then left her to put the boxes away again, saying he had to think about it. She was pleasant and helpful and neutral, just the way she would be with any customer. She had already turned away from the counter before he left. She wore red, startling with her hair, and looked wonderful in it.

The third day he bought the pearl drop necklace. He waited, looking at watches, while Patsy took the box away and wrapped it in a creamy paper and tied it with gold ribbon. He thought it was awkward for her to do that for him, but he did not have anything to wrap it in at home, and it was her job, just like his was hanging up pants and jackets all day long, and once in a while selling a shirt or a tie. When she gave him the box, he said it looked very nice. She shrugged, unsmiling, and for a moment he thought, hell, she was acting like that to make a sale, but when he reconsidered, he did not think she would be working for a commission, any more than he was. There really wasn't anything for her to say.

Outside the store he stood for a moment, taking in the bright winter afternoon, looking up and down the street. People were dashing in and out of shops, then hurrying along the sidewalks to their cars, their arms laden with boxes and sacks. He had bought his father a fancy ballpoint pen, his mother a scarf he could not think she would ever wear. He had not thought to get anything for Joyce Ellen.

Across the street, in the doorway of the State Farm office, he saw Saul. He almost raised his hand and called out, but then he saw that his father was standing with a woman in a green cloth jacket and a tight brown skirt. She was a young woman, with short curly dark hair, and David could see her face from the side. She was talking and gesturing animatedly, touching Saul's sleeve, leaning toward him as she laughed. As David watched, they moved closer and talked intensely for a moment. Then Saul squeezed the young woman's arm, and walked away whistling.

Whistling.

David was already at least five minutes late, but he ran over to Walgreen's and bought a Christmas card. They sold him a stamp at the register. Then he had to find a phone book, to look up Patsy Randall's address. The card was a picture of a medieval painting of the Madonna and child. Inside, the message wished the recipient a joyous and holy season. He wrote: I don't know about all that, but Merry Christmas. Below, he signed his name. He dropped it in a mailbox, and went back to work.

A couple of evenings later, she called him, speaking rapidly. "Is that you? I'm glad it's you, I didn't want to talk to one of your parents. That was a nice card. I don't send them out. I never had anybody to send cards to."

"I don't send cards either," he said. "I just sent that one to you." Sending cards was for old people, but this one had served its purpose. She did not speak. "It doesn't seem much like Christmas, does it?" he said. The sun had been brilliant every day. It frosted at night, but nothing stayed on the ground in town.

"Four more days on the chain gang," she said. "I'm going to buy some clothes in the after-Christmas sales."

"I'm saving up," he said. "Hey, I liked your red dress."

There was a long silence. Now that she was on the phone, he did not know what he wanted, except that he had wanted her to call, to save him the embarrassment of trying and being rejected. He did not expect Patsy to follow the same rules as girls like Glee.

"There are a couple of neat guys living in the motel now." she said. "One is from New York City."

"Interesting."

"I was thinking, maybe you'd like to meet them. I could ask them over Sunday afternoon." He could hear her take a breath. "You don't have a date on Sunday, do you?"

One of the men, James Notley, was a 1954 graduate of Basin High School. Tall, blond, crewcut, he looked like a West Texan, and he had a hard, strong look, too, from his time in the army. His roommate was Ari Finberg, with whom he had served in Germany. Ari, with his heavy New York accent, was a smaller man, wiry and dark and intense. He looked like Saul might have looked in his early twenties. Every time David looked at Ari, Ari was already looking at David. It made David uneasy.

James and Ari were spending the rest of the school year in Basin, attending the junior college on the GI Bill. James laughed about it. He said it was Ari's idea. Ari said, "He talked about Basin all the time. I thought it sounded exotic, something I ought to experience."

"And do you think it's exotic, now?" David asked. All of them laughed. Ari did not bother to reply.

Patsy had made some tiny sandwiches of pimento cheese, and had laid out pickles and olives on a saucer. When they had eaten everything, Ari said they ought to go over to their place, where there was a record player. "We've got a lot of platters," he said.

Their place was untidy and interesting, with books and records, jackets and shirts, magazines lying over every surface. The tacky little couch was covered with a crinkly length of fabric printed in an unusual, bright pattern. David sat on a cushion on the floor and drank a beer while they listened to Billie Holiday. David had never heard Billie Holiday before. He could not think of anything at all to say. He seemed to feel the singer's voice glide over his body, like a soft breeze that rustled the hair on his arms, and then when she moved onto a plaintive higher plane, he wished he were alone so he could cry. Patsy came with another cushion and sat beside him. She sang along for part of one song. "Isn't she fabulous?" He nodded. He wondered if she and Ari were lovers; he found that the thought distressed him. Ari was sure to know things

David did not, for he was a world traveler, an army veteran, a native of New York, a sophisticated man.

Ari and James said David would have to come again and hear more music. "You into music, man?" Ari said. David was dizzy and tired, and strained to find anything to reply. He nodded his head yes. "I listen to the radio all the time," he said, but he saw by the look on Patsy's face that that was the wrong thing to say.

The afternoon before Christmas Eve, David dressed up as Santa Claus and handed out stuffed animals in the pediatrics ward. Glee went along with him. She was charming with the children. She cooed and asked everyone's name. She sang "Frosty the Snowman" and "Jingle Bells," and told them all she knew they'd be strong and big and well in the new year. He was hot and claustrophobic in the silly costume, but the ambulatory children clung to him and crawled up on his lap. They whispered their wishes for tricycles and toy guns, doctor's kits and dolls and puppies. Nobody said he wanted to go home; they knew that was not in Santa's power.

Afterwards, he drove Glee to his house. While he showered and dressed, she straightened his room and sat on his bed, listening to the radio. After the gaiety of the children's ward, she seemed unusually quiet; she did not even try to kiss him.

They had dinner at a steak house. Although he tried to talk her into having the filet mignon, she ordered spaghetti. He had a New York strip. It took a day's wages to pay for the evening. He ate too fast and finished almost before you could even tell she had begun. He fiddled with his fork against his plate, while she chewed self-consciously, sometimes halting mid-bite to study his expression, until finally she said, "I can't eat, I'm not hungry anymore." He raised his water glass and proposed a toast: to the end of high school. Her eyes filled with tears and she put her own glass down. "It's only December," she said, not looking at him. "I'm sorry, I said the wrong thing," he groaned. Did she not look forward to the future? Did she not want to stop being a girl, a daughter and stepdaughter who had to ask for everything? As if he had spoken his thoughts out loud, she said, "I love school, Davy. I love my friends—and you. Us. I dread it ending."

"But everything's ahead, Glee!"

"I'll have to get a job. What will I do?"

"You could go to the junior college, or to secretarial school." Tears welled and spilled onto her cheeks. He could not stop himself: "You'll get married."

She left the table for a long time. He felt like an ass. He knew he had said a cruel thing. *He* would not marry her. He did not want to be married, not any time soon, and Glee, who was pretty and sweet as a girl could be, would never be the person he would want anyway. He thought about the Kimbroughs, about marriage as a contract to make lives work. A beautiful and wealthy woman, a powerful man. What had Saul and Marge thought marriage was? What it was for most people, sanctioned coupling? Of Glee he thought, we shouldn't be dating. I'm cheating her. I'm keeping her from other boys. But it was what she wanted. When he tried to back away she went crazy.

She brightened when he gave her the pearl. "I'll treasure it," she whispered, "always, always." She had his gift in her purse. It was a fountain pen, with his name engraved on it. He wanted to tell her, I'll treasure it, but it wasn't that kind of gift, and what was the use of a lie. If it had not had his name on it, he could have given it to Saul with the ballpoint.

He had put a blanket off his bed into his mother's car. He drove out of town, along a farm road, looking for a view of sky that caught his fancy. He did not feel like parking near a pump jack or a derrick. He wanted an open space, the way the pioneers might have found the prairie. It was bitter cold, and they huddled close with the blanket wrapped around them. He put his hand between her legs and held it there, as though it were only a way to keep warm. She leaned her head on his shoulder. "I wish you could tell me what to do," she said, but there was nothing he could say to that. She did not seem to want to be kissed. She did not have her hands on him.

When he said it was too cold and they should go home, she said that Evelyn Singleton was having a New Year's Eve party at her house, and they were invited. "You'll go, won't you? We'll go? All my friends will be there. It'll be the best party of the night."

Ari Finberg would play jazz records on New Year's Eve and make love to Patsy Randall. David's throat constricted and ached. He turned to Glee, pulling the blanket all crooked, and he kissed her forehead and cheeks, and he said, "Merry Christmas, Happy New Year, don't think it's you, that it was ever you that went wrong." He felt her tense. "What?" she asked anxiously. "What are you saying?"

"We ought to have as much fun as we can," he told her, backing away from whatever was inside him wanting to be said. "New Year's Eve, whenever." She relaxed. She said, "I keep thinking you're going to tell me you don't love me any more."

He touched her cheek, then bent and put his face in her lap. Her warm musky smell filled his nostrils. Her skirt absorbed his tears.

22.

His parents woke him Christmas morning with their quarreling. He moaned and pulled his pillow over his head. He heard his mother shout, "My house!" her eternal cry, and then, "your daughter." Saul yelled, "MY daughter! Now she's MY daughter," and David got up.

"It's Christmas, folks," he said. His parents had settled down. They were seated at the table with cups of coffee in front of them. They looked surprised to see him. "Hey, it's me, I live here," he joked, pouring his own coffee. He put bread in the toaster and took out the oleo, then sat down. "You going to Aunt Cheryl's today, Mom?" he asked, wording it like that so she would know he did not plan to go. She shook her head. She did not have the evening off.

"So are we cooking here?" he plodded on. He just wanted somebody to say something ordinary and civil, they did not have to say Merry Christmas. If there was food in the house, he would offer to cook it himself, if need be.

"I'm going to make that chicken with Campbell's soup, like Joyce Ellen likes so much," Marge said. "It's easy. We can eat early in the afternoon." Saul harumphed at her announcement. "I'm going to go get her as soon as I get dressed."

"And Kelton?" David asked. He could not believe it, a Christmas gathering, how about that. "Kelton is coming over, too?" He knew his sister could not get away otherwise.

Saul snarled. "I should have tied her up and locked her in her room for a year. Now I ought to lock her out."

His mother said, "Pete's still in Dallas."

"Still?" David asked.

"He's been there since the first of November."

He did not understand the charade his sister was playing, but he knew he could count on repercussions. His mother had a stubborn, gritty expression. She would prevail. "I don't understand."

"The Big Mouth doesn't want to have a baby," Saul growled.

"She's more pregnant than she said at Thanksgiving," Marge said. "She's nearly four months. When she told him, he went to Dallas. And he isn't coming back. Only she didn't know that. She called the station. He quit five weeks ago."

"This is not making sense," David said. Saul said, "Ha."

Marge shook her head. "You work fifteen years with crazy people. Maybe it sticks to your hair, you bring it home. Your daughter marries a madman." She did not look like she had slept much. "It's complicated, Davy. Too much to explain right now. He's not coming back, and she doesn't have any money. She needs us now." She started to cry. "She's barely seventeen."

Saul stormed out of the room. David ate his toast. Saul reappeared. "You go get her, all right. You cook cream of sick chicken soup. I'm leaving."

"Where are you going on Christmas?" Marge asked wearily.

"To the greyhound races."

"Juarez?" David asked.

"Right now."

David jumped up. "Hey Pop, I want to go. Can I go?"

"Move fast."

Marge shut her eyes. "This is Christmas?"

David kissed her on top of the head. "I'm sorry, Mom. I've got to go with Dad. You get Joyce Ellen. It doesn't matter what day it is, we can straighten it out later. Don't you see, I need to go? You and Joyce Ellen, you can have the day together. Hey, she's pregnant, she'll want to nap won't she?"

He ran to his room and dressed hurriedly. He put two twenties in his wallet from the stash in his sock drawer. Suddenly he felt happy. It was Christmas, and he was getting out of town.

They did not get to the races. They did not even find out if there were any. It took the rest of the day to reach El Paso, where Saul checked them into a motel, turned on the television, went for ice and 7-Up. He had brought a bottle of gin. They stripped to underwear and stretched out on the two double beds. "Now, this is the life," David said. The water glasses were gleaming, the pillows hefty, the bed like a rock. You could put a quarter in and jiggle yourself. There was a faint odor of disinfectant, sweetish and clean and anonymous.

His father raised his glass. "I should have been a traveling salesman."

"You were."

Saul slapped his thigh. "What a life it turned out to be."

On TV, a chorus was singing Christmas hymns. Saul turned the volume down to a murmur. In a while a movie came on with James Cagney. David never did know what movie it was, or what it was about. It did not take much gin for him to feel drunk.

"I've been thinking about marriage," he said, slurring only a little.

"Shit," Saul said.

"Not getting married. I'm not thinking about getting married. I'm just thinking about marriage."

"The way two people join forces."

"Against the world."

"They think they do at the beginning. Later they learn something about the scale of conflict in the world."

"It cuts off a lot of possibilities. Marriage."

"If there are any out there. Possibilities." Saul belched loudly. "The mistake young people make is, they think the possibilities are there, when they're not. They think they're doubling their odds because there are two of them. It's a condition of youth, naivete. Like acne."

"Something has to happen. Why couldn't it be good?"

Saul went to the bathroom. David got up and washed his face with cold water. He was shaky, hungry. When his father came out he sat on the end of the bed, with his feet between the two beds, and he asked him, "If it turns out to be a bad idea, do you just give up?"

"I thought so once."

"But you changed your mind." David thought, maybe he will tell me about the woman downtown. There was no way to ask. He did not want his father to leave his mother again. The quarrels were not that bad.

Saul lifted his glass again. "You kill the pain."

"That's not enough!" David cried.

Saul was amused. "You're too young to worry about life, son. You ought to worry about getting laid, and getting into college. You are one strange boy."

"Not the junior college." David had caught his father at an oddly communicative moment. He wanted some sort of support, some sort of commitment for his plans, however tentative they were. Saul waved the notion away.

The motel restaurant was closed. They drove all over town looking for something to eat. They finally ate in a truck stop, hamburgers, fries. They were messy and greedy and added an order of onion rings when they weren't even hungry anymore.

"I was going to give you fifty bucks for Christmas," Saul said. "But I spent some of it." He pointed at the remains of their dinner.

"I'd rather do this." David ate an onion ring in one bite.

"I don't think there's anyplace to get more gin."

"I could go to sleep, Pop. I'm pretty wiped out."

"We ought to call your mother."

"At the hospital?"

"Nah. Not up there."

"We'll see her tomorrow."

"Where you going to go, son? Austin?"

"Maybe so."

"I don't know if we can be any help. I don't know how things will be day after tomorrow."

"I'm not counting on anything."

"Hell, I could be in Florida," Saul said blandly, and took the check to the register.

"Florida?" David said in the car. "What's this Florida?"

"It's an expression," Saul said. David did not press the matter, though "Florida" was not an expression he had ever heard.

When they got home the next day, Joyce Ellen and Marge were cleaning the extra bedroom. Joyce Ellen's boxes were piled in the living room. "Oh Dad," she cried, and threw her arms around Saul. He was astonished. "Oh Dad what?" he asked. She stepped back. "I'm so happy to be home," she said, but her face was drawn and pale. She did not look happy at all.

23.

Leland heard that a fight was going to take place at the Fina station, and went by to pick up David. Sissy and David were both sprawled on David's bed, reading old magazines discarded by the school library. "Do tell," Leland said. Sissy wanted to go, too. They were in the dead hours of a Sunday afternoon, in the dead time between Christmas and New Year's. What was a fight but a convocation?

Leland drove out of town, along the bare expanse of caliche-bed farm roads, to a remote intersection where there were already more than fifty cars parked along the sides. Leland swerved the car around and went back toward the main road a hundred yards, and parked. "They're going to fight out here," he told the other two. "And the cops'll come, and when they do, I'm heading for this car as fast as my big feet can carry me, and when I get here, I'm splitting, riders or no riders, you understand?" Sissy was wide-eyed. David grinned easily. "You're a real shit, Piper," he said. "We'll stick with you, what's hard about that?" They pulled their jackets tight and fastened them.

It was not a gang matter, though there were two gangs out there. It was a fight between two boys. No one was saying what it was about; a fight, however public, could be about a private matter, of no concern to anyone but the combatants. A girl, a car, a dare, an insult? There was that dead time to fill. There was the eerie wintriness of the plains that, it was said, had driven more than one woman crazy. A lot of young people had come to watch. One of the combatants was leaning against the hood of his car, his jacket off, his black teeshirt tight on his biceps. Other boys stood nearby with their hands crammed deep into their jacket pockets. They were saying things to him, making one another laugh. The second boy nosed his car up as close as he could maneuver it, parting the crowd like Moses did the Red Sea in the movie. He got out. His friends clustered quickly, calling out jeers and insults from behind him. To him they said, "Say hey. Cream the bastard." He began to shrug off his Levi's jacket as he walked toward the other boy, but before even one arm was free, the first boy bent low and accelerated without warning, fiercely plowing into his stomach with the force of a moving vehicle.

Sissy clung to David. Leland stepped ahead of them, leaning toward the scene, breathing with his mouth open. "Jesus," he said. The boy had pulled his jacket back on. His face was bloody. At first it looked like he would never get started, but he found his own power, and knocked the other boy down and began to beat his head against the hard ground. The two boys rolled and banged on the caliche, their faces and arms covered with blood. After a minute or two all the booing and hissing and cheering from the onlookers had stopped. The boys fought in silence, except for their own grunts and the thuds of their bodies against one another and against the earth. In the sour winter light, the scene was tinged brownish-yellow. Little by little the crowd began to move back, as if it were dissolving. Along the edges, bystanders turned and went back to their cars and drove away. Only the close buddies stuck it out. David pulled Sissy back, and turned her and held her against his chest. The boys lay still on the ground. Some of their friends knelt by them. Leland turned. "Let's get the hell out of here," he said.

In the car, Sissy touched David's arm and his face, over and over, as if he were one of the injured boys. He said he was sorry. He did not know what he had thought he would see. He had been to drag races out there, once he had seen a wreck from which they took an unconscious driver, but he had never seen a fight. "I'm sorry, I'm sorry," he told Sissy. "What will you do now?" he asked when they pulled up in the alley behind her house. "Write in my notebook," she said. "Before I forget."

David, Ellis and Leland went driving around in Wayne Hansen's new Chevy with Wayne and some other boys, but nobody was out yet. They drove all the way out to the meteor crater and got out and stood around and speculated on what it must have been like when a chunk from heaven split the earth. They drank the six-pack of beer one of them had brought, wishing they had more. They piled back in the car and drove through niggertown. Jack Parrish said he heard that some of Stripling's gang had gone niggerknocking the night before: they rode slowly down the streets until they came up on a group of Negroes, then yanked out baseball bats and, picking up speed, roared by, getting in whatever licks they could.

Ellis said, "I've heard that ever since I first moved here, but I don't believe it. Who would do that? For what?"

Parrish said niggers were a change from rabbits. Leland said, "If you know there were white boys through here last night making that kind of trouble, I want to get out of here as fast as this cherry piece will carry us." Whooeee! they all yelled, and sped away.

There was talk about how to get more beer. Wayne said he thought his ID would pass. He was proud of it. He had spent hours slicing out the dates, transposing numbers, and sliding them back in, then laminating it. He passed the license around for them all to admire. "Shit," Leland said. "You've got the best yet." They bought malt liquor at a corner market, and parked behind the high school. Parrish said. "What this party needs is pussy."

"I know a girl that might go riding with us," Leland said. Ellis said, "I can't stay out much longer." He looked sleepy from the ale, or bored. He might have to go out with his father before dawn, to work.

The girl lived in a trailer down by the junkyard. Leland said she hung around with Nesmith and his buddies. That was how he knew her. He went up to the trailer door while they all watched from the car. She shifted her weight back and forth, one hip high and then the other, leaning against the door jamb. Someone must have yelled at her; she looked behind her, then stepped forward and shut the door. Leland stepped up close to her. He had one hand on her shoulder. She grinned and hung her head, then shrugged and followed him out to the car. She was wearing turquoise pedal pushers and a cotton blouse printed with kittens. She looked like she might be cold, but she had to sit on Leland's lap, and it was warm inside the car.

They went to the park and killed the rest of the beer. The girl chugalugged half a bottle while they cheered. Someone asked her what year of school she was in. Nobody remembered her. "I don't go no more," she said. "I'm in beauty school." There was a lot of grinning and rearranging of weight throughout the car. Parrish was sitting next to the girl and Leland's was the lap she sat on. "What do you do for fun, hon?" Parrish asked, and laughed loudly. He bopped Wayne on the neck. "Fun, hon!" he said again. The girl had twisted around, leaning against the car door, facing the carful of boys. "Whatever I feel like I guess," she said coyly, grinning. Parrish put his face over close to hers, stuck out his tongue, and slowly licked her chin and lips. The other boys went, Oooh, like a bunch of girls. Parrish fell against Wayne and the steering wheel. "Bring me a pillow, Mama!" he said. "Turn down the BED!"

David was in the middle of the back seat, between Ellis and a boy everybody called Bull, because he had no neck. Bull said, "I think we could have fun right here." He was a mean tackle who would not have anything important to do the rest of the year. The girl giggled. "There's so many of y'all," she said. She wrapped an arm around Leland's neck. "And I'm sort of with Piper, ain't I?"

There was a moment of clamor, Wayne, Parrish and Bull whistling and saying Piper wasn't going to hold out on his buddies. Leland was not saying anything, nor David, and Ellis, without a word, simply opened the car door and sprinted away. For just a moment Leland caught David's eye. He looked hapless, confused, half-pleased. David was disgusted, and bored, but the girl was asking for it, the guys were half-drunk, and he was trapped. If he made a big deal about this, they would talk about him all over school, what a bad sport, what a prude he was. He was not going to fuck her, that was the line, but what she wanted to do was her business. He did not think anybody would hurt her. What would they do that Nesmith's bunch hadn't already done twice over?

Parrish reached over and fondled the girl's breast. She had not said what her name was. She squirmed uncomfortably. He put his other hand on her thigh. "Hey man you are on my LAP!" Leland protested. Parrish pulled the girl briskly over onto him. She squealed, her arms flailing, then settled with them around his neck. Now when Leland looked back at David he had a panicky, silly expression; David wanted to punch him. Parrish was deep-kissing the girl, who rearranged herself to straddle him. Wayne threw his arms up in mock-horror, against the driver's window, like a man in a holdup, and Bull picked up all the ale bottles one by one to drain the dregs. There was a feeling like static in the car, like something might ignite.

"Out!" Parrish said suddenly. He shoved Leland's shoulder. "Let us OUT of here." The girl scooted into the empty space Leland left, looked around at the rest of them, then climbed out of the car. Bull called after Parrish as he climbed out. "I'm next." The girl stuck her head back in. "I ain't gonna fuck all of you," she said weakly.

"Man, this is lame," David said in a moment. Leland was back in the car, leaning forward, his forehead on the dashboard. Bull opened his window and, leaning out, aimed a bottle at a tree. He missed. "A horny man can't pitch worth shit," he said. It was not very long before the girl and Parrish came back. They were standing outside the door, talking. She said no, she wouldn't; he said she sure as hell would. In a flash Bull had left the car and had run around to where they stood. Now the girl was between the two boys, whimpering and fussing. David leaned over the car seat and said, "Let's go, Wayne. We've been out long enough." Wayne, always the follower, did not reply. Leland said, "She's friends with tough guys, this could make them mad." Wayne said, "Mad at *you*, shithead. This was your idea."

David leaned hard into the corner of the seat, still warm from Ellis, and closed his eyes. He did not think he was getting much air in the stale atmosphere of the car. His chest hurt terribly. Through the closed window he could hear the girl's muffled cries. He looked out. She was leaning against the front door, and Bull was pumping into her violently. "Jesus CHRIST!" David said. Leland, who must have felt the whole thing like a man sharing a bed, suddenly said. "I'm gonna be sick, shit, I'm gonna puke," and shoved the door hard, against the weight of the girl. He only managed to open the door partway; his vomit spewed over it inside. David got out of the car as fast as he could and shoved at Bull, who outweighed him by forty-five pounds. Bull shoved back and sent him sprawling, but the diversion freed the girl long enough for her to pull her pants up and hobble a few yards away where she fell to the ground. By now everyone was out of the car. Wayne caught up with Leland, who was leaning against a tree, and hit him in the face with his fist, then went back to his car. Leland fell to the ground like a sack of onions. Five yards away the girl was in another lump. Parrish caught David by the shirt collar and shook him. "Stick with pansies, asshole," he said. David steeled himself for a blow, but it did not come. In a moment the car, and the three buddies, were gone, leaving David, Leland and the girl. David threw his arms up toward the cold black sky. Then he went to see about the girl. She was weeping.

"Come on," he said gently. "We'll have to walk to Leland's to get a car." She held his arm and pulled herself up. Her mouth was bruised. "The big boy," she said, and started to cry harder. Leland staggered over to them, rubbing his face.

"You guys hungry?" David said. "You eat, I'll buy." Both Leland and the girl looked amazed. "What's your name?" David asked her, putting his hand out for her.

She squeezed it tightly. "LaVonne. Yeah, I'm hungry."

That night Ellis called. "You listen to me, Puckett," he said. "I don't ever want to know you do things like that."

David started to protest. "I didn't do—"

"Stuff it! If I ever hear of it—because it won't happen with me around—I'm not going to stand in the same sunshine as you, I will find another tennis partner. Do you get it? I'm not going to be partners with someone who takes girls on joyrides."

"It wasn't me."

"You sat back there like a wooden Indian, and you stayed, didn't you?"

David did not think it fair that Ellis hung up before he could tell him he took the girl home, that he bought her a hamburger first. LaVonne. At least he did that; he did not run away. Leland drove, and waited in the car, while David walked her right to her door, like a date. He even said, "See you sometime, LaVonne." She said. "Oh sure you will." She gave her butt a little twitch before she shut the door.

24.

"I'll understand if you have to say no," Beth Ann said. She did not sound the least bit worried. "I know it's short notice." It was the day before New Year's Eve. "But we'd really like it if you could come."

Excited, a little insulted, he was clenching his free hand into a fist. Beth Ann had called the day before the country club dance to ask him to escort her. "It's a family tradition. All the club families. Not just ours."

"I did have plans," he said.

"Well, if you can't change them—"

"What happened to your date?"

"He's not like a real date! Cliff Easterling, he's a sophomore at Princeton? He's like a *cousin* or something, our families are best *friends*." She took her time. "He's not who I'd ask, it's just *tradition*." He didn't help her out. He knew she would say something and then he would say yes, but she ought to have to say it. The day before! "I'd ask you, wouldn't I? He's sick, so I can. Even my mother said, now you can take someone you really want to."

He wondered who else she had called. "It's formal," he said. A prom for special people only. He could not go in his stained jacket.

"Oh yes, it's a big party, it'll be a lot of fun. There'll be champagne. My daddy is getting the flowers for Mommy and me. I'll have you a boutonniere here. All you have to do is come." She knew he would. "I'll pick you up, David. You will go, won't you?"

He called his father at work. A light snow was falling. "I haven't got any way to get to the store!" he said frantically. "You've got to come get me. I want to get a new jacket and pants. I've got my own money from the summer." His father wanted to know, where's the fire? He had to tell the rest. "The Kimbrough girl. I'm going to the club with her. It's formal." He held his breath, waiting for his father to say something ridiculing, but he did not.

All his father said was that he was busy; David's heart sank. It would take him twenty minutes to walk, in this cold. But his father relented. "I'll pick you up about 5:30, son, and bring you back. We'll have the store to ourselves."

"Do you think I'll still get a discount?"

"I'll see what I can do." There was a sound—a snicker, a sniffle? "Considering the importance of what you wear to the *club*."

"Thanks, Dad." He stopped worrying about what his father thought, and started thinking of what to tell Glee, and when to call her. He wondered if he should get a haircut.

At the store his father carried clothes back and forth, tucking and adjusting, seriously attentive, as to a client. David chose gray wool pants, a pale pink shirt, and a new white jacket. Bradley, apprised of the occasion, stayed to give advice, and threw in a bow tie for free. David viewed himself in the three-way mirror. The two men stood slightly aside surveying the net effect; David could not remember ever seeing them shoulder to shoulder like equals. He felt admirable, handsome, "likely to succeed." Wasn't his appearance working some sort of magic on employer and employee? "There'll be a band," Bradley said admiringly. He pulled his shoulders back. "The wife and me are going to the party at the hotel. We go every year." He winked at Saul. "I usually get away for a little craps upstairs." He straightened David's tie. "Anybody asks, you tell 'em where you got this jacket, hear? They don't come any better in Basin."

"Don't you know I'll do that," David said, with a perfectly straight face.

That night he took Glee to see a movie, and then he took her home early. He said it was too cold to park, and he wouldn't come in, he wasn't feeling well.

"You're not coming down with something?" He could hear the panic in her voice, and he suffered a prickle of guilt.

He followed her into the living room, then stood between her and the open door. "I can't go tomorrow," he blurted. "There's all hell over at my house, my sister whining, my mother crying, my father in a steam. There are—things—I've got to do."

"There are things you've got to do on *New Year's Eve?*"

"Really, Glee. You don't understand. You don't know what it's like." He pushed the door open behind him. "You'll still have fun, you know you will."

She ran out of the room.

Beth Ann scooped black jelly onto a cracker. "You'll like it better with sour cream," she said, and added some. She held the cracker as he bit into it. The taste was salty, sharp, fishy. "You have to cultivate a taste for it," Beth Ann said.

"I like it fine." He took another. They snacked from the trays of elaborately arranged foods and then returned to the dance floor. He could not have named half of what he had eaten, and he had not honestly liked much of it, but he was acutely conscious of what it meant to eat caviar at a party, instead of popcorn. Beth Ann was beautiful, in a long straight-skirted dress of deep rose silk. All the girls at the prom had worn crinkly dresses with big skirts, but here he saw elegant dresses, probably bought in Dallas on special shopping trips. The singer, who wasn't bad, was singing "Chances Are." David had begun to lose his stiffness, but he did not hold Beth Ann close. He held her in what he hoped was a courtly manner, as if he were a visiting knight. He had been careful not to assume too much. He was a guest; he did not belong. Yet the other kids he knew from school greeted him warmly. "Beth Ann! David!" they said, as if it were the most natural thing for him to be there. Such was the power of invitation. The club was lavishly decorated and lighted. It was Fitzgerald territory. The young couples looked more relaxed than anybody had at the prom. Kids he knew from school were wildly unfamiliar in their finery, as if they wore saris or carried Mau Mau shields. They seemed to be their real selves here, older and more beautiful, far removed from the world of Basin High and its hysterical social machinery. A sudden thought pierced him: They have always had this world to go to. They have always been visiting the world where I was living. None of it has ever mattered to them.

Beth Ann's cool fingers lay lightly on his neck. "This is going to be the most exciting new year, isn't it?" she said.

"When I think about going away, pledging a sorority, it makes me just tingle."

He pressed his hand into her back. She let her chin rest on his shoulder.

They were at the table with the Kimbroughs and another adult couple when the band began the drum roll that led to a moment of loud horns. Confetti poured over them as if by magic, the room was filled with the cheers and cries of the assembled. Both of the older couples kissed. David did not know what to do. Beth Ann smiled up at him. "Happy New Year, David," she said, and raised her face. He kissed her lightly on the lips. "Happy New Year, Beth Ann."

The four of them went back to the Kimbrough home and ate scrambled eggs and toast off pretty china dishes. Laurel Kimbrough wore a long embroidered apron over her evening gown. She smiled at David and said, "I hope you can eat, after all the food at the club. We always have a New Year's breakfast. It wouldn't seem right not to." He settled comfortably at the round table in their nook. Windows looked out on a garden, now bare except for scraggly bushes, and, farther on, onto a wall of stone or brick, now deep in night shadows. He tried to see the picture they would make to someone from outside, clustered around the table under a light that hung from the ceiling, but of course no one could see them, because they were at the back of the house, and there was the wall. The Kimbroughs chatted cozily, swapping observations of their friends, the food, the band, taking pleasure in recollection. They reminded him of Glee after a ball game or a dance, wanting to catalog everything she had seen, everything they had done. "Such a nice salmon paté!" Laurel said. "Didn't Carl Bentley look smug with his pretty new wife?" Hayden said. "I liked all the slow tunes," Beth Ann said dreamily. They did not seem to expect comment from their guest, did not seem to mind his presence or expect anything from him. They had allowed him into their "tradition" to make an odd number even. David thought, this must be what Cinderella felt like. He longed for his own room, his bed, he wanted to take off his formal clothes. He would want to think about the night, but suddenly there was too much of it. He felt foolish in his pink shirt. He wanted to be home.

Beth Ann took him there in her mother's station wagon. In front of his house she said, "I'm so glad you could come."

The motor was running and she had her hands on the steering wheel. She had thrown a long cashmere scarf around her head, giving her the mysterious air of an older woman.

"I had a wonderful time," he replied. There was nothing else to say. He stood on the edge of the yard and watched her drive away. He saw her glance into the rear-view mirror and wave her gloved hand. The station wagon did not look anything like a royal coach, but as it disappeared it was easy to imagine that if he ran after it, he would find a pumpkin.

He made his way through the house in the dark to his room. As he switched on his light there was a pounding at the alley door. Glee stormed into the room. She was wearing a wool coat over a dress. "I've been waiting for two hours!" she cried.

He glared at her, embarrassed in his white jacket and fine pants.

"You're a bastard! You lied to me! Where did you go?"

"It's none of your business. You have no right to spy on me."

"You lied to me."

The door from the kitchen flew open. His father was standing there in his baggy robe. "What is going on out here?" David moved quickly to shove his father back into the kitchen. "Go to bed. This will be over in a minute." He slammed the door and turned back to Glee, who was standing in the middle of the room. Her coat had swung open. She was wearing a dress he had never seen, something blue and shiny. On her high heels, her one ankle turned awkwardly, she looked dangerously off-balance. "You go home," he said menacingly.

She began weeping loudly, making pig noises with her nose. "I thought you loved me!" she shouted. "We've slept together a thousand times!"

He despised her for catching him. "That's because you're a whore, Glee," he said. He felt as if he had fallen through an elevator floor. His stomach jumped and his head throbbed.

Glee was wearing the pearl drop necklace he had given her. She tore it from her neck and threw it to the floor, screaming. "I'm a whore! A whore! Whores get paid, David. What did I ever get from you for putting out? What did I ever get from you?"

He hung up his clothes carefully, and draped a towel over the shoulders of his white jacket. He heard movement and voices in the kitchen, so he went in to see who was up. He was in time to see his sister disappear around the corner, back to bed. A lamp was on in the living room; he heard the groan of the easy chair as his father's slight weight settled in it. Marge sat at the table, sipping a drink with no ice. It was a little after two-thirty in the morning.

David poured himself some whiskey, added half a glass of water, took ice out for both of them, and joined his mother. She drank slowly as he told her about the evening. Her nose crinkled when he described the strange food, but by the time he told her about his one o'clock breakfast at the Kimbroughs, she was too blank for expression. Still he was certain she listened to every word.

25.

He spent all of New Year's Day with Patsy and her friends. They lay around on the floor on folded blankets, listening to Miles Davis, the Modern Jazz Quartet, Dave Brubeck. All the music was new to David. "Sketches of Spain" reverberated straight up his spine. Patsy kept smiling at him, as if to say, I told you so. The two men, James and Ari, treated her affectionately, teasingly, but David could not see that neither one was especially attached to her. That made him feel better about them. Patsy was at ease, though she did not have much to say. There was plenty of Lone Star beer, and pretzels, Fritos, fat pickles, and a chicken Ari had roasted on a bed of onions. Patsy encouraged her friends to talk. James told about the beer and sausages in Germany, the easy feeling his blondness gave him there. Ari told about the Philippines, where he was stationed before Germany. He said he had eaten dog meat.

David got up to stretch, and walked around the room. Books lay in no order: Lawrence, Kerouac, Buber, Pound, and others. David picked up books, held them and riffled the pages, read a line or two in each. He would have liked to ask Ari what he thought, but about what? His reading? Basin? The world in general? He wanted, really, to ask him: How do I get where you are? How do I know to have these books, and where to get them?

He could not think why the New York Jew would want to spend half a year in a place like Basin, a place *he* only longed to leave. James he understood better. He had gone away, to the army, and he had grown up. He had seen things. He knew how to order in a restaurant in another language, maybe more than one; he knew how to ride cheap trains (he told about visiting Italy that way) and find a room not too close to the station. Coming back allowed him to see what he had left behind, and to be glad of it; David did not believe James would stay this time. He would not want to lead a boom and bust life dependent on the vicissitudes of the oilfields. He would find a kind of work that he could do in the greater world, the world Ari had come from; he was lucky, to have made a friend to show him the way.

Later in the afternoon, after a couple of desultory games of Hearts, Ari changed the music. He played The Midnighters ("Work with me, Annie;" "Sexy Ways") and Chuck Berry, the Drifters, Little Richard. He had a trash bucket filled with 45's. He played LaVern Baker singing the original "Tweedle Dee," stolen by Georgia Gibbs. He talked on and on about the way R & B was changing the culture, how even though it had been 'whited up' we would all see that after Elvis, nothing would ever be the same. That made James remember that there was an Elvis movie, "King Creole," at the downtown theatre. Patsy ran back to her rooms to cook supper for her father; afterwards, they would all go.

David used the bathroom and washed his face. He tucked his shirt into his chinos and pulled himself up tall. He thought he was better-looking than James or Ari, their advantage was only age. He felt like he had spent the day in a museum (which he had never done); he had learned about culture, hadn't he?

Seated on the couch, his legs stretched out in front of him, he found himself telling his hosts about the fight he had seen a few days earlier. It was like scratching an itch and discovering a mass of bites. Once he started talking—he mentioned it casually, wondering what they would have to say—he grew more and more intense, searching for the right description, the right feeling for what had happened. "I felt like there was a glass wall between me and the fight. There was nothing I could do."

James drawled, "Nobody wants interference in a fight. That's for cops."

Ari said, "I must have had two or three fights a week the years I was in junior high. I lived in the streets. Then I looked around; boys had shot up, put on weight. I was never going to catch up. I had to get by some other way. I learned to skirt a fracas. I learned how much it doesn't matter. I've never had a fight since I was fourteen. Not in the army, either."

James laughed. "Hell no, Finny. Men were too scared of your sharp tongue."

David asked James, "What about you? In Basin? Did you fight?"

James yawned hugely. "I came very close one time and that was really it. I played football, there was plenty of bruising there. But this one time, I was in eighth grade. None of us could drive yet. There was a ruckus of some sort on the playground at school. I don't remember what it was about. A smart remark I guess. Some stupid junior high insult. There were two big groups of us who stuck together. Sometimes at recess we threw rocks, that sort of crap. Only this day, somebody said, Let's fight it out, shitheads. We agreed. As soon as school was out, we'd meet at the old windmill east of the school, out where the houses stopped and the prairie took over. I was scared to death, I wasn't very big—I had a big spurt the next year, surprised me most of all—but I couldn't not go when all my buddies would. The only thing was, I was wearing this brand new shirt my mama had bought me a few days before. I knew she'd kill me if I ripped it or got blood on it—this went across my mind and I was miserable at the idea. I was more scared of my mama than of the boys, so I said I had to go home and change first. My neighbor, Stevie, in my class, said if we ran home his brother would be home from high school and he would drive us out to the windmill. We ran off, I changed, then we had to wait maybe ten minutes for the car. When we finally got out near the windmill we could see all the boys in our class there, and as many more there to watch; we could hear shouting going on. Kids were shaking their fists and trying to menace one another, but nobody had had the nerve to start punching. And before I could get out of the car, we heard sirens coming from the other way. It wasn't going to happen! I could go home unscathed but not a coward."

Ari had enjoyed James' tale. "It's always like OK Corral with you Western boys," he laughed. "We had skirmishes. They happened where they began, nobody ran off to get ready. There would be blood, and we'd scatter, knowing there was always another time to come."

Suddenly David longed to tell them about LaVonne. There had always been girls like that. What did they do in cities? Duck into alleyways? Vacant lots? He would never have the nerve to ask Ari, but James was a local. David wanted to hear about Basin when James was still young and stupid enough to cruise with creeps, doing things he wouldn't be proud of in the morning. Casually, testing the water, he said, "So, James. If there's football, fights, and fucking, you've only told us about the first two. Were there girls to ride around with? Girls to—" He faltered, aware that James and Ari were looking at him with something very much like disgust. The laughs had all died away.

In a low casual voice, James said, "I didn't start dating till late. I didn't slum with girls, didn't think of them that way. You see, with girls, by the time I'd changed my shirt, so to speak, the scene was breaking up. I joined the Army and went off to life like men live." James and Ari exchanged looks.

David stood up and beat his chest like a monkey. "Jesus, we've been sitting around the whole damned day! I need to stretch my legs. I'll go see what's keeping Patsy." He was getting no encouragement from the two men. "We still on for 'King Creole?'"

"I never miss an Elvis flick," Ari said.

James said, "Tell Patsy it's my treat," and instantly David knew he would not. James had meant some sort of insult. David would pay for Patsy. If he had not gone off and lived *like men live,* whatever the *hell* that was supposed to mean, he did know how to act in Basin, Texas, with a girl his own age.

He spent most of the few remaining days with Patsy, Ari and James. No more was said about fights and girls, certainly not in front of Patsy. It crossed David's mind that it was odd, when he was alone with the men, that they never, even then, mentioned the women of Germany, Italy, the Philipines, New York. They asked no questions of David, as if he lived a general life, the details inconsequential, the broad outline available to anyone who looked out on the flat streets of Basin, and beyond, onto the dun prairie. They talked about books and music and politics. Occasionally, they politely entertained comments from David (he had very little to say on any of their topics, but sometimes he had read a pertinent article), then returned to their odd little duet of comments. Their sighs and glances arose out of two years' shared com-

pany, the fortune of foreign travel, and the confidence of
youth moved into adulthood, still unburdened by debt, ambition, and authority. They were a happy pair, and David
envied them both their experience and their friendship.

26.

David attended an opera performance in the school auditorium. Not a whole opera, but pieces—what were they called? arias?—from "La Boheme," "Madame Butterfly," "La Traviata," and others he had already forgotten. Five performers from the Houston Opera were going to Santa Fe, and a local music-lover had arranged for them to stop in Basin. Mrs. Schwelthelm told them about it in English and then Patsy called him and asked if he wanted to go with her and Ari.

The singers were an intriguing group. Two of them were Negroes, a woman and a man. The woman had a massive chest and a fascinatingly huge mouth. The white men wore their hair rather long, combed in an almost womanish way. All their voices were amazing. There were moments in the songs that gave David a chill, but at other times he had to fight his desire to yawn and stretch. He had no idea what they were singing about, though the program summarized the selections. Sometimes he could see the singers' throats trembling.

By the time the singing was over, he was starved. Ari had bought the tickets, and would not let David repay him, so David offered to treat the trio at the Stockman Cafe.

They were eating hamburgers when the five performers came in and took the big circle booth in the corner of the busy cafe. All the customers stared. At the counter, a couple of redneck types cawed, "Look what the cat drug in," and then called out to Mick, the cook, "You gonna serve niggers in here?"

The pleasant clang and buzz of the cafe came to an abrupt halt. David could not remember ever seeing a Negro in the Stockman, though, technically, he believed Negroes were supposed to be able to eat where they wanted. In fact David could not remember being in the same room with a Negro in his whole life, unless you counted the times they were in the grocery store, or Sears, where they had their own water fountain in the back by the bathrooms. His heart was thudding. Patsy, seated beside him, took his hand. The waitress looked like a statue, her hands on the back edge of the counter. After several moments, a man in the back said, "Any chance of getting more coffee back here?" and the waitress jumped as if he had goosed her. David watched the performers speaking in low voices. The hicks at the counter started up again. "You smell something!" one of them said. The other coughed and gagged. A couple of good ole boys sitting two booths down from the performers got up and made a big show of skirting the corner booth. Patsy was squeezing David's hand hard. Ari had a bland, interested look on his face; hadn't he come, after all, to see the natives?

The performers stood and quietly eased their way out of the booth. All of them left except one, a tall white man, who went to the counter, near where David was sitting, and asked the waitress if he could get an order to go. One of the men at the counter said, "They don't serve no collard greens here." The waitress, red-eyed, fled into the kitchen. The man from the opera group turned and looked out at the customers, as if he were going to speak, then shook his head and left. David sighed, Patsy sighed, they smiled at one another nervously. At least there had not been a fight. The waitress came back from the kitchen with the cook.

The two men from the counter were standing in the aisle, adjusting their Levi's and sucking on their teeth. "Maybe the Stockman ain't the place to go no more," one said. The other said, "You figger that? Eating with niggers?" His pal replied, "They was queers, you see that hair?" One of the other customers said, "Where do you think they're from, not knowing no better?" Another man joined the group, chewing on a toothpick. The cook said, "They're gone now, how about a piece of pie, on the house?" He had the steady neutral gaze of a school administrator. One of the men, a sandy-haired roughneck type, said, "I'm full up," and hitched his pants to make his point. A man at the register, fiftyish and tired-looking, waved his hand at the little gang; "Aw, go home, you jerks, the world is changing." When he opened the door they could hear the sluggish chugging sound of an engine not quite turning over. Ari, turned so that he could see out the window, said quietly, "Our friends are having car trouble, bad luck." He scooted out of the booth. "Let's see if we can give them a push or something." David fumbled with his wallet at the register while Ari went outside. The men, still loitering at the counter, caught on. The car labored, then sputtered and died. "Looks like they're gonna need a little help getting outa here," the sandy-haired fellow said. The other men snickered and guffawed, and like a sticky lump of insects, went out the door.

David and Patsy followed. Ari was leaning in the window of the station wagon, talking with the Negro driver. The men from the diner strolled to the wagon, one at each bumper. Ari straightened up. "Hey man," he said. "We can take care of it." One of the men gave the bumper a hard shove, grunting furiously. Then another did the same, and another. In half a minute they were rocking the wagon violently. The driver tried the starter again. It almost made it. "Shit!" David said. He was still back by the cafe door with Patsy, wondering what to do. Ari started shouting, "You stupid jerks, leave them ALONE." He was holding onto the edge of the window pane, like a man in a cartoon clinging to a flying airplane. The men paid him no attention at all. He ran to his own car and started it. David and Patsy panicked and ran toward the car too. Ari leaned out of the window, waving them back, "Wait!" he shouted. "Get back!" By now the station wagon was rocking dangerously. The men shouted something back and forth, and the rocking slowed. Two of them came over to the same side as the other two. "They're going to turn it OVER!" Patsy said. She turned around twice, like a confused dancer. There were at least a dozen onlookers from the diner in the parking lot by now. The cook was at the door, wringing his apron. "Do something?" Patsy shrieked. The four attackers, cursing and laughing, were positioning themselves to lift the side of the station wagon.

There was a frightful clank as Ari's Ford hit the back of the station wagon. His engine revved fiercely. The driver of the wagon cranked the starter again. The four men were shoving the side of the car. The wheels on that side were just off the ground when Ari managed to give the car enough push to lurch forward, and in that instant the motor turned over, and the bucking car drove away. One of the men had been thrown onto the pavement by the movement of the car. David grabbed Patsy's arm and yelled, "Come ON!" Ari screeched up to them, and David and Patsy both managed to jump in as he accelerated.

David let out a long noisy exhalation of breath. "God DAMN, Finberg," he said. "You were slick as spit back there."

Ari shook his fist in the air. "You don't have to fight people dumber than you." He was laughing. "If you're in a car and they're not."

They could not get inside fast enough. They ran from Ari's to Patsy's apartment. There they clung to one another. They were inflamed by what had happened, by the near-miss of it, like passengers out of a wrecked car. "God I hate this place!" Patsy cried. David clasped his arms around her and kissed her neck. There was no one else he would have wanted to be with at the cafe scene.

They lay on the daybed, on the faded chenille spread. He did not stop to think about the ways this was different from the first time, the comfort of her house, the sweet easiness of it. They were together, as they had to be, like exiles.

That was on a Thursday night. Friday he went up to the hospital to help his mother. Saturday he watched TV at Leland's. At home, when the phone rang, he jumped. He did not call Patsy. There had to be some time to let things settle down again. He did not want to make too much of what had happened.

He had just squeezed out of one girl's clutches, he told himself. He was not ready for another. But Sunday was long and dull, and he went back to Patsy's. She had a copy of "Antigone," which they were casting soon. For an hour he listened as she told him the story and read long passages to him, while he stared at her and wondered who she had been with before him, where she had learned not to be scared.

After a student council meeting, Beth Ann said, "David Puckett, aren't you going to ask me out? Or are you waiting for me to call you every time?" Stupid and surprised, he stood with his mouth open. She laughed and invited him to dinner at her home the next weekend. Going out isn't any better than staying in, she said. He supposed that was true, if you had her house.

The house was in a cul de sac, further hidden by a brick wall eight feet high in front. An arch curved over the front of the long drive; there was no gate. He had not remembered how grand the house was. After the club party, they had entered the kitchen from the garage, and he had seen only that room. This time he stepped down onto flagstones in the entry way, and followed the Negro maid through a room lined with books and paintings, to a sitting room where the family was gathered. Laurel Kimbrough sat at a small teak table, folding a creamy piece of paper into an envelope. Hayden had a fat book on his lap. Beth Ann was stretched out on a chaise longue, half a dozen glossy magazines spilled onto the floor beside her. David had a moment of complete bewilderment, as a person must feel upon entering a room where another language is being spoken. He felt overwhelmed by the variety of patterns and colors (however subtle) in the room; the chairs were upholstered in rich fabrics and the walls were flocked or embossed with an intricate covering. He sat down most gingerly on the offered chair, feeling his awkwardness as a great weight on a delicate surface.

They ate in the dining room, served by the Negro maid. He said thank you when she ladled soup into his bowl, but the Kimbroughs did not acknowledge the service, and he decided to do only what he first observed. He ate lightly, for him, out of self-consciousness. There were certain obligatory questions about his family, which he answered with a briskly polite brevity. His father was a tailor, his mother a nurse. There was the sister, married to a "radio executive." The answers seemed to satisfy; he was not required to elaborate. There was of course no way for him to ask the things he wanted to know, details about Hayden's role on the bank board, the nature of his law practice. It was like dining with Africans and never mentioning the home country; not having traveled, he did not know enough to formulate inquiry. Beth and her mother moved their food around on their plates, eating little, and though the maid said there was a cobbler, they declined dessert. Hayden said, wouldn't that make a good snack later? and David of course claimed to be altogether too satisfied with the meal to have another bite. He wondered if the maid took leftover food home, or if the

Kimbroughs threw it away. Glee had told him her mother was once fired for taking a ham bone home from a cafeteria.

Beth Ann's parents excused themselves and disappeared into a far wing of the house. Beth Ann took David into a large room with a white tile floor, pool table, couches, a bar. The high ceiling was crisscrossed by dark beams. One wall was broken by French windows, looking out onto the same gardens as the breakfast nook. Near the windows stood an easel with a canvas, covered by a length of muslin. Stacks of board games filled two shelves behind the pool table. Beth put on a stack of records, and they danced. Perhaps half an inch taller than he, she was a light and graceful dancer who seemed to anticipate his every movement. They danced as they had at the club, politely. When he said he thought it was time for him to go, she kissed him. Her lips were cool. He felt like a boy with a fever being soothed. And he was surprised.

"But why me?" he blurted.

"I'm bored with them. I understand them perfectly, boys who grew up like me. I don't understand you."

Later at home, as he was undressing, he noticed the fleshiness of his belly. He had been eating like a starved man. Soon, with winter winding down, he'd be able to play tennis again, and he could swim before class. He fell onto his bed smiling. You could be confused as hell, and a girl could interpret it as mystery, when all along, the mystery was the girl herself. He felt he had survived an initiation. He would wait to see what happened next.

When he saw Glee, he ducked or turned or pretended not to see her. She walked in a mass, surrounded by her girlfriends who, when they saw David, moved in closer. (But hadn't Jenny Weaver stood in the cafeteria line flirting with him when Glee wasn't around? Hadn't Betsy been friendly as could be at "Antigone" tryouts? Wasn't he "available" again?) He had not met her eyes since the night she threw his pearl on the floor. At first when he saw her he was pinched with regret, but it had already faded; he did not want to think about her. And suddenly he was very busy. He did start swimming early in the mornings before school. There were always a few guys from the swim team, and they all joked and splashed and then got down to serious laps. The mornings he swam, he felt lean and sharp; he was losing that embarrassing ring of belly fat he'd built up over Christmas break. Then "Antigone" was cast and he was Creon. Often on weekday evenings he took Patsy home and they dissected the rehearsal. Sometimes they did schoolwork, sometimes they made love. On Friday nights he took Beth Ann to the movies, or, once in a while, to the Teen Center to dance. "See you tonight?" he would say at council meeting, and then that night, "See you tomorrow?" She smiled and nodded, like these were silly questions, but they had no understanding. Sometimes she did have other things to do. One weekend he did not see her, and then on Sunday in the paper were photographs of a "Black and White Ball" at the club, and there she was, with her mother, and Amos Lawton, home from Yale. Usually on Saturday he went to her house and they watched television or played cards and listened to records. And talked. Mostly, *he* talked. She listened sweetly, she smiled at him, but she did not really have very much to say. He had never heard her voice a strong opinion about anything. Maybe opinions, like meals, were to be served in tiny portions, something to do with good manners, with breeding. He thought he ought to be more reserved with her, but if he stopped talking, their evenings would consist of dead space. They were most chaste.

There was still often a bitter wind, and an occasional rain, but now and then the day was bright and clear, and David and Ellis began practicing tennis again. They laid bottle caps on the court and aimed serves at them. They played each other for hours at a time. They ran. The team began to assemble after school for workouts; winter was winding down. Some days he went straight from the court to rehearsal, skipping supper altogether. He liked to go late at night to the Stockman for a hamburger. He could not lose the feeling that he was an alien, visiting a local waterhole. Since the incident with the opera singers, he found a curious pleasure in watching the other patrons in the cafe. Most of them were laborers, coming or going from a job, or sensibly having a bite before hitting the bars. He thought you could tell by looking what any of them would say about white and Negro friends eating together. What you could not tell was how far they would go to make a point. In January a spurned lover had burst into a cafe like this in Andrews and shot two people dead. Any of these customers could be capable of such an action: one night a customer, the next a murderer. Any of the customers could be victims, himself included. All it took was a moment of insanity, a storm of anger, a gun.

Leland started dating Sissy. David had told him that her father was working pipeline in New Mexico, and on David's dare, he had called her, while David listened. When he hung up—"She said, 'That'd be nice!'" he was sweating drops so big he looked like he had come in from the rain. Sissy had cut her hair in a short style that made her look more like the other girls and less like a waif. David thought she was putting out signals. He was too busy to spend time with her, and he did not want to encourage any fantasy she had about the nature of his friendship, but for some crazy reason he wanted to help her out. She had never once talked about wanting to belong, but who didn't want that? If it did not matter to her, he could admire her solitary pride, but she had to be lonely. He suggested that she work on "Antigone," where anyone could be useful. She was assigned to props, and was helping build the sets. Some evenings he didn't see her; she was like a mouse, you only caught a glimpse of her if she moved across your vision. Leland complained that she wanted to talk about David when they went out. "But what about me?" David asked. Leland shrugged. "'What would *David* think of that? Did *David* ever do this or that?' Like I'd know everything about you." He did not seem to mind all that much. His tone was jocular: "I can't get to first base with her, there's Puckett in the road." David did not think Leland was serious about bases with Sissy. The little joy ride with LaVonne and the boys had scoured a lot of the brave vulgarity right out of him. David thought he and Sissy were a good pair. He tried to get Leland to describe their dates, but there did not seem much to talk about. They went to movies, they drank Cokes, they kissed goodnight. Evidently Sissy did not read her notebook to Leland. Maybe, David thought, she had given it up, as, it seemed, he had. His notebook lay on the floor by his bed, and there were times when he picked it up, but he could not manage to write anything, as if his hand had grown too heavy to move across the page. He had lost patience with his notes, and he was awed by the challenge of attempting a real story. Maybe next summer, he told himself. Maybe in college there would be a writing class. Maybe a writer had to live first and write later. There were innumerable reasons for avoiding his notebook. When he was at Patsy's, though, he often noticed that she had a lined pad out on her table, stacks of pages covered with her scrawl. He thought she probably wrote every day. He wanted to say to her, I thought you wanted to be an actress! Her discipline was accusing; she flaunted it.

One Saturday afternoon he spent an hour with Hayden Kimbrough in his shop. He had admired the teak table where Laurel liked to work on correspondence, and Hayden had revealed that he had made it. David sat on a bar stool that matched the set in the den, while the older man puttered at the bench. Kimbrough was finishing a small cherry wood stool. They spoke of inconsequential things—the weather, sports, the likelihood that Basin would build a new high school next year. All the while, David longed to ask him real questions: What does a board chairman *do*? Did you always know it would be like this, your life? Did it all come naturally, because you are who you are? *How can I be more like you?* Kimbrough was the son of a judge, and the judge the son of a sheep rancher who had moved into liveries, hardware, freight drayage. Beth Ann had told David that her mother's family had bought school land for a dollar an acre, then raised cattle, cotton, and sorghum. She showed him handsomely bound books stuffed with photographs and clippings about the families. Being old family seemed as important as the wealth. You could find a way to make money, but how could you make up for being nobody from the start? What would Kimbrough tell him about that?

David ran his fingers down the silky wood. Kimbrough said, "This is the one thing that makes me stop thinking. It's not social, I don't have to talk, there's no strategy, just the craft of it." He clapped David's shoulder. "A hobby gets important when you have a home and family. It's your retreat."

David thought of his father in his easy chair, his feet propped on the hassock. "Beats drinking, for something to do," he said. He wished he had not. Kimbrough gave him a quizzical look, then switched off the lights and led them back into the kitchen where the women were drinking cocoa.

That night David sat with Beth Ann in the den, she curled

up against him on the couch as they listened to music. They sat in shadows, the only light a small lamp across the room. He was saying how good it felt to start playing tennis again, how much he looked forward to the spring competition. He did not say what he was thinking so much lately, that he wanted the chance to be somebody, to show what he could do. Whatever had appealed to Beth Ann in him might soon wear thin, without fresh accomplishment. Kimbrough often mentioned the successes of men in his acquaintance: one appointed to a judgeship, those who won major cases, a friend who was likely to be the Republican candidate for district congressman. Of course no one expected a boy to walk on water, but if you could not get by on who you were, you had to be what you did. These people admired tennis; they would admire him if he won. Beside him, Beth Ann said, "Mmm." Her father was going to organize a tournament at the club in April, she said; David would play, surely. She snuggled closer. He laid his arm across her shoulders gently. He was suffused with the sense of rightness, being there, of the surprising fit of himself and this girl. He wondered why he kept seeing Patsy at all, and decided it was only the play, that threw them together four nights a week. She was beginning to get on his nerves. Always he felt there was something she wanted from him, something she was waiting for that he might or might not have to give. They had some unspoken pact not to talk about sex. It happened now and then, and they felt close for a little while, though there was never the intensity of that night they came back from the opera. Was he ignoring signals from her? Had it gone so far now that she *did* expect something, some outpouring of feelings, verbally, to make the sex mean more? Wasn't she the one who wanted to run off and live like a bohemian? Didn't that let him off the hook, let her off, too? Then there were her damned poems. They lay there like indictments: where were his stories? He did want to write, but it wasn't so easy. You couldn't write if you didn't yet have a story to tell.

"There's probably a stage, in becoming a writer," he heard himself telling Beth Ann, "when you haven't found the language for the stories yet, when what you have inside you is more like this, this *awareness*. You see the world in a different way from other people; you watch, like it's your job to take notes, but the words to shape what you see aren't there yet, because you need to keep watching a while longer. Lots of writers didn't even start writing until they were thirty or forty years old. You can't rush it. Maybe it's not till you escape. Like Conrad going to sea, those English poets going to Italy, men going to war." He had never told her he wanted to be a writer. This was all out of the blue. Maybe she had guessed; didn't she say he was different, didn't she say that was what she liked? He didn't know if the Kimbroughs would think as much of writing as of tennis, though it was hardly a matter of one or the other. He stretched one leg, to ease a cramp that was starting in his calf. From where he sat he could see the French windows, a flat black against the night. Wasn't it dangerous not to have any lights out there? Were they so confident no one would want to come in here, take things out of their beautiful house, maybe hurt them?

"I have to get out of Basin," he said with a fresh spurt of intensity. For a moment he lost the good feeling about where he was; he felt confined by the darkness, oppressed by the beams overhead, crowded by the girl on his arm. If she wanted him, she would have to understand, he had a lot of feelings that collected in him like steam and had to get out. A lot of those feelings were about this awful town. "I feel closed in here, which is pretty crazy, isn't it, with all that huge sky, the land? Once last summer I was coming home from Fort Stockton. I parked the car out at the sandhills, and walked a far way from the road, so that I didn't see lights anymore. I went down in one of the little gulleys and took my shoes off and sat there. The moon wasn't bright; it seemed to say, I'm tired, I'll shine some other night. But the sky was like cloth, close enough to touch. I sat there, kind of burrowed down in the sand, and I just knew, for that little while, that I was part of—part of everything. That if I put my hand out, what it touched was far away from Basin, far away from my whole life right now. It made me feel calm. I realized, if I just hold on, I'll find out what I'm supposed to do. I've thought of being a lawyer, like your dad. That would be a good career. And I think I could be a teacher. Maybe I could be a college professor, that's not so bad, is it? It sounds ok, doesn't it? Professor Puckett?" Suddenly he felt his face flaming. On and on he had jabbered, like a crazy person, and saying how terrible Basin was, when her parents' families had been here for generations. She probably expected to make her life here, just like them. What did she care if he wanted to write?

Beth Ann didn't say anything. He pulled his arm free and she slumped against his chest, her hair falling down her neck, her mouth slack. She hadn't minded his rambling monologue; she was asleep.

He and Patsy, talking about Antigone and her stubbornness, ended up talking about what it meant not to fit in. "You don't know," she said. "Look at you, Likely to Succeed." He thought she sounded almost resentful. "But that doesn't mean anything!" he protested. "Kids saw something that isn't even me, some outside-David—" She interrupted him. "They saw how you stand apart and the distance is just right to make you look good. That's not like being left out, not at all." The sharpness of her voice stung him. "It's not like you make any effort to fit in!" he accused her. In the play, Antigone defied Creon, even though it meant a terrible death, suffocation in a cave. You could look at Patsy, playing the part, and know Antigone would never, ever give in.

She spoke without the edge of anger that had cut him. "I wouldn't want to. Not belonging hurts, but it's only now, and now is going to pass. I look at the other kids, and I know they don't know what I know. They don't know that the not-belonging leads to something else—"

"Yes?" he asked eagerly. *Why did he keep thinking she knew something he needed to know?*

"But I don't know what it is!" she cried. "I just know I have to look for it away from here. And sometimes I feel afraid I'll find it—that place that leads to my true self—too soon. What if I'm not ready? What if the place is just a metaphor?"

"What?" he pressed. "What metaphor?"

"For love. What if someone important comes in my life before those other things? What if he were here, in this awful place? What if you could love someone, when you haven't been anywhere? What would you love with? Dreaming? Wanting?" A stillness fell over them. She had brought love into their conversation; how would he set her straight? He pulled away from her. "You're being melodramatic," he said coldly. "You sound like you're working at being a poet."

Angrily, she retorted, "At least I work at what I want to be! At least I'm not afraid of my true self."

He went home agitated and paced his room. What did Patsy mean? Was he supposed to talk circles around anything sensible, to feed her fantasies about an artistic life? Was he supposed to match her writing, maybe make himself look bad if it wasn't up to her standards? *Was he supposed to love her?*

He thought of Beth Ann, asleep against his chest. She didn't really care what he thought all that much; she just liked it that he was a thinker. It was like being tall. As for her, he had no idea what went on inside her head. She did not have a compulsion to reveal it. She knew that what she had on the outside was enough for David, for any boy.

27.

For Valentine's Day he had bought a box of Whitman's chocolates for Beth Ann. As he cut across the back of the courts, he caught up with Sissy heading home. She was cheerful and glad to see him. "You're always so busy," she said.

He had heard from one of the kids in the play that she had been asking around if anyone had sleeping pills. He asked her if that was true. "I have a headache sometimes," she said, in the same cheerful voice. "I thought if I took something, when I woke up it would be gone." He did not think it was his place to lecture her. When they got to her house she said, "Come in, I'll show you something." They went in the back door. She called out a hello to her mother and took him in her room. She took her notebook from under her mattress. He asked her if she was still writing. She looked surprised. "Of course." What she wanted to show him was a clipping she had cut from the newspaper, about a girl in Iowa who committed suicide on Christmas Day. "It says two hundred kids came to her funeral. She wasn't a cheerleader or anything, she was just a girl who killed herself, and they all turned out." She tried to show him the clipping, but he said he didn't need to see it, he believed her.

"Can you come to my house?" he asked, impulsively. "I've got something to show you now." He could see she was pleased. She ran to tell her mother.

He got the box of chocolates out of his closet. It had a wide red ribbon tied around it.

"Is that what you wanted to show me?" She looked disappointed.

"Why not?" he said. "Do you like the nuts? The nougats?" He let her choose first. They each ate several pieces. Then he asked her again about the sleeping pills. "You worry me sometimes," he said. "It sounds like you want to hurt yourself." He wondered if she had ever thought of getting away. Maybe it seemed too long until it would be possible; she was only a junior. Maybe it seemed harder to a girl. Where would she go?

She was sitting on his bed, backed up into the corner. She pulled a pillow in front of her and hugged it, and giggled. "You know, David, if you were my friend, you would shoot me if I asked you to. My daddy has a rifle and a shotgun, too." She had this silly grin. No way was it funny.

"Go on, Sissy," he said. "Things can't be that bad."

She threw the pillow down and leaned her elbows into it. "Think what a story it would make," she said in a teasing, playful way, like they were talking about putting toilet paper in someone's tree.

The comment about the story irritated him. Suddenly she felt like a big weight around his neck. He took his time picking out exactly the right piece of candy and popped it in his mouth. "You think I'm up to that?" he finally said, trying to sound teasing himself. She said, "I thought you'd know how to do it right."

He said he had someplace he had to be. As soon as she was gone he rushed to the drugstore to buy another box of candy for Beth Ann. She was picking him up to have dinner at her house. He gave her the candy on the way. For some reason he did not understand, he told her about the first box, embellishing things a little. He told her about knowing Sissy from the hospital, about being neighbors. According to his story, he gave Sissy the whole thing, after they each had a piece. "I feel sorry for her," he said.

Beth Ann acted bored. "Heavens, I don't care who you give candy to, David Puckett. But I don't see why you want to be around that girl. She's too weird for words." Actually, he was surprised that she knew who the girl was, and said so. "Well, who else looks like her? Like a little lost *bird*?" Beth Ann said, tossing her beautiful head. It bothered him, that Beth Ann discarded the subject of Sissy so disdainfully. What would she say if he told her, I see a lot of what she sees, I get afraid and desperate, too, only I'm a little stronger, a little luckier. Not such a *lost bird*. After dinner Beth opened the candy at the table, but only her father and David ate any. Her mother made a nice show of choosing a piece, then barely nibbled at one corner of it, which, David supposed, was more polite than refusing. He wished he had bought flowers. There were always flowers in this house, in tall vases.

When he got home he called Leland and asked him if Sissy talked funny on their dates. Leland said, "She never says anything funny."

"Christ!" David said. "I mean, anything *strange*. Does she talk about murder, suicide, that sort of thing?"

Leland laughed heartily. "She reads the paper just like me, did you know that? She always knows what crazy thing happened. Did I tell you about the couple that couldn't get their kids to sit still for Christmas pictures—?"

"Aren't you the perfect match?" David interrupted, and slammed down the phone.

He took his father's car and went to Patsy's. He had something for her, too, a copy of *The Prophet*. It was only eight o'clock, but she was in her pajamas. She said she was studying. She took the book and thanked him. They were both standing by the door. "Guess I'll go on then," he said, embarrassed by her lack of enthusiasm. What had he done to her? Brought her a present!

He left her place, kicking the dirt. If he had taken a copy of a romantic book to Glee Hewett, she would have been thrilled to death, even if she never did read it. He had given two girls gifts on Valentine's, and neither one had shown any particular appreciation.

He felt a gush of pure lonesomeness for Glee. He had seen her less and less, almost as if she had found a new route around the school. Once she had come in during his library aide time and checked out a book from him, and she acted like he was the old maid librarian.

He parked a few houses down from her house and got out and leaned against the car, thinking about seeing her. The lights were out in the living room; either they were watching TV, or everyone had gone to bed. It was not so very late. Stealthily, he walked across her neighbors' lawns and went along the side of the house to the back corner where her room was located. He did not want to frighten her, but he did not want to go to the front door, either. He picked up a pebble and threw it lightly at her window. Her curtain was drawn. He waited a minute, then ran back to his car.

She called him a little while after he arrived home. "Were you at my house?" she asked timidly. "Were you just here?"

"Did I scare you?"

"Somebody running in your yard in the middle of the night, isn't that a reason?" she said, her voice a little stronger.

He thought she was teasing him, and laughed. "It's not nine o'clock," he said. What would it hurt to see her again?

Her voice came out in a long strangled noisy rush. "I want you to leave me alone, Davy! I'm dating somebody else now—"

"Dickie Huber!" he said. He had seen them in the halls.

"Yes, Dickie Huber, and it's none of your business, you hear? I don't want you to even say hello when you see me. I want you to leave me *alone*, finally and for good, so I don't go around hoping you'll come back again. So I'll know you're really gone, now that you're screwing Miss High and Mighty Beautiful Kimbrough!"

He was so shocked he held the phone out from his ear an inch, as if it were hot. He could hear her sobbing. "Listen, Glee," he said, "Beth Ann Kimbrough doesn't screw around."

"What you never understood was that I don't either. Only you did. You're the one who screws around."

He practiced tennis furiously. One day he slammed a ball right into Sandy Holt's thigh. Hey, lighten up, Puckett, the other guys said. The wind blew every day. It made them all giddy. The kickoff tournament of the season was right there in Basin in March, the West Texas Relays, originally a track meet, since expanded to include tennis. It was the one meet at which West Texans had an advantage. They practiced in the biting wind, they batted balls with grit blowing in their faces, they knew the ragged courts like their own back yards. Boys from other schools got red faces and their eyes streamed tears. How do you stand it? they asked.

Ellis was working out with Burt Lasky, too, playing singles. "What's with Lasky?" David asked one afternoon. He felt just the least bit deflated when he played without Ellis. They all rotated among themselves, everybody played everybody sometime, but this Lasky business was getting to be a steady thing. Ellis was casual about it. "He comes at me stronger than the other guys," Ellis said. David realized his partner was as serious about the singles competition as he was about their team. Ellis boxed at his bicep. "I know all your moves, Puckett." David was peeved, he could not help it. "I'll see what I can do about that," he said.

28.

He saw his father with the young woman again. They were going into Woolworth's, where there were booths in the back and a snack bar. He waited on the sidewalk for them to come out. His father went back to the clothing store. The woman walked down the block in the other direction. As soon as Saul was inside, David ran to catch up with the woman. She pranced along snappily on her high heels, giving the illusion of speed, but in fact not moving so quickly. A lot of her motion was side to side. She was wearing a big full skirt and a crinoline that made it stick out stiffly. He came up behind her and called, "Miss, Miss." He knew it sounded stupid, but what could he say? He came up beside her. "Excuse me," he said, just about out of breath. "Could I talk to you a minute?"

She stopped so abruptly he almost lost his balance, stopping too. "Who are you?" she asked, calmly; she knew a person would have a reason to want to talk to her. When he told her he was Saul Stolboff's son, she did not look the least upset. If anything, she had a concerned look, like a nurse. She was not as young as he had thought at first, she was maybe twenty-eight or twenty-nine. "My car's right here—" she pointed. "Why don't we sit in there and talk." She had a pleasant voice, almost free of twang; she had to have come to Basin from some other part of the country. He climbed into the car, relieved that it was so much easier than he expected. Then, when he realized she was waiting for him to speak, he could hardly breathe for the anxiety he felt. She had that same patient, almost worried expression, but she wasn't exactly helping. Why did he have to say anything? How could she not know what he was thinking? *That's my father you were with.*

"Your father is a serious man," she said.

He thought of Saul reading *War and Peace*.

"A sensitive, special man."

He could only stare.

"I know this must be confusing for you, but you must see, it's not your business. It's nothing for you to think about."

It was as if she had pulled a cord that opened him up. "Of course it's my business!" he said. "My father left us once. He could do it again."

"Do you think that would be up to me? That I could make it happen or not happen?"

He thought about that for a long moment. If you were stuck in your life, you might not see another way, unless a person came along to show you. "My mother—" he began, and faltered.

"Your father is a philosophical man. He sees the way life hands you your cup of pain. Of course there's all that history, with your mother."

"Nineteen years."

"But when you've drunk it, you don't have to sit there holding the cup, waiting for more. Life isn't a sentence handed down to you."

"I think he thinks it is."

She smiled, a little smugly, thought David. "Another person can make you rethink your convictions. That's a benefit of dialogue."

"And is that what this is about—you and my father? An affair, about philosophy?"

She said sharply, "Love is based on respect. I think your father is a very intelligent, very sad, very good man." She did not say, *sexy*, but the word was in the air.

"It is an affair?"

She took her keys out of her purse and put them in the ignition. She had wonderful legs. "I need to go. David, isn't it? David, you can't stop things that are in motion. You just don't have that kind of authority in your father's life. This doesn't have anything to do with you. It doesn't even have to do with your mother. It's all about Saul."

"And you." His voice croaked, embarrassing him.

She started the car. "Do you want a ride somewhere?"

He opened the door. "How long—" he stumbled, finding his nerve. "How long has this been going on?"

She smiled at him. "I met your father in the library, over a year ago. David—?"

"Yes?"

"It won't help to tell your mother. Really, it will only hurt."

"Listen, one thing. Did he ever talk to you about Florida?"

She had a merry look. "Oh heavens, we're always talking about the ocean! Isn't there some place you'd like to see?" She pulled away.

He ran toward home, his heart banging in his chest. Damn! he thought, as he arrived at his door. What the *hell* is her *name*?"

He was afraid the woman would tell his father that he had approached her, and either his father would attack him— maybe even physically—or David's effrontery would some- how precipitate a decision, an action, which might be worse. If you made someone choose sides, there was always the possibility you would be sorry. But Saul said nothing, a week went by, it was clear the woman had not told him.

David seldom saw his father. Since Joyce Ellen had moved back in the house, Saul had withdrawn, or disappeared, avoiding the company of his swollen daughter. David had anticipated scenes in which Saul railed at his daughter for her stupidity, her fecundity, while Joyce Ellen snuffled and lowed like a farm animal. But Saul was absorbed and indifferent, less quarrelsome than ever. There were small exchanges, skirmishes that revealed a thread of his contempt, but he had moved beyond this bothersome household, David now knew. He floated in some intoxication brought on by talk and sex and fresh dreams. He was easier to live with. He bought a second television and installed it in his bedroom, where he sometimes took his supper and did not come out again. He seemed to be drinking less often, though when he did drink, he did not stop until he was stuporous. Many nights he simply left the house without a word, coming back within minutes of his wife. He seldom took the car, for which David was grateful, but confused. Where could you go in Basin, carless, especially a grown man? After David met the woman, it occurred to him that she must live nearby, within walking distance. There was a newer apartment complex half a dozen blocks away. David drove by slowly a couple of times, think- ing that a new apartment would be a nice change from an old house. One night, coming home from rehearsal, he drove around and around, looking for her car, a white Studebaker.

He thought he saw it in one of the parking spaces, but someone drove into a nearby slot and David drove away. He had noticed nothing about the car's interior. There would be no way to confirm that it was hers. And what would it matter? He already knew it was.

He wanted to talk to his mother. He wanted to warn her. He had the idea that if he could *say* the right thing, Marge could *do* the right thing, and this threat, embodied in a younger woman (embodied, indeed, very attractively), could be brushed away. But there was no right thing to say. And it was hard to find a moment alone with his mother. Joyce Ellen was like a big sausage, lying about the house, sleeping much of the time her mother was gone, waiting for her mother's company, and when Marge was home David was in school. On Sunday, when everyone's time off overlapped, they crowded one another in the small house. David went off to play tennis or to spend time at Leland's. He seldom spoke to his sister, though he pitied her, and wished her life were different, arranged in a way that would please her and please their mother and take up, somehow, less space.

He managed to catch his mother for a few moments one Monday evening before supper. Saul was in his workshop. Joyce Ellen was beached on the bottom bunk in her bedroom. Marge was seated at the kitchen table, looking through the baby section of a Sears catalog. David sat down across from her. There was no good way to say what he had in mind. Instead, he said, "Do you think Kelton will ever come around on this? Won't he want to see his kid? Is he sending money?" Marge looked up almost dreamily; she had not been paying attention to the catalog pages at all.

"He was adopted, you know," she told him. "He never knew anything about his mother. He has terrible thoughts about her, an awful woman who did this bad thing, and then gave him away out of shame. He told Joyce Ellen about it. It made her love him, a man with a mysterious past, a lost mother. But it's a sickness with him, this bitterness. When Joyce Ellen told him she was pregnant, he turned her into his mother. He said it wasn't his, she would have to give it away."

"Why, he's nuts!"

"Oh, precisely. Nuts. We have a lawyer now, but of course Joyce Ellen doesn't want to be divorced before the baby is born. We are advised to wait, but then it will be settled, he will have to give her something." She sniffed. "It's cost me two hundred dollars so far."

"It's awful!" David exclaimed, truly sorry for his sister, amazed at this dramatic story, which he would not have thought to invent. He felt almost pleased.

Marge sighed and closed the catalog. "A young girl with a baby. She isn't going to have an easy time."

"She should get her diploma," David said. "She could study now, while she's waiting. She could work on her equivalency."

Marge smiled. "She's very lazy now."

"Mom? Would it be easier someplace new? If we all moved, she could say she was divorced—she will be divorced—or even that she was widowed. She could say anything she wanted, in a new town."

"She can't go away! She's seventeen!"

"No, I didn't mean her, you weren't listening. Us. All of us."

Marge was perplexed. "Go where, son?"

"Anywhere. California! Galveston, maybe." He was thinking of the ocean.

Marge laughed mirthlessly. "You can't move away from your troubles."

David rushed in with his thesis. "Maybe Dad would be—happier—if—." It was too hard to say, he had not thought it through. "Maybe it would be better if you started over, in a new place."

"Such a strange idea."

"I mean it, Ma! Like plowing under last year's stubble, planting a new crop—"

His mother set her mouth. "What ideas has he been *planting* in your head?"

"It's not like that! It's my idea. I thought—if you changed your lives—"

Marge got up and took lids off the pots on the stove, peered in, banged them back down. "Nonsense."

"Think about it."

She turned and glared at him, a hard look in her eyes. "This is what he married. Right here, this is what."

"Not *what*, Ma! *Who! You!*"

"*What*," his mother said again. "This is it."

Later, with Beth Ann, he remembered the whole conversation. Of course he could not bring it up with Beth; he could not think aloud. He thought: It is what, and not who. He looked at Beth Ann. In Texas, you can work very hard and make a lot of money, if you are smart and lucky and not afraid to be mean, but you can join the world of her family, the world of the Kimbroughs, if you have not been born to it, only one way, and Beth Ann is the way.

He felt a thrilling chill along his spine. It was possible. Something in him, something he did not understand but other people saw, made it possible.

And his dreams changed. He stopped thinking about the city, about little offices looking out on green campus lawns, about his name on the spines of books stacked in the windows of bookstores. He thought of himself in a house with a flagstone entryway and a greenhouse, where he might grow orchids, or bright peppers and cherry tomatoes in February. He thought of himself in suits you had to buy in Dallas, of coming home at night and changing to go out again to dinner with friends. He felt himself catapulted by the surprise of his father's dreams: a woman who talked like a book, thoughts of life on a coast, things David had not guessed. He was thrown headlong into his own fantasy, and it was not impossible, it was not foolish, it was the first thing that had made sense. Hayden Kimbrough would advise him; he was a man without a son. Hayden wanted the best for his daughter. Maybe David could rise to that. It was worth a try.

He caught his father one night on the front steps. "Wait up!" he called out. Saul was impatient in his old-fashioned short wool jacket. It was already almost too warm for wool.

"Yes, what is it?" Saul pinched his nose, squinted. "What?"

David had practiced what he would say. Very evenly, in a voice as neutral as he could make it. "What's her name, Dad?"

Saul's gaze was thick, like something sticky, heavy with hate. David steeled himself for a blow, his father's curses, but he had to let him know he knew.

His father gave him a false, condescending smile. "Hope," he said, and spun on his heel and was away.

29.

"Watch!" Ellis said as they started the last set. It was the finals. They had made it. "Watch!" he said, he always said that. All around them, people were watching *them*. His father was there, his sister looking like Dumbo's mother beside him. The Kimbroughs were there. But Ellis meant *watch what they do. Watch me.* Because in tennis, as in chess, you had to have a plan. You had to be ahead of the other players. You had to think: I'll do this so he'll do that, and then wham! he'll be sorry. But David thought, at that fraction of a moment before Ellis watched the first serve across the net: I have to watch Ellis, he always gives me the cues. I need him.

They were like an instrument, playing together. All the parts fit. Yet there was something different in Ellis' play this year, a greater aggressiveness, a tendency to take a little more of the credit, with shots that made the crowd go *Ahh!*, the way they sometimes did for David, who was showier, if he had the right set-up. Ellis was stronger, this year, with a look of joy and determination. He had become ambitious.

David asked the coach, when all the yelling was over, when there had been hugs and handshakes: "Who was watching?" He wanted to know about coaches and scouts. The coach named three schools, disappointingly small. "There's a lot ahead, still," he said, catching the expression in David's eyes. "And it's not football," he added, ruefully. David tasted a bitterness in his mouth, which was still gritty with sand. The real tennis was played on club courts, he knew. This high school shit—who was he kidding? There were boys his age headed for the US Open. He was already behind.

But this was what he had.

He found Ellis again and they threw their arms across one another's shoulders. First there was a shower, clean clothes, then the barbecue at the fairgrounds. Even with the wind and sand, the city would turn out. There were so many winners, in so many events. The locker rooms were full of shouts and moans and congratulations, the aftersounds of competition among the young.

Ellis' whole family was at the fairgrounds, except his father, who was working. David and Saul met up with them and went through the long lines to get meat and beans and coleslaw on big paper plates. They sat at rough wooden tables and gorged. "Here we go, partner!" David said, slapping Ellis on the arm. He had thought he would feel more exultant.

Then someone came looking for the Whitteys, and suddenly all around them there was a terrible silence, a parting of the crowd, people staring and moving back slowly, giving the Whitteys room. There had been an accident in the oil field. Ellis' father was at Basin General, it was bad. David said he would take the younger children home, so that Ellis and his mother could go to the hospital, but Mrs. Whittey said no, they would all go. She pulled two young sons close to her hips. "We have to be together," she said. You could see in her eyes that she knew the worst had happened. The man who came to get her had said, you have to come, it's bad, but hadn't he said, on the way, let me through, someone's been killed? Give me room, I have to find the widow. Couldn't she tell, by the look on his face, on the faces of the people he had passed on his way to her? Ellis' father was dead.

David and his parents huddled at the table to read the newspaper account. He could not think when they had been so close. Joyce Ellen, who could have cared nothing for the Whitteys, lay on her bed weeping.

Mr. Whittey had been struck by a drilling tong and his head wedged against a corner of the derrick he was working on. "Listen to this!" David said indignantly. "Listen to the last line of this article: 'The rig supervisor said the rotary table kicked out of gear and stopped the kelly before much damage was done to the equipment.'"

"What's a tong? What's a kelly?" Saul asked drily. His wife gave him a long look. "What do you care?" she asked. "What does anyone care, except whoever owns the equipment?"

The family went to the funeral together. There were three dozen people in the church, most of them kids; anyone who had wanted to go was excused at school. It was a funeral

Mass, long and dull and in Latin. They sat a couple of rows behind the Whitteys. Just in front of David was Betty Leyerbach with her mother; both of them cried all through the service. When the Whitteys entered the aisle behind the casket, Ellis looked at Betty in passing, and as David saw Ellis' face, so full of misery, he clasped his own hands hard, into two white-knuckled fists.

The next weekend "Antigone" was performed. David had not talked to Patsy in almost two weeks, except at rehearsals. He told himself it was because of their parts, the antagonism and tension between Creon and Antigone. When she looked at him, he saw how remote she had become in her resolve, how capable she was of anger and spite and self-punishment, all to defy authority. When he looked at her, when he heard her fiery denunciations, he felt his spine stiffen and his temples pound. How dare she, he thought. How dare she.

He went to the cast party at Mr. Turnbow's house alone. Beth Ann had gone with her mother to Houston to a baby shower for a cousin. She had not said anything about missing the play. David was shocked; all along he had assumed she was impressed by his leading role in a classic play, but it was obvious that it meant nothing to her. The play was merely something for him to finish up, so he would have time for her when she had time for him. At least his own family was there; his mother took off work on Saturday to come. Afterwards she kissed him and said, "I knew you had it in you." Saul shook his hand and said, "What are the wages in this line of work, son?" David, hurt, said lightly he had no idea. "Acting is for fun," he said. "I'm going to be a lawyer." His father did not comment.

Of everyone, Sissy was the most excited. "I love theatre!" he heard her say over and over at the party. Her eyes were glittery. She never sat down or stood still for long. David asked her how she was getting home; he had his mother's car. She said Leland was coming for her. "Well, then, I'll say goodnight," David said. They were in a corner of the kitchen. Someone had spilled a Coke on the counter and it had run toward the sink, a rivulet dripping over the edge onto the floor. She saw him looking at it. "Yuk," she said. She looked around. She took a damp towel from the table and wiped up. She rinsed and wrung out the towel, then hung it over the faucet. All the while, he leaned against the refrigerator, watching. She turned around, close to him. "Sissy," he said. He put his hand on her shoulder, leaned toward her, and kissed her mouth. It was a sweet kiss, the kiss of a friend, it was his admiration for her tidiness and generosity, her kinkiness and independence, it was his appreciation for her dating Leland. It was a gift.

"Gee, now I can die happy," she whispered.

He touched the lobe of her ear with his thumb. It was soft and faintly downy. "You deserve a lot more than that," he said. He was suffused with a feeling very much like shame.

Ellis did not come to tennis practice. David felt lost. The coach paired him for doubles practice with Burt Lasky. They did not make a good team. David played badly, resenting Burt's smug competence. The coach slapped David on the back. "This Whittey thing is bad business," he said.

David felt like throwing up. "I'm going in to shower," he said.

He went straight to Ellis' house. His mother was in the kitchen setting biscuits. When David let himself in, she smiled and told him to sit down for a minute, and she would get coffee. "I don't want you bothering," he said. "I just came to see Ellis. I wondered when he's going to come to practice. I thought it might help if he played."

Mrs. Whittey wiped her hands slowly on a big white towel, then sat down at the table across from David. "Ellis is what we have now," she said. "You have to understand. He isn't thinking about tennis."

David was embarrassed. "I didn't mean—"

She patted his hand. "You meant well. I know you love Ellis. But he's the man of the house now." She got up and poured them coffee. David put too much sugar in his cup, and gulped the coffee down. "I wish I knew how to help," he said, pushing the cup toward the middle of the table. "I wish it hadn't happened." He felt tears welling, his face burning. Mrs. Whittey leaned over and laid her open hand along his cheek. The cool feel of her flesh comforted him. Her belly pressed into the table's edge.

Ellis called late that night. "I'm not going back to school. I'm going into the field, just like my dad. I'm starting in the morning."

"Oh shit, man," David said. He felt rigid with fear, as if Ellis were calling to him from a pit of quicksand. Don't go under, he wanted to say. Don't leave me by myself.

"What else can I do?" Ellis said. "My mother can't work, with the baby coming."

"Didn't they give you anything? Wasn't it somebody's fault?"

"His supervisor brought a ham," Ellis said.

At the country club meet, David lost to Burt Lasky early, a humiliating defeat. Lasky went on to quarterfinals and lost to a kid from a little town with no team sports. David slunk away without speaking to any of the Kimbroughs. He felt that Ellis' father's death had brought him bad luck. If there had been a little more time, he told himself. If he had had a little more time to get his game together.

He opened the car door and reached across to lay his racket on the floor. For a moment he held it in his hand, wondering if it was his, it felt so strange to him. He laid it down and drove to Patsy's.

"I thought you might have come to the tennis match."

"You didn't ask me."

"It's a public meet."

"At the country club?"

He shrugged. "I'd have asked you later. This was just the first stage, the good part should have come after. Only I'm already out. I lost. I played like a real amateur."

"So now you know you aren't going to have everything you want."

He could not believe her cruelty. "What, you're glad? You wanted me to lose?"

"Of course not. But you can't win everything. You can't succeed at everything." He thought, maybe she does mean to sympathize, but she added, "You don't try hard enough."

He remembered the note on his locker door the day he was elected Most Likely to Succeed. *At what?* it said. He realized it had been Patsy's writing, he was sure of it.

"You've been angry with me all along, haven't you?" He was amazed at the truth of it; he suddenly saw her for what she was.

"I've just had enough," she said.

"Enough of what!"

She spoke in a maddeningly calm, even tone, almost as if she could not be bothered to muster up energy for him. "I kept waiting for you to take me out. I bought a dress with my Christmas savings. I thought, sometime we'll go to a movie. We'll go out to eat. But it never happened."

"I've spent so much time with you!" he protested.

"At my house!"

"I thought—"

"You didn't think. You just tagged along. You didn't think I might like to be seen, like any other girl, on a Friday or Saturday night. You thought I was thrilled just to be your weeknight fuck."

"Patsy!" He was shocked at her language. It was something she had picked up from Finberg, that New York Jew. "Where did you learn that?" he had to say. "From your big city lover?"

She laughed at him. "Ari is homosexual, you baby, don't you know anything? *Don't you pay any attention?*"

He was sitting in her lumpy armchair. He simply could not make his muscles pull him to a standing position, not yet. He felt like a cripple. "Then who?" he asked. He was confused. He had thought he had it figured out.

"After that night at the courts, I decided to get rid of my virginity," she said coolly. "It was easy."

He shook his head. He would have liked to cry. He felt such a sense of loss; it might have been him.

"You want me to choose," he said. "You can't make me choose." Beth Ann never asked what he did on week nights. She never showed any interest in what he did away from her.

Sadly, Patsy said, "You are going to have to learn to treat people better, David. At least you would have to treat me better, though I think it's too late now. I have learned a lot from Ari, you know. He's a true friend. That's what I wanted from you, really. Your friendship. I want out of Basin as much as you, you know. I'm no Glee Hewett. But you made me feel like an alley cat. One day I said to myself, why am I putting up with this?"

"You never said anything—"

"We didn't talk about anything important. It didn't matter anymore."

He thought: She looks older. She's grown up this year. She looks like someone who's been away and just come back to visit.

Everybody's leaving, he thought.

Hayden Kimbrough was casual about David's loss. "Listen, David," he said. "Put it in perspective. What's tennis good for? You never wanted to go on the circuit. It's a social skill, like bridge. You're a good player. It'll stand you in good stead all your life. You don't want to be so good nobody wants to play you!" He put his arm across David's shoulder. They were standing in the garden, where Hayden and Laurel had been pulling weeds while Beth Ann sat in a lawn chair, her skirt hiked up to bare her legs to the warm spring sun.

"Are you sending out your college applications?" Hayden asked. He stepped around in front of David. "Am I intruding here?"

"Oh, yes sir. I mean, no sir!" David laughed uneasily. "I'm applying to UT. I've got all the stuff at home."

"No problem there."

David took a deep breath and then said, "I'll have to get a job. I'll have to pay for it myself."

"Ahh," Hayden said. "I thought as much. That's why I brought it up. We've plenty of time to discuss this, but I'm glad it's come up. I can help, you know. I know a lot of people down at the legislature. No need for you to work at something mindless. You can start in the right lane from the very beginning." He smiled broadly. "With your looks and brains, and my pull—" He did not have to finish the sentence.

30.

They drove to the sandhills in a convoy of souped-up cars
and motorcycles. The girls liked the bikes best, broad and
humming between their thighs. At the dunes, everyone
pitched in to carry cases of beer, bundles of kindling, ice
chests with hotdogs inside, sacks of buns and mustard. At
midafternoon the wind died down, and there was the clear
hot brilliance of a spring afternoon. Everyone, among
friends, was happy. School, work, adults were forgotten;
there was no one to tell them what to do, no one to bemoan
their bad language and bad grooming and bad manners and
bad attitude.

They did not worry about the sand; they burrowed in it,
lounged on it, dug in it with bare toes. They sprawled on it in
a gulley between dunes, drinking and talking, telling terrible
jokes. Some of them would feel the sting of the season's first
sunburn by nightfall, would stand in front of bathroom mirrors pasting on Noxzema, grinning, before they went to bed.

At dusk the wind picked up again, and it was sharp. The
gang clustered in the hollow and built fires. They ate messy
hot dogs and washed them down with beer. Here and there
couples lay stretched out on blankets or towels, or only on
sand, seeking the warmth of one another's bodies. One boy
slipped his arm around the girl next to him. She snuggled
closer. Tentatively, he kissed her, then looked around, embarrassed. She lifted her hand to his neck, drew close, and
kissed him back. Someone close by yelled, Way to go! Let's
hear it for making OUT! The boy and girl drew apart, faces
hot in the dark. All around them boys started to make
smooching sounds, laughing, maybe meaning well, calling
out, Come on, you can DO it. Girls, giddy with their sophis-
tication and opportunity, placed warm hands on their boy-
friends' crotches; boys slid their hands up under shirts and

inside the legs of shorts. Still the boy and girl sat side by side, now barely touching. Aw, they're shy! someone said. So, go over the hill! someone else yelled, and suddenly kids were tugging at the girl and boy, pulling them to their feet, while the chant built: *Over the hill, over the hill.*

He led her up a high sand dune, stumbling and sliding, laughing with self-consciousness. At the top, they paused, they looked at one another, laughing again, a bit bravely, and then they went down the other side. *Awww!* they heard the kids behind them cry. *Awww!*

In a little while the group low in the crevice of the dunes wondered about the boy and the girl. They laughed and squealed and mimicked what they thought was going on over the hill. Someone said, we could go see. Giggling and stumbling and falling and climbing and growing more and more hilarious, they made their way to the top of the hill, and there, suppressing their laughter, then growing utterly quiet, they made a line along the crest. The wind was cold. The sky blazed with stars. The kids stood for a long while atop the dune, hugging their arms, watching.

David went into the bathroom and found his sister in the tub. She was lying back, her head against the enamel, her belly stuck up like a huge mound of risen dough. He groaned loudly at the sight, stumbled back a step, and knocked against the door behind him. Joyce Ellen wailed loudly. He turned and fled into the tiny hall, banging one fist into his other palm. "You could have locked the door!" he yelled. She shrieked, "What do you think it feels like! I'm a big blubbery whale! I know what you think!"

Mrs. Whittey had had her baby, a girl she named Rita. David took her a flannel blanket his mother had bought for Joyce Ellen. The baby looked like a pink prune. Mrs. Whittey seemed almost happy, sitting in a rocking chair with the baby in her arms. The children were in the yard and out in the street playing.

David sat on the porch steps with Ellis, sodden with pity. "What's going to happen, man?" he asked. Ellis shrugged and said something about taking it a day at a time.

"What about Betty?"

Ellis flinched. "She's going to go to secretarial school after graduation. Six months. Then she'll get a job, what else?"

"You guys want to get married?"

Ellis moaned. "I don't see how. I don't see it happening."

"You could get a bigger house."

Ellis spread his hands on his thighs. "You get married, and then there's another baby."

"You're smarter than that."

"I'm Catholic! She's Catholic!"

"Who'd know?"

Ellis shook his head. "She believes all of it. Mortal sin and excommunication and hell. Sex is for making babies."

David wheezed with his next breath. He coughed noisily to cover it. "I'm sorry," he said.

Ellis jumped to his feet. "There's a reason for everything! My mama says. The priest says. God sees ahead. It will work out."

David wanted to put his arms around his friend, but he could not see his way to it. Awkwardly, he stuck his hand out, and Ellis pumped it twice. "See you," David said. "See you," Ellis said back.

David told Beth Ann, "Sometimes I don't think I can make it one more week. One more day! It's already over. All this winding down is a waste, it's boring, it's driving me crazy." They were seated in lawn chairs in her garden, under a big pink and white striped awning. Her eyes were closed. He thought, if she's asleep, I'm going home right now.

Beth Ann stretched one arm up lazily. "You get so worked up, Davy." His neck prickled at the name she called him. When had she started that?

He leaped up. "Let's get out of here. Go for a ride. Want to go out to the dunes?"

She made a face. "Too sandy," she said, and they both laughed loudly. She held her arm out to him.

He drove them in the station wagon, out to her grandparents' old ranch house, ten miles east of town. He had never seen the place. The old couple lived in Midland, but the whole family went out to the ranch for summer barbecues. Everyone came for July 4th. A Mexican couple lived out there to keep it up.

Within sight of the house, the station wagon came to an overheated, steaming halt. Beth Ann sat placidly in her seat while he looked under the hood. He knew next to nothing about cars, but he could see the radiator boiling over, and he knew they were not going to drive anytime soon. "Damn!" he muttered.

"It's not so bad," Beth Ann drawled. "Luis will know what to do." She took his hand and led him to the drive and up to the large white clapboard ranch house, with its long graceful veranda. A Mexican woman came out of the front door, banging the screen. She shaded her eyes to peer down the drive. Beth Ann called out, "It's me, Maria. Beth!" and the woman broke into a huge smile.

Luis said it was the fan belt, and set off for town in his pickup to get one. Beth Ann led David around the house. All the old things were dusted and arranged, as in a museum. Kerosene lamps and dainty dishes, crocheted antimacassars adorned polished tables; family photographs and paintings of Western scenes hung on the wall. In the bedrooms, the iron beds were covered with quilts in complex patterns of bright cotton.

Beth Ann sat down on one of the beds, and motioned for David to sit beside her. "Just think, this was the best of the best at one time."

"It looks pretty nice to me right now."

"When I was a little little girl we still had an outhouse, even though they had plumbing by then. It was like a monument. I tried to imagine going out there in February, or in a dust storm."

"They had to be hardy people, ranchers."

"I'm glad I live now."

He pecked her cheek. "I'm glad, too, because if you'd lived then you'd be an old hag and I wouldn't love you."

She looked startled. "Do you love me?"

It was he who was startled, as if grasshoppers had jumped out of his mouth.

"Do you?"

He kissed her seriously. She had a sweet, toothpasty taste. She pressed against him for a moment, then pulled away. "*Do* you?" Her hair was disheveled and her breath uneven. For the first time ever he thought about taking her clothes off, seeing her naked. He wondered if she would be so haughty, so perfect, then.

"You know I do," he said steadily.

She lay back on the bed, smiling at him. One finger idly

traced a block of stitching on the quilt. He imagined her hand on his body, a cold thrilling thought. She said, "Sometimes I think about us in a little apartment in Austin. There's a bed with lots of pillows, and one of my grandmother's quilts."

"I didn't know you thought like that."

"You don't?"

"I don't *have* anything," he said, almost angrily. The future was far, far away. He had been a fool, thinking it would burst upon him, sparkling; what he saw now was a long grind, and nothing sure at the end. Beth Ann would not know about working for what you wanted, or about doing without.

"But you will."

"It's a long way off."

She yawned, collected again. Even the disorder of her hair looked arranged. "I know it is. I want to pledge my mother's sorority. There are things you just have to do or you'll be sorry ever after." She sat up, and reached for his hand.

"So you're going to go to Austin, too?" he asked.

"I might go to SMU for a year. That's where my mother went. But I could transfer whenever—"

"Whenever what?"

She ducked her head shyly. He thought the gesture looked almost rehearsed. "You still didn't say, Davy."

"I did."

"You answered a question. That's not the same."

He slid to his knees in front of her. He took her hands, looked up at her, and said, "Beth Ann Kimbrough, I love you." His heart was pounding hard. They had just been talking about marriage, hadn't they? What would her parents say?

"Let's go see what Maria's got in the kitchen," Beth Ann said brightly. "There's bound to be beans."

They sat at a table in a room with windows looking out on a vista of sand and sky. In the fields he could see half a dozen pumps. This was how ranchers got rich. The table had a red and white checked cloth on it. They ate bowls of pinto beans, tortillas, and hunks of fresh white cheese. He felt like someone in a Western movie, the house like a set.

Maria brought in a pitcher of lemonade that clinked with ice. David drank two glasses straightaway. Luis came in to say the car was ready. "Muchas gracias," David said impulsively. Luis replied gravely. "De nada, señor."

When they had driven out of the ranch roads onto the highway, David asked Beth Ann, "When you think about the bed in Austin? What are we doing in it? Do you think of that, Beth?"

She reached over to run her fingers lightly down his thigh. He moved her hand away. She arranged herself primly and said, "I want to be a virgin when I marry."

"Of course."

"I'd like it if you became a lawyer."

"Like your daddy."

"Yes."

"Whatever you say, Beth Ann." He meant to tease, but it came out utterly serious. They glanced at one another, then looked away. He thought they understood one another. It did not seem any of it had been his idea.

31.

Sissy was waiting for him on his back step. A small fist of anger struck inside his chest, seeing her there. She would want something; they all wanted something.

She looked sad and tired. She had a light sunburn across her cheeks and nose. "You're pink," he said gently.

"It doesn't hurt."

"I'm beat, Sissy. I was going to take a nap."

"That's okay. I just wanted to give you this." She held out a spiral-bound notebook. "Could you keep it for me?"

"Your notebook?" He held it gingerly; something told him this was not a good idea.

"We're doing spring cleaning. Turning the mattresses, taking down the curtains. I don't want my ma to find it. You can read it, if you want."

He felt sorry for her. "We haven't talked in a long time, have we?"

She shrugged. "You're busy."

He opened his door. "I'll keep it for you."

She stood there as if there were something he had forgotten to do. "You can read it."

"Yeah, you said that."

He waited until she was in the alley before he went inside.

It was quiet in the house. A pot of something was simmering on the stove. He peered into the living room. His mother was sewing a button on a blouse. She saw him and smiled. "You hungry?"

"Not much."

"I made soup, eat it any time."

"Where is everybody?"

"Saul's gone to play poker. Joyce Ellen is lying down."

"Is she okay, Ma? Earlier, she was all upset."

"Be patient, son. It's very, very hard to walk around with thirty pounds of baby and water and extra flesh."

"I'm going to my room."

He meant to sleep, but he was curious about Sissy's notebook. Each entry was dated and neatly written. Sometimes she wrote only a line or two:

Mr. Wickers farted in history class and turned beet red, but he kept right on talking.

I think my dad hit my mother last night. I heard her squeal. I hope he gets another job away from home.

Other entries were long and detailed. Turning the pages, he noticed his own name sprinkled throughout the book.

I saw David today but he didn't see me.

David's really good in the play. He makes you see how hard Creon's responsibility was. I wouldn't want to be somebody who has to make people do things.

When did David break up with Glee?

And later:

David kissed me at the party. He acted silly about it, but he did kiss me. He wanted to.

There was a long entry about a boy named Jerry Cooper. David knew him. He was a junior, a boy who seemed to have a lot of friends. Sissy was remembering something that had happened at the municipal pool the summer before. She had watched Coop goofing around on the high board; he tried a fancy dive and did a belly flop. He must have come up stunned with pain, and everybody laughed at him.

David could imagine the scene: the hooting and good-natured shouts. You made points with your friends when you laughed at yourself. Coop was popular enough. They wouldn't have been making fun of him, but they would not have cared either, if he was really hurting. They would not have seen it the way Sissy did, from the sidelines. She wrote:

I wanted to go up to him and say I was sorry, but I knew he would think I was kissing up. I wouldn't mind kissing up, either.

Then there was a page where she wrote something he realized he had known, and ignored. She wrote: *I want to die.*

Jesus, he thought, slapping the book with the flat of his hand.

She wrote that her baby brother had spit up on her new blouse. *Oh well,* she wrote, *I think I'll wear my pajamas when I go, anyway.*

David's chest felt tight. What the hell? he thought. What did she want him to do?

I don't have the nerve to do it without help. David won't do it. He'll see the danger in it for him. I can ask Leland. He wants so much to have an adventure.

He turned the page. There was only one line written on it, and it was underlined.

They watched.

David crammed the notebook under his mattress, shoved his pillow under his chest and his arm under his face, and shut his eyes. He would give it back to her tomorrow. Whatever she was trying to do, trying to make him do, it wouldn't work. Everybody wanted him to *do* things. Everybody had ideas.

One came to him. He sat back up. He retrieved his dusty notebook from the floor by the bed and wiped it with a corner of his sheet. He turned the pages slowly. There was a lot in it, he just had not taken any of his story ideas far enough. He was glad he had written what he had, because it would be there when he needed it, when he was ready.

There was a man who painted china, he wrote. He was thrilled by the sentence, because he did not know where it came from. The story appeared, whole in his mind.

The man lived and worked in a small town in Europe—France? Italy? He was a craftsman. On his own time—and there was not a lot of leisure in his life—he painted canvases. He played with color. He fell in love and was married. Then his troubles began, because his wife, who was herself only a peasant girl, had fallen in love with the man who painted.

She imagined that his experiments in color would become great paintings, that they would hang in museums and galleries. He would be famous. She told him the parable of Jesus about the man who did nothing with what he was given. Like your talent, she said. God expects you to paint. The man laughed at this; he thought his wife was young and foolish, tender and dear. He liked his work at the pottery factory. He painted flowers and herbs on china plates, for people to take back to their fine homes. He thought of families seated at the grand table, eating from the china he had adorned. But his wife thought his work was beneath him. She wanted him to paint. So he told the owners at the china factory that he had to quit. He could not explain to them. He went home, and began to paint. First he painted blocks of primary colors, then he painted windows and doors. He tried to paint his wife's portrait—she loved sitting for hours—but he could not capture her beauty or petulance. Then he began to paint pictures of china dishes, and the dishes were painted with flowers and herbs. The wife had to work as a laundress, because their money was gone. He painted bowls and platters on dark plank tables. He worked all the hours there was light. He painted cups on window sills drenched with sunlight.

David's heart was pounding so hard he thought someone in the room would have heard it. He read what he had written. He wondered if he should show Mrs. Bodkins. He wondered if he should give the man a name, and if it was important to find a village for the story, or if it was enough to tell the tale, simply.

He fell back on his bed and tucked his hands behind his head. He smiled at the ceiling. He had forgotten Sissy's notebook. He had forgotten Beth Ann's coy demands. He was seeing the paintings, stacked against the cool stone walls of the man's cottage.

You can make the world anything you want, if you make it up, he thought. It's like Patsy said, you use everything. He laughed aloud. Obviously he had used her in this story; she was the heckling, pushy wife, he the reluctant painter.

Did the paintings sell? Did the man stay with the wife?

He did not know the answer. He could not see that much of the story. He could not know what lay ahead.

32.

A car was parked on a little road near the stock pond. A girl and boy sat in it for a while, talking, then got out and walked down to the edge of the pond. It was a clear, cool, starry night, and they had no problem making their way. The girl was dressed in pajamas and slippers. The boy was carrying a shotgun.

At the edge of the pond, the girl paused. She seemed to be studying the shallow, muddy water. She said something, then ran back to the car and took out a sweater—a pale blue lambswool cardigan—and put it on. She went back down to the pond. She stood on her tiptoes to give the boy a quick kiss on the mouth, then took her slippers off and waded into the water.

David would have liked to stay home the next day, to work on his story, but he would have to give his mother some explanation, and she would scowl, and his sister would be around all day, too. Besides, during his library hour he could see if there were any books about china, something he could look at to help him describe what the painter did.

He was in first period about fifteen minutes when the vice principal came to the room and asked for him. This was unusual, not sending a student, and David wondered wildly what it was about. You did not get collected by the vice principal if you were not in trouble. Unless someone had died. Maybe his father had had a heart attack in the shower. Maybe his mother.

The administrator, Mr. Calloway, stopped a few steps from the door to his office and spoke in a low voice to David. "This isn't anything you've done, son. Don't be scared. But there's a problem, and they're hoping you'll know something to help them." Mystified, David followed Calloway into his office.

Two policemen were standing there. The principal was seated at Calloway's desk. He motioned for David to sit across from him. David did so, gulping air.

"They want to ask you about Cecelia Dossey," the principal said.

David blinked and looked at the policemen. They moved closer to him, so that he had to crane his neck and look up at their faces.

"Sissy?" he said.

"Sissy Dossey, yes," a policeman said. He had a pad and a pencil, and he seemed to have checked something on a list. As if "Sissy" were an alias.

She had disappeared from her house sometime in the night. Her parents called the police when the mother went to wake Cecelia for school and found her missing.

They wanted to know if he had seen her.

Reluctantly, he said, "For a few minutes yesterday afternoon. About four."

"What did she say?"

"Nothing. Nothing I can remember. She just dropped by to say hello. I said I was sleepy, I was going to take a nap, so she went home." He did not think they needed the notebook. What would it have to do with anything?

"And then? After that?"

"Why are you asking me?"

"Her mother said you're friends."

"I don't go out with her. I don't see her very much. We live near each other. We worked on a play together. Why are you asking me!" *Where was she?*

"We're going to talk to everyone we can think of."

"I don't know where she is." The policeman with the pad wrote something down. David coughed. They all continued to look at him. "Sometimes she went out with Leland Piper." He spoke so softly, they asked him to repeat what he had said. "Piper," he said. "You ought to ask Leland Piper."

Because it was Monday, his mother was home after school. He found her napping on her bed. He said, "Mom? Mom, I need you," and as she turned over, he sat on the edge of the bed. "I think something has happened." He was scared, but he didn't think it showed.

His mother sat up. "Oh no. Not again."

They heard it on the news at 5:30. They had taken Cecelia "Sissy" Dossey's body from a stock pond. They had arrested Leland Piper, 18, who had admitted to the shooting and had taken officers to the site. David and his mother sat up until after two in the morning, drinking. They watched the same news on the ten o'clock broadcast. There was film of Leland being taken into the police station. He did not look like anyone David had ever known. Saul came home as the news was ending, and went to bed without speaking. "Just as well," Marge said, when they heard the bedroom door shut. Neither she nor David had much of anything to say. David stumbled to bed quite drunk. He dreamed of Leland and Sissy. He saw them sitting parked in Leland's car. They weren't doing anything. In the dream, he knew he ought to talk to them. They needed advice. They needed somebody to remind them of what was sensible. He did not know where he was in the dream. He did not know how to reach them.

The next morning the paper's headline was: BASIN GIRL PAYS THE PIPER WITH HER LIFE. The details were spelled out: the pond, a few cattle nearby, the pumpjack. Her slippers on the ground, her father's gun in the water with her. They quoted the Piper boy. "I didn't think how much it would upset my mother. It wasn't my idea. I didn't think about it enough."

David did not go to school. Terrified, he hid Sissy's notebook under his mattress. He slept fitfully through the day. Once, jerked out of a dream, he jumped from bed because he thought it was on fire. He thought the notebook had ignited. He wished it had. He was afraid it would ruin his life.

"I knew she was weird," Beth Ann said later that day on the phone. "Both of them, really weird. Your friends."

"I need to talk to you," he said. "There's something I need to show you."

He went to her house after supper. They sat on the couch in the family room and he took out Sissy's notebook.

"What's that old thing?" Beth Ann asked.

"It's a notebook, like a diary. It belongs—it belonged—to Sissy."

"Why do you have it?"

"She gave it to me Sunday afternoon. She wanted me to read it."

Beth Ann shook her head in disgust. "You shouldn't have taken it."

"I didn't know she was going to get killed! She had a reason, it wasn't a very big favor. Beth, there's stuff in here about Leland. She asked him to do it. It was her idea. It might be important for his lawyer to see it. It might show what really happened, that it wasn't all his fault."

Beth Ann made a noise, something like a belch.

"I have to decide what to do with it."

She saw right to the heart of the matter. "Are you in there too, David?"

He nodded miserably.

"I don't know why you wanted to hang around with some-body so pitiful. So notorious."

"We were friends, in an odd way. Maybe because we both wrote things down."

"Oh God. You mean, you've got stuff written too? About her?" She looked horrified. "About *me?*"

"She wrote for herself, a way to let things out. But when she decided to—do it—she must have wanted somebody to read what she had written. She wanted me to. Maybe she wanted to leave something."

Beth Ann's beautiful eyes narrowed. Her mouth twitched. "My father would never stand for it."

"I'll get rid of it," he said quietly. All along, he had known he would. Now, though, it was partly Beth Ann's idea. He had not decided all by himself.

Driving home, he thought about what happened to the painter. He became obsessed with the paintings of china dishes. No one bought them, of course. They wanted por-traits, and landscapes. His wife became pregnant and could not wash laundry anymore. The painter went back to the china factory and begged for work. They had replaced him, but they gave him a lower job, glazing the raw pots. Where once he had been happy at work, he was now desperately unhappy. He stopped painting at home. He put the paintings around the cottage. At night he sat with them. One night he realized he could reach into the painting, he could take out the dish. He threw it against the wall. He took a platter from another painting, a bowl and saucer, he took all the dishes, and one by one smashed them. When he was done he sat in a rubble of china.

On Wednesday they let him see Leland at the jail. Leland wore blue jeans and a blue work shirt. He looked tall and haggard, but he said, "Hey, man, you came to see me!"

"This is a mess, Piper."

Leland shook his head. "She was driving me crazy, David. She begged me. Practically since our first date. At first I thought she was joking—"

"Sure, I know. She said nutty things all the time."

He wondered if Leland knew about the notebook. "She was unhappy." Surely Leland would say.

Leland put his head in his hands and said something David could not hear.

"What? What did you say?

Leland looked up again. "My dad's getting me a good lawyer. I'll probably get out of here by the weekend. It's not—murder."

"Guess not."

"They act like I'm the crazy one. They act very careful with me."

"They probably don't know what to think."

Leland bobbed his head. "That's probably it. It's not like what they usually have to deal with." A deputy said it was time. Leland stood. "Hey, David. Did you save the newspaper?"

He could not bring himself to destroy the diary. He kept it under the mattress. Late at night he took it out and read it again and again. *They watched.* Who were they? What did they watch? He dreamed about Jerry Cooper on the high board. He thought, good for him, he's going to try it again. He did not assume that Cooper would flop this time. Saul used to say, "An example is not proof." Next time, Cooper might glide through the air like a bird. But in the dream, he stood there motionless, he did not dive. David wondered why he waited, what he saw. There was only water below. He only needed to leave the board.

33.

Leland's father (and Marge) had gone to school in Monahans with a boy who had become a rich and famous lawyer.
His name was Carroll Dale Crawford. He had practiced in
Basin, then moved on to Houston. He came to Basin for
Leland's arraignment. The paper said he would spend several days in town, laying the groundwork for a defense. He
was able to arrange Leland's release.

David went to see him at the Alamo Hotel. His suite was at
the top, seven stories up.

"Have you been to see the Pipers?" Crawford wanted to
know.

"No sir."

"Not a close friend, then?"

"I went to see him in jail." Crawford was a large, tidy man,
very well-dressed, with the shrewd look David had expected.
His perusal made David very uncomfortable. "Maybe he
didn't have close friends," he mumbled.

"*Doesn't,* young man. It isn't Leland Piper who's dead."

"We all know that," David said. He felt fourteen.

"And the girl? You were her friend, too?"

"No special friend. I knew her. We lived near one another."

"Leland says she asked him to shoot her. It was her father's
gun, she had brought it along."

"That sounds right. I can believe it."

"Why so?"

"She was long-faced. Sad."

Crawford considered that for a moment. He had been
about to make himself a drink when David arrived, and he
went ahead and did it now. He gave David a glass of ginger
ale and ice, and motioned for him to sit at a small round
table. He sat down across from him. "Walking down the hall,

say you're on your way to—physics? English?—and you see Cecelia Dossey, and you remark to yourself—*long face?*"

David's own face was turning red. He was sorry he had sat down. "Something like that," he managed to say.

"Did she ask you to shoot her, too?"

"No sir."

"Why Leland?"

He wants so much to have an adventure. He said he did not know.

Crawford set his glass down with a thwap! against the table. David bounced in his chair, startled. "What do you want, David Puckett? Why have you come to see me?"

David took a moment to collect his wits. He reminded himself that he had starred in two plays that year. He knew you breathed to stay in control. He said, "I want to know how Leland is." His voice sounded all right. "I thought you could let him know."

"He's at home. You could go see him yourself."

"I thought—he'd be busy. I didn't want to disturb his family." He did not want to go over there. He had a vivid picture in his mind of Sissy at the cast party, wiping up Coke. And Leland had not called.

The lawyer shifted in his chair and took a long drink. "He and I have a lot to talk about, ourselves."

David took a deep breath. "And I wondered—why you? The Pipers don't seem that—well off."

"Shorty Piper and I played football together. We shot rattlers together. Sat out in the flat hot sun and drank ourselves blind. We go way back. And this is an interesting case."

David nodded, approving, understanding, hoping he did not seem stupid.

"What *I'm* wondering is, why *you?*" Crawford was staring at David intently.

David felt perspiration begin to trickle down the inside of his upper arms. "Why me what?" he stalled.

"Why you come to see me. You want something."

"I wish I could help."

"You can."

"Oh."

"Tell me what the girl was like."

"I told you. Sad."

"Depressed?"

David felt a vague thrill, cold and stirring. This must be like court, he thought, his questions coming at me like Ping-Pong balls. He had no sense of strategy. "I guess you'd say she was depressed." He felt engaged, though; they were adversaries.

"She talk about death? Love? The Cold War? What riled her up?"

"I don't see how that would help."

"She ask you to shoot her?"

"I said no, sir."

"She talk about it?"

"Not to me."

"Leland says he met her with you. She was in the hospital. You took him up there. You talked him into dating her."

"You already had my name?"

"I tell a client, 'Tell me everything.'"

"He did do it."

"There are words. Mitigating. Temporary this or that. States of mind. That comes later. I start with—history."

"My mother worked at the hospital. I was killing time. Leland and I hang out together."

"Try this, Puckett. She wants to die. She talks about it to her friends. To you, to Piper. She plants the idea, like the idea for a play. Like a play, she keeps it in rehearsal. Over and over she talks about it. Till you're all sick of it."

David could hardly speak. Crawford was uncanny. David felt as if his skull was sliced open. The lawyer could read his brain. If David had wondered why he wanted to see him, he knew clearly now. It was an instinct that had served him well. "She didn't talk about it to me," he said.

Crawford stood, walked over to the windows, and pulled the drape shut. Not turning around, he said, "You remember what she did say, you come back." He went back to the bar and poured himself a fresh drink in a clean glass.

"Sir," David began. His chest was like a band of steel. "Are you going to call me up on the stand?"

"How's that?" Crawford held the glass high in front of him, waiting to drink until David answered. The glass was like an extension of himself, a fist.

"I'm wondering, under oath, what name I say." David had not planned this. He had not even thought of it until this moment. He felt himself let go of some of the tension; air came more easily to his lungs. Crawford could not know what was coming.

"How's that?" Crawford said again.

"Puckett is my mother's family name. My dad's name is Stolboff. Now, testifying, under oath, I'd have to say Stolboff, wouldn't I?" He wondered what Crawford thought of Jews.

"You think that matters a rat's ass to me, Puckett? What's your story? You come here to be sure I don't call you? You ashamed of your friendship with Leland? He's not as pretty as you?"

"Look here."

Now Crawford drank. He sloshed the liquid around in his mouth before he swallowed, and then he said, "You think he would say, 'Puckett knew about it, and didn't do anything to stop it?'"

"No way."

"Or is it that you want to be called? You want your big minute on the stand, everybody watching?"

"I'd have to say, I don't know. I didn't hear. I'd say, *Not me.*"

"Why? Because she did ask you? And you're ashamed, you didn't care, you didn't talk her out of it, you were home in bed when she went wading in that caliche pit? You have a conscience, young man?"

"I wouldn't be any help. I came to tell you that."

"Don't you worry, Sholfobb. I won't call you."

"She was depressed!" David cried. "She was melodramatic. Ask around at school. Lots of other kids can tell you."

"Name some."

"Kids in 'Antigone.'"

"In what?"

"She worked backstage on a play we just did. She spent time around other kids. Look, Mr. Crawford, I don't understand Leland doing this. I don't see how she talked him into it. But it had to be her idea. He wouldn't have any reason."

"I had a client once, I asked him why he shot his wife. She was in bed with his partner, they owned a Conoco station. He said, 'I wanted to see how big a hole it would make.'"

"She would watch Patsy in the scene where she knows she's going to go into the cave, she's going to be shut up to die in there. She would say—Sissy I meant—'That would be so slow. It would be so scary.'"

"Very good, Puckett. Stawfobb."

"Other kids heard her say it! We all talked about how it would feel. But she was—she was crazy. Don't you think she'd have to be?"

"It's Leland Piper they're wanting to try."

"She didn't ask me."

"She'd know you'd be too smart."

The phone rang. "Yes?" Crawford said. "Just a minute." He put his hand over the mouthpiece. "Don't you worry, Shawfart. I won't call you. You wouldn't be any help at all."

34.

Leland's mother gave David a long look when she opened the door. He blushed; it was the first time he had been to the house in the weeks since the shooting.

There was a four-drawer dresser in the hall outside Leland's room. Inside, what was left of Leland's belongings was piled on or next to the bed, and the walls had been stripped bare. Leland was by the window, hunkered down, painting along the sill. The room was now a pale green, the color their classrooms had been in elementary school. Did Leland remember that?

"Do I know you?" Leland said.

"Come on, Piper," David said. "This is tough."

"You tell me."

David gestured at the walls. "Funny seeing them so bare. What'd you do with everything?"

"Tossed it. This is the new Leland Piper. Orderly, clean—"

"Green."

They laughed, the tension eased a little.

"I'm going to my uncle's in Big Spring in a couple of days, to work construction. The trial's set for August."

"That'll be good, huh. Being busy."

"Make some money."

"Sure."

Leland laid the brush down carefully on a piece of newspaper on the floor. It was awkward, the two of them standing looking at one another across the mess on the bed. He said, "It all seems a hundred years ago already. Or like it was somebody else and I read about it. I can't believe it happened."

"Yeah."

"I wish I could undo it. This has just about killed my mother."

"Do you think about Sissy? Do you see it?" He knew he sounded ghoulish, but he really wanted to know.

"Nah. It's more like, I don't know, like it was a kitten you put out of its misery. I don't know if she was ever real, you know? To me, I mean. I don't think anything that ever happened with her was my idea. I was always following along."

"My pop's gone," David blurted. For a moment he thought Leland didn't hear, or understand, but then he said, "Gone where," without the energy to make it a question. David could see that Leland was somewhere in another universe. He was the only person David could think of who would understand what this meant, but he wasn't that person anymore. He was the boy who had killed Cecelia Dossey and that was the sum of his identity. It made David angry. He shrugged. "Florida, I think. Since Joyce Ellen had her baby, he stopped coming home lots of nights. He said he was staying at Chasen's, but he had a girlfriend. Then he didn't come home at all. We got a postcard from someplace in Louisiana. It said, 'Maybe it's not too late.' My mom reads it, tosses it in the garbage, says, 'Fat chance, Stolboff.' And that's all she's said."

"When did he go?"

"It's been a week." Talking about it made his throat ache.

"Tough," Leland said. He seemed bored.

"It's hard all over," David said. He could not keep from feeling resentful. Both his friends had disappeared down a rat-hole. And Beth Ann—you didn't pour your guts out to a girl like that. It wasn't like that between them. When he told her about his father leaving, she said casually, "You two aren't very close, huh?"

"You've got the best of the best lawyers," David said, wanting badly to leave. "It'll work out." He did not want to say, or hear, anything about the case. The idea of somebody he knew being "a case" was so strange, he would rather forget it. If Crawford was not going to bother him, he did not have to be involved. It was all so sad and pointless anyway. Sissy had wanted to be dead, and now she was. Leland was a sucker. They would never let him in Rice now.

Leland dipped into the paint again, stooped to brush the wall below the window. With his back to David, he said, "My dad says we have to live through the publicity, through the trial, and then everybody will forget. He says when it's over I can work at the store with him and nobody will care." He turned around. "Crawford's going to say I was crazy. That's how you get out of it. You say something came over you."

"Didn't it?"

Leland went back to painting. David went home.

He sat on his bed with the two notebooks, his and Sissy's, on his lap. He was thinking about the story he'd wanted to write last summer, about the woman who loved the boy, and then killed herself. What if she, like Sissy, had wanted to pull someone into it? If she had been beautiful, tragic, like Teresa, maybe that could have happened. You could talk someone into believing in your sadness. Sissy had not tried hard enough with him. She had not had a good enough story. She and Leland, they had been the right pair after all. He held the notebooks a long time, not opening them, trying to empty his mind. Then he put them under the mattress again. They aren't hurting anything, he told himself. Nobody cares about them. He thought of them as a matching pair.

The Kimbroughs took David to dinner at the country club. It was cozy. They sat by glass doors looking out onto a patio and a vast expanse of lawn. At the far end was a pumpjack. A few years ago someone had had the idea to see if there was oil on the club property; that hunch had made every charter member rich.

By this time of year, Beth Ann spent a lot of every weekend at the club. She didn't ask David along. He supposed there was a limit to how many times you could take somebody who wasn't a member. So Beth Ann went out, with her friends, her *other* friends, to swim and play tennis and have lunch, and then, later, she got together with David. Things had changed between them since the ride to the ranch. Beth Ann had dropped the coyness. She called and said, "Can you be here at seven?" She said, "Next weekend we'll want to see this movie." He told himself that being taken for granted was a high form of security, though it chafed him. He thought, more and more, of making love to her, but he never made the slightest overture. The lines had been drawn from the beginning.

There was going to be a lot of catch-up work if he was going to be anybody in her life.

They had a meal, served family style on platters, probably unremarkable to the Kimbroughs, that was the best David had ever eaten: a slab of standing rib roast, dripping blood, with a snowy mound of horseradish; potatoes that had been fried or baked so there was half an inch of brown crackly crust; and sweet long stalks of asparagus, which he had never tasted. They were so casual about the food; the women, like always, moving things around on their plates while they gossiped, Hayden eating in a steady, pragmatic fashion, as though all the dishes had the same taste. David could hardly keep from moaning with pleasure. He ate more than anyone at the table, slightly embarrassed to do so, but unable to stop himself. He lived on canned soups, cheese and bologna sandwiches, and hamburgers. There was never a real meal at home. Joyce Ellen drank gallons of juice, and ate from the refrigerator in the middle of the night, keeping her mother company while she drank after work. Marge had eyes only for the baby, who cried constantly, unless held and walked. Every time David came through a door he saw one of them parading through the house, cradling the baby, shushing and fussing and cooing to keep him happy. Meanwhile the place filled with filth and clutter. David felt squeezed into his room, and he knew Joyce Ellen wanted even that. The bitter, bitter thing about Saul's defection was that he did not stop to think that his son might want to go. Or worse, he did not care.

"Look, it's Helen Shaw back from Italy," Laurel Kimbrough said. "And Missy, home from Wellesley already." She slapped her hands together lightly. "We've *got* to go say hello," she told her husband. "We won't be two minutes." She went off, trailed by Beth Ann.

Hayden smiled indulgently. "Are we putting odds on two minutes?"

"Not me, sir, I don't gamble," David said, hoping he sounded easygoing and humorous, rather than stupid.

"Not on trivial matters, anyway, hey, David?"

"Sir?"

"Life's a gamble. I say you ought to take a chance or two. The West was built on risks. And I'd say the odds are in your favor."

David was lost. He tried to show no expression at all, while he searched for something to say.

"I'm glad to have a moment with you. Two minutes, as they say. I've been meaning to talk to you."

David wondered what Beth Ann had said. He swallowed hard.

"I get down to Austin every month or so. How would you like to make a trip with me, say in June? I could take you down to the legislature, see what might happen for you in the fall. You are set to go to UT, aren't you?"

"On paper. I guess I will, if I get a job, find a place, all that." He could not imagine how he was going to last that long in the house with the baby.

"We could look around."

"That would be great. I appreciate it."

Hayden studied David. "You're wondering why, aren't you?"

David squirmed, though he hoped it was not noticeable. He felt itchy and hot. With effort, he smiled. "Beth Ann—" he said.

Hayden waved his hand. "Not Beth Ann. You. Laurel and I have grown fond of you. We see things in you." He leaned his elbows on the table, closing the gap between them. "We look at some of the boys we've known all their lives, and we see boys without intention, boys without spines. Not all, I'm not saying our friends don't have fine youngsters! But there are some. They lack sinew. They've had it too easy too soon."

David wheezed.

"Besides, the world can't be run by a tiny elite. You have to have new blood."

"I'd like to be that," David said, finding the courage for a certain heartiness.

Hayden sat back in his chair. He waved at a waiter and asked for two brandies. The waiter looked at David. "My wife will be right back," Hayden said patiently. The waiter nodded and came back with the snifters. He set one in front of Hayden, the other at an empty place. Hayden smiled. As soon as the waiter turned around, he passed the glass to David. The first taste made David's nose and throat burn, but the second made his chest warm pleasantly. He could not think of anything to say. He hoped he looked casual about the brandy, and about Hayden Kimbrough's little speech, which might or might not be over.

"It's different for girls," Hayden said. "Beth Ann will go to college, study something not too hard, pledge a sorority. She'll grow more beautiful, more sophisticated, more like her mother. She'll make a fine wife one day."

David's face flamed. He had not finished the brandy, but he could not take another swallow. He set the glass down gently on the tablecloth. "All in good time," he said.

Hayden smiled broadly. "Exactly. That's it, young man. All in good time."

David flushed deeply, then relaxed. He had merely stumbled on the right phrase, but with it said, he could see clearly what Beth Ann's father had on his mind. A small hand-out, a bit of caution. No promises. It was not quite a contract, was it? But the door wasn't shut. Here's a leg up, Puckett, see what you can do with it.

What more could a poor West Texas boy ask for? Even Saul would say it was a fair deal. All David had to do was work hard and grow up, while Beth Ann matured with some less effort. Then they would see.

All David could lose was Beth Ann. He could gain a better life, the one his classmates thought he was headed for.

He picked the snifter up again and drained the glass. "Thank you, Mr. Kimbrough," he said. He was pleased with the nice dark timbre of his voice. "I am truly grateful."

"Don't you think it's time you called me Hayden? Look, here come the girls."

David and Beth Ann sat on the patio while her parents had a drink with friends in the bar. It had been a hot, summery day, and though it was much cooler now in the darkness, there was a pleasant smell and feeling to the air. David could feel the brandy. His toes seemed far away, but warm.

"What did you and Daddy talk about?"

"Not about. Around. We talked around you."

"What did you tell him?"

"That I'm a patient young man. That I know you'll want to do better if you can."

"David, you didn't!"

"Around. We talked around these things."

"They know I like you a lot."

"I like them too. I always supposed rich people were arrogant, but they're not."

"Arrogant?" Beth Ann said idly, as if it were a foreign word she only wanted to pronounce.

"Though it's hard not to mind."

"Mind what?"

"Where other people start from."

She didn't comment. Someone blinked the yellow patio lights.

"Maybe we should go in."

The lights went out. "I like the dark," she said. Through the glass doors, the dining room, now empty, seem to glow softly like a bowl of fireflies. They sat side by side on lounge chairs, their legs stretched out. She reached for his hand. "Davy, what did you do with that girl's diary?"

The feeling in his hand, one second before so warm in hers, went numb. He could still feel his toes, but not his fingers. He pulled his hand away, sighed, adjusted his position in the chair.

"Stop squirming and answer me."

He could imagine why men hit women. She would have to stop talking to him like that, sooner or later.

"I hear Mommy and Daddy talking about it. The case, not the diary. Of course they don't know about the diary."

"Notebook. She called it a notebook."

"Daddy says Mr. Crawford will say that Leland was crazy when he shot her, that she made him crazy, but that when he woke up in the morning, he was all better. It was all out of his system. Kids at school, they say she was weird. She bugged people. Daddy says Mr. Crawford can make it work. There'll be a hearing about it, it won't ever go to trial."

"That's what the notebook shows. The way she was."

"But they know all that already! You're being stubborn and *stupid*, David. They don't need her *notebook*. It would just be embarrassing. It would make you look just awful."

"You're the only person besides me who knows that it exists."

"So get rid of it! And yours, too."

"Mine?"

"What do you need to write things down for? You're going to go to college, you're going to go to law school. What's to write down? That's all high school stuff. She's dead. *You're my boyfriend now.*"

They heard Laurel's soft voice calling them. "Beth Ann, David. Are you out there?"

As they stood up, David pulled Beth Ann against his body. Over her shoulder he could see her mother standing in the open door, peering out into the darkening evening. He kissed Beth Ann quickly, hard. He thrust his tongue into her mouth. She pulled her face away. "Over here, Mommy," she called. "We're coming." To David she whispered, "I want to see it. Her notebook. I want to read it." She was panting lightly.

"I thought you didn't want anything to do with it."

"Before you destroy it. I want to see it. There's no reason not. I already know, don't I? Don't I?"

35.

He felt like an alley cat. When night came, he wanted to prowl. He felt he might explode. He wanted to swim at school, but he did not have an excuse anymore. The coach had moved him out of tennis practice last hour into general P.E., a class he cut repeatedly. It had been a mistake to drop tennis so precipitously. He had not thought it through. Maybe he would not have won big. Maybe he would not have won at all. But he would have looked like someone with guts, plowing on when his partner defected, and instead he looked like a tuft of milkweed. The galling thing was, nobody cared. They did not miss him. He got word about his transfer out of tennis by student messenger, a little slip of paper with numbers and times and his name on it. He literally had not spoken to the coach again. The other players acted like they did not see him. They were doing fine. Maybe not sweeping the state, not like that, but in every tournament somebody made the cut. Lasky came in fourth at the San Angelo invitational.

I could have found my stride, if I'd kept at it. Thinking that, he ran sweating through the streets at night. When he had worn himself out—otherwise he did not know how he would ever get to sleep—he walked, sometimes slowing down so that it was a matter of one foot in front of another, like an old woman. He imagined himself as Saul, roaming these streets, escaping the house. He walked again and again to the apartments where he was certain *she* had lived. *I would have understood,* he cried out in the night to his father. If only Saul had talked to him. Then what?

Then I would have been in his confidence. I would have said, *"Good luck."*

Back in the house, the night before graduation, the baby

was screeching. Marge was not yet home from work, and Joyce Ellen was just about at her limit. She glared at David as he walked through the livingroom. "Jesus," he said, "what do you want me to do?"

He showered, thought a moment about going to bed, then dressed in clean chinos and shirt. The baby's energy was amazing. He squalled for ten, fifteen minutes at a stretch, took a breather for five minutes, then screamed some more. He was named Ward, after Marge's father. Screaming Ward.

"Do you take him to the doctor?" he asked Joyce Ellen. She was walking around and around the table in the kitchen. The baby was seated on her palms, tucked back against her chest. He looked pleased, for the moment, drowsy and self-satisfied, the little tyrant. David knelt in front of the open refrigerator, looking for something to eat, finding only crusts of unwrapped cheese, a curled single slice of bologna, a row of eggs. He slammed the door. "Isn't he SICK or something?"

Joyce Ellen began bawling. The baby's eyes opened wide, as if in amazement, then he set in yowling again.

David stormed out the front door and around to Saul's storeroom. There was everything, as if Saul would be back in an hour. A dark gray thread in the sewing machine, the scissors partly open, a saucer of pins. David picked up the scissors and threw them across the little room. They bounced off the wall and fell into a box of kitchen towels.

Boxes of clothes and fabrics were piled against the wall. There might be a thousand dollars worth of goods left. David would have to go back to Fort Stockton, and make the circuit. He could make more money off this, his father's leftovers, than from any kind of job he could find for the summer. And, item by item, he would be rid of the remnants of his father.

Had Saul planned it carefully, over weeks? Had the two of them sat huddled on her bed (he in his tattered underwear?), laughing and figuring it out? Or had something struck him like lightning, set him aflame, so that he suddenly just *had to go*? Nobody had known it was happening. Saul had come home sometime late that evening, but not so late that Marge was home. He had packed a suitcase, taken some of his things, not all, clothes and *War and Peace* and *Anna Karenina*. He had slipped the suitcase into the yard through the bedroom window, then strolled back through the house, not saying a word—it would look like another of his walks—and outside he had collected his belongings and walked to meet her.

David went into the house again, banging the screen door behind him. He did not know what to do. He thought he would wait for his mother, and drink with her. He would say it was a celebration. His last night of childhood, if you thought about it. Tomorrow, graduation, adulthood. Why did it all seem to swirl around him, why did he seem to be sinking into it? He had grown up on the plains; he wanted to look out and see the future as a great undulating landscape of good fortune.

Joyce Ellen had turned off the lights. He stepped into the living room and paused for a moment. The light on the top of the stove in the kitchen shone eerily across the two rooms. He stepped toward it. From the little bedroom came the sudden piercing wails of baby Ward, followed immediately by the sharp shriek of Joyce Ellen, who had been sitting in the dark, in her father's easy chair. She sprang for David, and pounded him on the shoulders and neck. "He was asleep!" she screamed. "He was asleep!"

"You're crazy!" David shouted back, pushing her arms away, and rushing across to the kitchen. He looked back at her. "You need to be in Mother's unit, Joyce Ellen."

"I need sleep!" she yelled back. "I lie in that bunk bed and the baby is six inches away, I hear his breath whistle, I hear his little poots. You don't know, you're off in the luxury of your private world. I WANT YOUR ROOM. At least then I can put him across the room from me. I can look at him across space. I can go to sleep!"

David moved quickly to his room and slammed the door. He leaned against it, gasping. He had to get out of there. He could not take it, not all summer, not one more night. He had to get out of there, right away. He pulled a duffel bag out of the closet and began to stuff clothes in it, knocking his drawers onto the floor. He packed until the bag was too full to close, took out a pair of aged jeans, and drew it shut. He threw it at the back door, where it thudded and shivered still. He grabbed his pillow and a blanket off the bed and threw them onto the duffel bag, took his cash out of his sock drawer, then stood staring at the bed. He remembered that Poe story, "The Telltale Heart," with its beating heart—and an eye? Did an eye beat too? That was what the damned notebook was like. It lay under the mattress, pounding.

He pulled the mattress off partway onto the floor, and grabbed both notebooks and stuffed them up under his armpit. The cunning little bitch, he thought. This was why she had given it to him. She could not get to him alive, but she had him, dead.

He carried his things around the house and threw them into the station wagon. He backed into the yard, right up to the door of the storeroom, and began hauling boxes out and shoving them into the car. He worked in a frenzy until he could not fit anything else in, then slammed the back door shut and jumped into the car. He pulled out of the yard, his wheels whining, and hit the street with a skid.

He had no place to go. He slowed down. He drove to Ellis' and parked with the motor running, staring at the dark quiet house. They probably all went to bed at nine, because Ellis had to. He would be up in the dark, driving off toward Roswell or Farmington or who knows where.

He cruised the streets, driving around the high school, then back past Leland's house. There was a light on there. David imagined Leland's mother sitting up with a magazine on her lap, staring off into the terrible vision of her son's crime.

He drove to Patsy's, parked and cut the motor. The house was dark. Across the way, there were lights at Ari's. Maybe she was there. Maybe they were drinking wine and listening to jazz. She had reason to sit up, reason to celebrate. He had heard from Mr. Turnbow, not from her. She never spoke to him. She had taken the bus to Dallas to a regional competition, and had placed first. There were people there from drama schools. Afterwards, she sent tapes and photographs and Turnbow called directors. She was going to California—Pasadena, wasn't it? A drama school. Going where her mother was, wonder what she thought of that.

Last he went to Glee's. He parked down the block and walked to her house. He crept down the side, to the back, and stood beneath her window, as he had done before. He was careful not to make any noise. There was a faint light in her room, not enough to be a reading lamp. He thought it was probably one of those lights you plug into the wall because you're afraid of the dark. Had she always done that? Had she always dreaded night? Or was it something that had come over her this spring, something to do with ending her days as a girl? Was she afraid, too?

Beth Ann would be sleeping soundly, afraid of nothing, rosily confident of her pampered future.

He headed to the Kimbroughs'.

He pulled the car along the curve of the street in front of their house, a car-length short of the arched open gate. He climbed out and walked onto the drive. There was an ornate gas lamp near the gate, smaller than a street lamp, and the porch light was on. In between, there were pockets of dark along the driveway, and his feet crunched gravel and sent bits of it off to make a pinging sound.

There were several lights on in the house. One, near the front, was probably in the entryway. Upstairs a light shone through a tiny window, perhaps a bathroom, and two rooms farther, a lamp in a window showed clearly, for the curtains were drawn back. Someone reading in bed, he thought. He had never been upstairs in the house. The bedrooms ran along the top on one end of the house; the rest of the house was a single story, sprawling in an L that cut around the courtyard in back. He did not know where Beth Ann slept.

He thought he would drive to Fort Stockton that night, or as far as he could go before he was sleepy. He could pull over anywhere and sleep in the front seat of the station wagon. In the morning he would go to see Teresa's grandparents, see if the beauty parlor was empty for the summer, see the preacher about tables, eat at the Brite Spot. Maybe he would ask how Teresa was doing, maybe not. He would stay a week, then drive to some of the other little towns. Maybe he would go farther south this time.

Missing graduation was nothing. It was like not picking up your receipt when you bought a shirt. You had the shirt, what did it matter?

He had been watching the front of the house, while slowly walking backward, as if to take in as much of the house as possible in his view. He backed out of the drive, and his heel caught against the slight rise of the curb, so that he slid and had to shuffle and throw his arms out to keep from landing on his buttocks. His maneuvering sent gravel in all directions. He landed on both feet, backed against a rose bush, caught his breath, and realized what jeopardy he had put himself in. He had to get out of there.

The front door was suddenly flung open and there stood Hayden Kimbrough, a pistol in his hand. He was wearing a plaid bathrobe over long-legged white pajamas. "Who's there?" he barked. David didn't think the light shone on him. He stood in silence, hoping Kimbrough would go back in, but the man stepped forward, making an arc with his body to search the yard. "Who the hell is there?" He stepped out, in David's direction. David's heart clunked.

"It's me, it's David Puckett," he said as calmly as he could. He took a single timorous step forward, but it was enough to find the light.

"What the hell?" Kimbrough's arm fell, and the gun pointed down along his thigh.

David walked toward him. He was mortified and desperate, too flustered to think of anything to say. "I'm sorry, I'm sorry," he mumbled.

Kimbrough's anger faded. He reached out and put his hand on David's shoulder. "What's wrong with you, son?"

David felt tears welling, felt his chest tighten and burn. He put one hand up in front of his eyes. "This is awful," he said.

Kimbrough pulled him into the house. David heard voices and movement in the house. They went into the kitchen, Hayden flipping light switches as they passed through other rooms. He motioned to the table. "Sit," he said, and left the room. Tears spilled over onto David's cheeks. Hurriedly he wiped them with the back of his hand, then wiped his hand on his pants. He would rather be dead than caught like this, spying and lurking. Why had he done it?

Hayden returned with Laurel. She had a worried expression. She knelt in front of David and took his hand in hers. "Whatever is going on?"

David shook his head. "This is awful," he said again, and he began to babble about the baby, and Joyce Ellen, about going to Fort Stockton and skipping graduation. Laurel rose and filled a kettle and put it on the stove. Hayden pulled a chair closer to David and sat in it, facing him, their knees almost touching.

"I know how late it is, I don't know what I was thinking," David said.

"Shush about that," Laurel said gently. "I'll have coffee in a minute."

"Are you hungry, David?" Hayden asked.

David realized he was starving. He was shaky with hunger. He did not answer, but his eyes widened. Laurel moved to the refrigerator and began to pull out food: a platter of sliced roast beef, some pieces of chicken, a block of cheddar cheese, mustard. She opened cabinets and suddenly there was bread, all this food spread out on the table in front of him.

Hayden took a small slice of meat and began to chew it vigorously. He told his wife, "I'll take a cup, too," and in a moment the coffee appeared, steaming, in front of them. David ate.

"I didn't know it was so bad for you," Laurel said, sitting across from him at the table. She leaned on her elbows, her soft silky robe falling away from her arms.

David chewed and nodded.

"I'll put you in the guest room. It's down here, you'll have your own bath. You stay here tonight, David. We'll talk in the morning."

He shook his head and swallowed a big lump of bread and meat. "I couldn't."

Hayden clapped him on the bicep. "You can't go prowling around any more houses," he said jovially. "And you don't want to go home."

Beth Ann appeared in the door of the kitchen. She looked sleepy, but she had dressed in cotton pants and blouse and had combed her hair.

"Are you okay, Davy?" She leaned against the door. "Did something happen?"

He put his hands on the edge of the table, as if to shove it away. "I'm okay, except for making a fool of myself."

Laurel touched his cheek with her delicate fingers. "We're family, David."

He stood up quickly. "It's hot," he said. He had worked up a sweat, eating. He surveyed the mess he had made, the empty cup. He had not even taken time to put sugar in his coffee.

"We could go out on the patio," Beth Ann said. She glanced at her parents. They looked at one another, then rose.

"I'll put fresh towels in the bathroom," Laurel said. "Beth Ann can show you where the guest room is."

Hayden said, "I'll see you in the morning." David wondered where the gun was, then saw it lying on the corner of the cabinet, near the breadbox. Hayden was not angry. David wondered if he pitied him, or if he thought he was mad.

"I need to show you something," David said to Beth Ann. Her parents paused in their exiting. "Could we—" his eyes flitted to Laurel, Hayden, then back to their daughter. "Could we go for a ride? It's like summer."

"It's late," Laurel said.

"I'd like to, Daddy," Beth Ann said.

Hayden glanced at the watch on his wrist. "Not yet midnight," he said. He put his hand on his wife's arm. "Let's go to bed and leave them." He remembered the gun then, and picked it up tenderly, as if it might easily bruise, and took it with him. "Not too long," he said as he left the room. "And lock the front door when you're back."

David gulped. "Thank you sir. Thank you both."

Beth Ann took his hand. The moment her parents were out of sight, she said, "Where do you want to go?"

"Do you have some matches?" he asked her. "Get some matches, and I'll show you."

36.

He thought he remembered the place where he had pulled off the road to pee that August afternoon when he had first seen Sissy, but everything looked the same in all directions, once he was off the highway.

Beth Ann acted a lot more concerned about what he had done than her parents had. When she got in the station wagon, she made a big fuss about all the boxes. "What is all this stuff?" she said, getting on her knees and pawing at what she could reach. "What are you doing?"

He told her to sit down. The notebooks were on the floor at her feet. She said, "What's wrong with you? I like to died, seeing you in my house at that time of night. You're lucky my daddy didn't shoot you."

He turned off on this lease road and then that one, backing out, hardly seeing where he was going. "What are you looking for!" Beth Ann demanded shrilly.

He drove around for twenty minutes, a whole crisscross of dead ends and false leads. He could not find the stockpond where Sissy had died. Finally he pulled up not far from a thumping pumpjack and turned off the motor. The night was clear, the sky high and milky with stars. He got out of the car. There was a little pond there, but it was not much more than a puddle. It couldn't be the one where Sissy had waded in to await the blast from her father's gun.

He ran back to the car, on the passenger's side, and pulled the door open. "Davy!" Beth Ann cried, as he reached down to grab Sissy's notebook. She followed him out of the car, down beside the puddle of dank, dark water. He squatted on the ground and tore out a page.

"That's her notebook, isn't it? Give me that, David Puckett!" She grabbed, he pulled it out of reach, she fell abruptly onto the ground. "Ow!"

He struck a match and the page caught fire immediately. He held it for a moment, then dropped it onto the ground in front of them, where it was quickly extinguished.

"I want it!"

"You said to get rid of it. Here I go."

"I wanted to read it first."

In a singsong voice, he said, "David kissed me and he wanted to. I saw David in the hall today. I want to die. I'm crazy, crazy craz—"

"Oh stop it, stop it right now!" She put her hands over her ears.

He had several pages wadded into a ball on the ground, he tore out more pages. Soon he had a little pile, for a bonfire. He struck several matches, trying to light it, but they blew out. He lit a single page, then held it to the pile until it caught. With a whoosh! the balls fell apart, one of them burned for a moment, then they were all out. The smell of smoke made his nose itch. "Damn," he muttered. Furiously he tore out more pages and ripped them into tiny pieces and threw them into the air. There was a breeze, and it caught some of the pieces and took them a few yards away, but mostly the paper fluttered down around them like heavy snow.

Beth Ann reached for the notebook and tore pages out, too. She ripped them into long strips, as he remembered doing years ago in school, for a papier maché project. They had made little dinosaurs with pipe cleaners for the skeleton, then pasted on the wet newspaper strips.

He kept lighting matches and setting pieces of paper alight until the matches were gone. Some pages caught and burned to ash. Most burned part of a corner away, then sputtered out. He was too hasty, too careless. He could not make paper burn!

He picked the notebook up, what was left of it, and grabbed sheets of paper that were loose, he took up all he could hold and went over to the water and shoved all of it under with both hands. The cold water shocked him. He saw himself at the edge of the puddle, pushing under Sissy's notebook, and he saw himself for the idiot he was. Beth Ann crouched beside him. "Will it rot in there?" she whispered.

He grabbed her shoulders. "No, summer will come and the water will dry up, and the pages will still be there, and they'll dry too, and a dusty wind will pick them up and carry them all the way back to town!"

She began crying.

He got up, pulled her to her feet. "Of course they'll disintegrate in there. And what if they didn't? Who goes around oil leases looking for things to read? Snap out of it. I've done what you wanted me to do." He snapped his fingers. "Wait, done half of it." He ran to the car and got his own notebook, then ran back to the water. He took his shoes and socks off, and then, on second thought, stripped off his trousers, too. He waded to the center of the little puddle and laid the notebook on the water's surface. It floated, one end dipped, very visible in the starlight. He lifted his foot and stamped it down. The water was about eight inches deep, and muddy. His feet sank into the soil.

He came out of the water and took a length of fabric from one of the boxes in the back of the station wagon, and used it to wipe his legs and feet and hands. All the while, Beth Ann followed him around like a dog. She had picked up his clothes. Silently, she handed them to him, and he dressed.

He started the car and dug out fast. He turned right on the highway and headed towards the sandhills.

"It's good you did that," Beth Ann said in a few minutes. Her voice was clear, almost piping, like a child's.

He drove as fast as the car would go, which obviously was not as fast as a Kimbrough car, because Beth Ann did not protest. He pulled off at the base of the hills and they got out and headed off into them. He trudged ahead of her, until she called to him to wait for her. She had taken off her expensive flats and carried them. His shoes and socks were gritty with sand. They came over a small crest and down into a valley between the dunes. From here, there was sand in all directions, sand and sky and stars.

If he had been alone, he would have lain in the sand and thrown his arms out and given himself up to the night. He would have slept and waited for morning.

He kissed Beth Ann hungrily. He knew he was frightening her. He felt her body grow tense. Her hands on his back dug into his flesh, not with passion, but for balance.

He began to sob. Soon his body was racked. He fell away from Beth Ann, to his knees in the sand. He put his face in his hands. He wept for all the sadness, the cruelty, the awful *resolution* of his friends' lives.

He wept for himself.

In a little while he was tired, and dry. He sat back, his eyes closed, his hands on the sand by his hips.

"Davy," Beth Ann said softly.

He opened his eyes. A few yards away, she was taking off her clothes. She did this slowly, letting her blouse drop off her shoulders like liquid, letting her slacks fall down around her feet. She stood above him in her white bra and panties. Her hair was loose around her face and shoulders. She smiled at him, then ran past him and started up the dune.

He crawled up onto his knees facing in her direction, part of his weight on his hands flat in front of him. He felt the force of gravity holding him there.

She reached the crest of the dune, and walked along it slowly, putting one foot in front of the other carefully, toes pointed, like a performer on a high wire. She stopped, reached behind and unhooked her bra, and let it fall down onto the sand below her. Her white panties gleamed. Her breasts shone, as fish do deep in the sea.

"Davy, Davy," she called. She held her arms out. "Come up here with me, Davy." She was long and slim and straight, like a blade of prairie grass.

He said nothing. There was a long moment. She pulled her arms back to her body slowly, crossed them in front of her breasts. "Davy," she called again, her voice quavering. She stuck her head forward a little.

He sat back on his heels, staring at her. She looked ghost-like, beautiful, up there. He felt dizzy. As he stared at her she seemed to be receding, as if the dune ebbed, like a wave on the sea that once was here. She floated away. He blinked, and the dune was there again, in front of him. She was riding its crest.

"You come down here," he answered. "You come to me."

DUTTON

CONTEMPORARY FICTION

☐ **CRIMINAL SEDUCTION by Darian North.** A man and woman who never should have met . . . a brutal murder that defies comprehension . . . an eccentric life veiled in layer upon layer of secrets . . . and a maze of mystery and passion that spans the decades and the globe . . . all come together in this stunning novel. (937404—$22.00)

☐ **ANNA, ANN, ANNIE by Thomas Trebitsch Parker.** With the elegant economy of scenes glimpsed from a moving train, this extraordinary novel portrays one woman's trajectory through life in episodes as haunting as dreams remembered. "This disturbing story of an uprooted woman's struggle to assert herself against the overwhelming tide of male history and male aggression is also a heartening attempt by a male author to put himself in a woman's shoes—and heart." —Susan Faludi, author of *Backlash* (936076—$21.00)

☐ **FORBIDDEN ZONE by Whitley Strieber.** Every small town has a special place like the mound—but in Oscola, New York, the mound is dangerous. Even in their most private imaginings the community cannot conceive of the power they will confront and the vengeance it can wreak on any who oppose the invincible evil beneath this mound. Only an impossible gamble will give the town a chance to prevail . . . and only Brian and Loi know the stakes. (936831—$21.00)

Prices slightly higher in Canada.

Buy them at your local bookstore or use this convenient coupon for ordering.

NEW AMERICAN LIBRARY
P.O. Box 999, Dept. #17109
Bergenfield, New Jersey 07621

Please send me the books I have checked above.
I am enclosing $_____ (please add $2.00 to cover postage and handling).
Send check or money order (no cash or C.O.D.'s) or charge by Mastercard or VISA (with a $15.00 minimum). Prices and numbers are subject to change without notice.

Card # _____ Exp. Date _____
Signature _____
Name _____
Address _____
City _____ State _____ Zip Code _____

For faster service when ordering by credit card call **1-800-253-6476**

Allow a minimum of 4-6 weeks for delivery. This offer is subject to change without notice.